A PERILOUS QUESTION

Barry Finlay

A Perilous Question
Barry Finlay

Published by Keep On Climbing Publishing

Copyright © Barry Finlay 2016

Cover by ShokVox Productions

Cataloguing data available at Library and Archives Canada

ISBN: 978-0-9938910-5-2

ACCLAIM FOR AWARD WINNING AUTHOR BARRY FINLAY

THE VANISHING WIFE

"His characters are well-developed, the scenarios are believable, and there are dozens of twists and turns throughout." – Amazon reviewer

"I had a hard time not just giving up the rest of my life and reading this in one sitting." – Vaughan Hopkins, Amazon reviewer

"I never knew where the plot was taking me, and I was swept along for this roller coaster read." – Kare, Amazon reviewer

KILIMANJARO AND BEYOND: A LIFE-CHANGING JOURNEY

"If you're the kind of person who can usually find any excuse to talk yourself out of a great idea this book is the inspiration you need to get out of your comfort zone and make things happen." – Helen Osler, Author, *Cameras of Kilimanjaro*, Australia

"…at once so inspirational and courageous, so human and humane, and so deeply personal that the reader feels they are climbing right along with this small and highly determined group." – Reverend Dr. Linda De Coff, Author *Bridge of the Gods*

"*Kilimanjaro and Beyond* is a beautifully written tale about a spiritual journey, a physical embarking, and so much more." – GoodbooksToday.com

I GUESS WE MISSED THE BOAT: A TRAVEL MEMOIR

"This is an exhilarating read." – Grady Harp, Amazon Hall of Fame reviewer

"*I Guess We Missed the Boat* is a fresh, ironic and jovial travel adventure novel in which each traveler can recognize himself or herself. It is a travel book that is amusing and practical at the same time." – Reader Views

"I really enjoyed this book! I think this is a great read. It definitely lightened my day…" – Shirley Priscilla Johnson, Amazon Top 1000 reviewer

Dedicated to the tireless efforts of organizations
working towards improving the lives of youth.

ACKNOWLEDGMENTS

There are so many people who have bought my books, provided feedback and reviews and given me moral support for my writing. I can't possibly thank everyone who has contributed in one way or another to making a passion so enjoyable. However, there a few that I would like to name specifically.

My first thank you goes to Sergeant Cory Robertson of the Ottawa Police Service. Cory was a tremendous help with the police procedural aspects of the book. Any errors, omissions or exaggerations related to police procedures are strictly mine.

Thanks also to Innocent and Joyce Mwabebe from Tanzania who helped me through the Swahili translations.

Karena Marie provided enthusiastic and supportive feedback on an early draft of the book. Thank you, Karena!

Tom Nickerson, ShokVox Productions, designed the artwork for the cover. Tom was, as always, very easy to work with, provided professional advice and willingly accepted multiple changes until we were both happy with the result and for that, I'm very grateful.

Thanks to Ron Melanson for the profile picture. It was fun working with Ron on the shoot and I'm thrilled with the result.

A huge thank you goes out to my wonderful editor, Kip Kirby. Kip challenges me and forces me to think long and hard during the editing process. She is incredibly conscientious and the end result is always a better book.

Magdalene Carson did the layout of the interior and the work to convert to ebook format, and I'm grateful for the effort. It's not an easy task, and it was handled quickly and efficiently.

Finally, to my family who are the biggest supporters for my writing and any other adventures that I might dream up in my senior years. My wife Evelyn provides unwavering support and dedication, reading through the manuscript countless times and pointing out things that I never seem to see. Her patience and support are invaluable.

Tanzania, Africa

Chapter 1

Shoni Batanga stepped back to examine her handiwork. The outline was barely visible in the indigo shadows of the room, but the moon peeking through the window cast just enough light. She inspected the profile from a distance because that's what the patrolling teacher would do. *Perfect.* Her lips turned upwards in a small smile of satisfaction. The mound in the bed, built of rolled-up bedclothes and hidden by the flimsy sheet that normally covered her as she slept, would go unnoticed until morning.

She cocked her ear to confirm the room was quiet. Shoni knew that at this time of night the fans that whirred noisily in the darkness to keep the temperature tolerable stopped automatically to preserve electricity. She cast her eye nervously at the bunk of the new girl, Aziza. In the darkness, she could barely make out the tiny girl's body curled up underneath the sheet. Even *she* seemed to be sleeping, although she had been awake many nights since she arrived. Shoni's heart was thrumming against her chest as if it were a moth trying to escape from a sealed jar. It pounded in her ears, and it occurred to her that it might be loud enough to awaken everyone in the room. She had done this before but the stakes were higher now. No matter, I'm doing the right thing, she thought.

The room was long with bunk beds aligned on both sides and a narrow space to walk between. When the head teacher, Mrs. Adimu, entered the room to check on the girls, she would be coming from the end of the room farthest from Shoni's destination. The teachers had separate quarters attached to the dormitory, and the door between the two rooms was always locked from their side to prevent the students from entering. The door leading to freedom where Shoni was headed was locked with a key from the inside. The teachers said it was so that the lock could not be picked by the male perverts that prowled from sunset to sunrise. Shoni and her classmates were told it was for their protection, but she was convinced it was to keep them from discovering what life was really like.

She crept stealthily past the rows of beds that held her sleeping classmates. Her body was tingling, her sharpened senses acutely aware of everything around her. She could hear only heavy breathing coming from all sides. She paused momentarily to listen for unwanted footfalls. Then she saw it – a movement out of the corner of her eye. A chill shimmered through her body like a sudden draft, and Shoni gasped and whipped her head around to see what had caught her attention. A scan of the room revealed nothing unusual. The door at the far end was still closed. Then she realized it was only shadow puppets dancing eerily across the wall, manipulated by the moon through the trees waving lazily in the breeze outside.

Shoni sighed quietly. As she continued, she deftly avoided the dark shapes that designated the lockers holding each girl's worldly possessions at the end of the beds. Her own extra clothing was in a small bag slung over her shoulder. She glanced at her best friend's bed located on a lower bunk and could see a mound similar to the one she had constructed – but Irene Sembaza was nowhere to be seen. Shoni's eyes narrowed and she pressed her lips together in agitation.

I have to keep moving. Mrs. Adimu always makes her rounds later, but this is the one night she could be early.

She arrived at the door that would take her to a better world. She sensed the fingers of freedom beckoning to her from the other side of the obstacle facing her, but a gentle twist of the door knob confirmed it was locked, as usual. Mrs. Adimu made sure the girls saw the chain with the key at the end that she carefully tucked inside the top of her dress. There was no way that anyone but The Gatekeeper, the name given to Mrs. Adimu by one of the girls, was going to access that key. But Shoni reached inside the pocket of her dress and pulled out two hairpins that had been twisted into unusual shapes by her boyfriend, Samuel.

Conflicting thoughts raced through her head.

He's not really my boyfriend, even though we kissed a few times and I even let his hands roam over my uniform once. She smiled inwardly. *I probably shouldn't have allowed him to do that. But there are better things awaiting me now. Oh, how I will miss all my friends, including Samuel.*

I have to concentrate.

Snapping back to the present, what Shoni really appreciated about Samuel right now was the trick he had shown her with the hairpins. The teachers hadn't talked about anyone picking the lock from the inside, and Samuel had shown Shoni that it was pretty simple to unlock the door so she could sneak out to see him. She had successfully used the pins twice and knew she would be able to do it again. One pin was bent at a 90 degree angle and the other had just a slight bend. As Shoni faced the door, she could barely make out the handle in the darkness. She set the small bag containing her meager belongings on the floor. Leaning forward, her eyes a few inches from her target, she fumbled with the handle until she found the tiny opening. The pin with the right angle bend easily slid into the bottom of the lock as she applied pressure. Her lips pursed as she focused on the task at hand. A drop of sweat rolled into her eyes and she blinked away the sting. She leaned back and rotated her shoulders, trying to relieve the tension. The second pin vibrated in her left hand as she leaned down again to insert it in the lock above the first.

She dropped it!

As the pin slipped from her trembling, damp hand to the floor, its fall was accompanied by an ever-increasing sick feeling descending into the pit of her stomach. The click of the pin bouncing on the concrete floor was magnified by the stillness in the room. Shoni bent down on her knees. The smooth concrete floor was cool to her touch. No pin. She brushed the floor deliberately as the last thing she wanted was to push it under the door. The hairpin moved under her sliding hand. She grasped it, straightened, and started the process again.

A hand came out of the darkness and touched her shoulder. Shoni jumped. "Kak!" She swore under her breath in Afrikaans, even though she had told herself the professional lady she was soon to become would never use bad language. In one motion, she tucked both hairpins into her pocket and whirled around to find her friend Irene looking at her sheepishly. "Sorry, I had to pee. I'm sooo excited," Irene whispered. "Have you got the door unlocked?"

"Shhh! Almost!" Shoni hissed at her friend as she listened to see if their muted utterances had awakened anyone else in the room. Everything remained still. The silence was only disturbed by the soft noises of their slumbering classmates.

Shoni wiped her clammy hands on her dress and once again fit the bent pin into the lock. As she turned it to the right and applied pressure, she inserted the second pin. It slid in easily at first, but then she felt the familiar resistance. "You have to disengage the five tumblers," Samuel had explained when he told her about the mechanics of the lock. She wiggled the second pin until she heard a click, followed by another and a third. She knew from previous experience that there would be only three clicks as two of the five tumblers had been worn down by age and use. Her breathing was labored as she leaned back, brushing against Irene who was pressed against her shoulder. Shoni noticed that Irene had picked up the bag with her belongings. She turned the handle, pushing the door open. Hot, humid night air rushed into the room, enveloping the two girls like cellophane.

Crossing the threshold to freedom, Shoni and Irene exchanged glances, hugged briefly and ran away into the night.

Chapter 2

The two girls held hands as they raced from the grey concrete cinder block building they had shared for the last year with 98 other female students. It was a dormitory at a rural community school just outside of Tanzania's most prominent city, Dar es Salaam. It had been funded by donations to an international development agency; and those lucky enough to have been chosen to stay in the dormitory were grateful for the building. The 400 or so other girls who hadn't been chosen (and all of the more than 500 boys) were a bit resentful and prayed that one day someone would fund more dormitories to make their lives easier as well.

Dust kicked up with every step as they ran, even though it had rained the previous day. The odd step splashed in some leftover water. A knot formed in Shoni's stomach. She was thinking about how much she would miss that building. She would even miss the monkeys clattering on the corrugated metal roof they used as a launching pad to start their trek from tree to tree at dawn each day. No need for an alarm clock, she thought. The building had become her home. Only two years ago, at the age of 15, she had been accosted in the dark on the 5-mile trek home from school. The man had done unspeakable things to her but she had no one to tell when she reached home. Her parents had both died of HIV AIDS and her siblings were all older and away from home, so she was totally alone. She hadn't spoken to anyone about her ordeal. But she had resolved to find something better.

It had not been an easy life. When Shoni got home from school each day, there was always an accumulation of dust that had to be swept. She had to walk a mile each way to carry clean water and she scrounged her food wherever she could, mostly from the local church that provided handouts. The dormitory was such a godsend for the many girls like her who had no parents or who had the furthest to walk to school or for the ones who had disabilities – like Irene.

Shoni's friend had a noticeable limp, which was even more pronounced when she ran. Irene once told Shoni she had been born with one leg shorter than the other and doctors had said it was likely caused by malnutrition when she was in her mother's womb. Irene's mother had died at childbirth, and her dad was a drunk who abused her. Like Shoni, Irene's brothers and sisters were older and had moved out of the family home. Lately, Irene often complained about not feeling well. Shoni felt sorry for her new friend. Their lives were similar in a lot of ways, and the two instantly became inseparable.

As they continued to run, Irene pitched forward on the uneven ground but she managed to regain her balance and forged on. When they reached the gate, Shoni and Irene squeezed through a small opening between it and the wall separating the grounds from the road. They hunkered down with their backs against the wall and sat silently in the shadows of a baobab tree, waiting for the taxi that was supposed to pick them up. Shoni thought to herself that they would be expecting one passenger, not two. *I hope that doesn't cause any problems.* She didn't say anything to Irene.

They listened for the one guard who slowly patrolled the large grounds on which the school sat. His approach was not difficult to hear, as the bundle of keys he carried on a chain jingled with each step. Shoni leaned around the corner and saw him rounding the dormitory and slowly shuffling along on his path around the grounds. It took the elderly gentleman forever to make it all the way around. She felt bad for tricking the kind old man. He was always friendly to the students but he was actually there as a good will gesture by Mrs. Adimu to give him employment.

After the guard had passed, Shoni looked down at her dress and frowned. Even in the shadows, she could see that spots of mud from the rain the day before had splashed on it during their run. She glanced at Irene and saw hers was the same. She nudged her friend and pointed at the marks. Irene looked at the spots and then back at Shoni with her nose wrinkled and eye brows knitted deeply together in an exaggerated frown. The two girls giggled nervously with their hands covering their mouths.

Shoni pressed her head back against the wall and recalled how their vibrant dresses were also the result of their friendship. At the end of the last school year, the head teacher had rewarded the student with the highest marks with a traditional African dress. It was obviously a hand-me-down, but Shoni didn't care. The greens and yellows were so vivid that Shoni brightened every time she wore it, enlivened by the dress. Later, the teacher had surprised Shoni by telling her she actually had two dresses and the young girl was allowed to give one to a student of her choice. There was no hesitation by Shoni. She had chosen Irene, and the two had chuckled as they shared a pair of scissors and reduced the two long dresses to what they considered to be American length, just above the knee.

As Shoni sat with her friend, she thought about how she had spent all her free time dreaming about something better beyond the walls of the dormitory. She knew the answer to her dreams lay in America. Visiting westerners who toured the new dormitory sometimes brought magazines, and the girls got to see pictures of the beautiful clothes, cars and houses. When the television was on in the cafeteria, they saw how Americans carried themselves with such confidence. It was obvious to all the students that Americans were rich.

So Shoni had devised a plan. She was one of the leaders in her class and had excellent language skills acquired through her studies – and by reading any English language books and magazines she could get her hands on. As a result, she got to lead tours of visitors from the West through the dormitory and around the grounds. The tourists always contributed in some way to helping Africans, confirming to Shoni and her fellow students that America was indeed the land of opportunity. Shoni understood they wanted to tour the dormitory to see the results of their contributions. She would patiently answer their questions. Then she would ask questions of her own as innocently and sweetly as she could. Her first question was always, "Where are you from?" If they were from North America, she would eventually ask, "When are you going to take me to Canada?" or "When are you going to take me to the United States?"

Her question was usually met with a chuckle or a dismissive, "I'm sorry, I can't do that." The tourists always thought it was a cute question, not to be taken seriously. But Shoni persevered. A week ago, she had hit the jackpot. Two Americans had visited within days of each other. The first was a pretty black woman who was so nice. Shoni had related easily to her and wanted so much to be like her. She was a perfect example to Shoni that a woman of African descent could thrive in America. The woman was dressed beautifully, was polite, smiled easily and yet Shoni had recognized a strong independence beneath the surface that she had come to recognize from seeing successful African women on television.

Nearing the end of the tour, she had posed her questions. The woman, who had said her name was Marcie, froze momentarily at the question and then politely declined. They had talked more. Shoni learned the lady lived near a place called Tampa, Florida in the U.S. and she had advised Shoni to continue studying and good things would happen. Shoni wished that were true – but so far nothing in her life had given her reason to believe it.

Then the second tour had happened two days later. It had been with a tall, good-looking man whose clothes and actions made Shoni think that, like all visitors to the dormitory, he had a lot of money. The scent of his exotic cologne had drifted over Shoni as she posed her questions. He stood before her in an open-necked white shirt and tan pants. And those shoes! It would take an African six months' salary to pay for those shoes. She had steeled herself for the usual response as he looked at her without saying a word for about 15 interminable seconds. His eyes had zeroed in on hers. They were gunmetal grey and they had pierced her soul as a hawk might set its sights on a wayward rodent. Shoni had never seen or felt anything like it, and her pulse had quickened.

The man had placed his hands firmly on her shoulders, held her gaze and simply whispered, "There will be a taxi at the gate on Tuesday at 4 a.m. Get in it."

Shoni couldn't believe it. She remembered how her mouth had gaped like a fish on dry land as she had tried to step back, but the firm hands had held her in place. The eyes had been unwavering, and she recalled shuddering involuntarily. From the corner of her eye she had seen the ever-present Mrs. Adimu, who had been hovering out of earshot, advancing towards them, her face a mask of concern. The man had removed his hands from Shoni's shoulders and said as he turned towards Mrs. Adimu, "I was just thanking this young lady for the wonderful tour. She has a lot of potential to go far in this world. Congratulations."

Mrs. Adimu's frown had deepened but she had remained quiet. Shoni was sure the message was meant for her as much as it was for Mrs. Adimu. *Potential to go far in this world.* Shoni had watched him leave, excitement cascading through her. *Please don't let this be a hoax. This is the chance I've been waiting for.* And then – *I have to take Irene with me.*

Shoni had thought long and hard about whether she was doing the right thing. She wondered if she had seen evil behind those eyes. But this was the chance she had been waiting for. Although she had always hoped she would get the opportunity, she never believed it would actually happen. Now, here it was. She had weighed the options available to her if she stayed in Africa versus those in America. The answer kept coming up the same. She had no family to keep her here. Her parents were dead. She never saw her brothers who were doing their thing only God knows where. As she saw it, her future in America far outweighed anything she might be able to achieve in Africa. Even better, she could get an education and earn money in America and come back to help out in her native country.

Shoni was brought back to the present by dogs howling in the distance, distraught at something passing in the night. The moon had been obliterated by a leaden mist that descended on her and Irene like a cold, damp cloth. The girls pressed against each other to try to stave off the chill in the air, but their clothes were slowly becoming wet and heavy. Quivering from the dampness and excitement, they held hands, willing the taxi to show up. The girls leaned with their backs against the damp wall as the ground accumulated moisture beneath them. Shoni fidgeted, crossing and uncrossing her legs. After about an hour, a rumble could be heard and lights danced in the sky, dimmed by the mist hanging in the air. The lights wavered shakily as the approaching vehicle rocked back and forth on the bumpy dirt road leading to the school. *This is it!* Shoni transmitted her silent scream of delight by squeezing Irene's hand so tight the other girl grimaced and yanked it away.

The girls hustled into the taxi and were driven away toward a new life of opportunity.

Or to one with deadly consequences.

Chapter 3

A cloud of dust swirled in the wake of the truck rolling into the suburbs of Arusha, Tanzania. The lower half of the white vehicle had been transformed to grey by a coating of dirt that made the Arusha Safaris decal on the door panel nearly unrecognizable. The top that had been open to offer the passengers a 360-degree view was now latched to keep out the sun and dust. The driver and three occupants rode in an uncomfortable silence as they made their way to a hotel occupied primarily by Westerners.

The sights and experiences had been incredible. The occupants had met some Maasai warriors wanting to sell them old tarnished machetes for American dollars – their apparent knowledge of global economics belying their meager existence. The tourists had been treated to sightings of the "Big Five" animals, among many others. A male lion had been spotted in a ravine, even though the guide had warned them that they hide this time of year. Further along the route, the driver had noticed a large dark object in the distance. He had picked up the binoculars from the seat and handed them behind him to one of the occupants who adjusted the focus until a black rhino came into view. It could have just emerged from the Triassic period a few hundred million years ago. A white bird hitched a ride as the huge animal lumbered across the short grass plains. Elephants presented themselves along the way, casually munching on shrubbery in their path and seemingly oblivious to the trucks passing by. The guide had pointed out Cape buffalo standing knee deep in small pools of water or in the shade of the odd acacia tree. Towards the end of the first day and only a few hundred feet from the vehicle, a life and death struggle had unfolded as the fifth animal comprising the Big Five, a sure-footed leopard, raced in full flight on the heels of a gazelle that was relying on its speed and a jagged pattern to survive for another day.

The tourists had been captivated by the animals roaming in their natural habitat, undeterred by the shimmering heat rising in the treeless areas. The migration of hundreds of wildebeest and zebras slowly shuffling across the plains in search of their next water and food supply had elicited gasps of excitement from the travelers. The sun was temporarily blocked by the clouds of dust kicked into the air by the thousands of hooves ambling along on their seasonal journey.

But the occupants knew that all good things must end and now that the tour was over, the truck was headed back to its starting point. Situated near the Kenyan border, Arusha was an overnight stopover for the African American woman seated in the back of the truck. Her 5'6" frame slouched in the seat, and she stared through the mud splotches on the window. Even in the Africa heat and dust, she was stunning. At 43, she was strong and independent. She had recently allowed her dark hair to grow nearly to her shoulders, a style she hadn't worn since her teens. It was definitely more effort to maintain than the close-cropped style she had worn for many years, but she liked how it accentuated the rest of her features. Her almond-shape eyes turned up slightly at the outer corner, giving the impression that the lower lid was slightly longer than the upper. The shape caused her dark brown irises to pop. Her lips were full, a feature that many women admire but one which often can only be acquired through expensive chemical injections. In short, she had the striking features of a model.

Right now, her dark eyes were unseeing as she stared, preoccupied by thoughts competing for her attention. She had flown to Arusha from Dar es Salaam for the safari and would be returning in the morning. Then she planned to go to Zanzibar for three days. After that, her vacation would be over and she would make the long journey back home to St. Petersburg, Florida. She had seen some wonderful sights in this beautiful country she had chosen for her vacation, and she knew she would be returning to the African continent soon. However, two things bothered her.

The first was the couple seated in front of her. They were the source of the uncomfortable silence that draped itself over the inside of the vehicle. He was in his mid fifties and he said he was from New Jersey. His frame carried about

50 pounds too much and had been adorned for the last three days by a bilious green Hawaiian shirt that was trying valiantly – but failing miserably – to meet the top of banana-yellow Bermuda shorts. A heavy gold chain around his neck and a Tilley hat topped off the ensemble. He had a young trophy wife or mistress from who-cares-where all over him during the safari they had just concluded. The material missing from her shorts should have been used to lengthen either the bottom of his shirt or top of his pants but sadly, such was not the case. Marcie Kane, who by contrast was wearing modest but attractive beige shorts with a caramel-colored top, didn't care who they were although in her mind she dubbed them New Jersey and the bimbo.

New Jersey called her "Mahcie." The bimbo didn't call her anything, which suited Marcie just fine. Marcie just knew she was embarrassed they lived in the same country she did.

During the introductions on the first day of their three-day safari, the bimbo had immediately removed any doubt about her I.Q. by saying to her companion in a high-pitched childlike voice, "Isn't it nice that we will be on safari with two black people in their own country?" She was referring to Marcie and their guide. Then turning to her companion and lowering her voice to nails-on-blackboard levels that apparently Marcie was not supposed to be able to hear, she said, "But how can *she* afford to go on a safari?"

Marcie successfully shut them out of her space as much as she could. Those who knew her well were aware of her directness, but she strived to keep a civil tongue. She recognized her travel companions as the nightmare tourists that show up on every organized trip anyone has ever taken. The driver, who also served as their tour guide, was a handsome man in his early thirties. To Marcie, he showed amazing restraint in dealing with the public and people like New Jersey and the bimbo. A discussion with him the first night confirmed that he had seen their kind many times before and that it was better to let them be. So, as much as she wanted to let them have it rather than let them be, she refrained.

Marcie had enjoyed seeing the animals in their natural habitat or, at least as natural as it could be given that they shared their home with a myriad of vehicles full of tourists. But the final affront had occurred this morning when they had a rare sighting of a cheetah, in Marcie's mind one of Africa's most beautiful animals. New Jersey had leaned towards the driver and said, "So why do they call it a cheetah? Did it take steroids before it ran or something?" The driver had stared stonily ahead. New Jersey had slapped his leg and laughed uproariously while looking at the bimbo expectantly. "Cheetah. Cheater. Get it?" But even when he had explained it, the New Jersey accent pronounced "cheater" as "cheetah" and the bimbo's blank stare had remained unchanged. Finally it seemed to dawn on her that she was supposed to laugh, so she joined in with a noise that, to Marcie, would be made by one of the animals they were watching during rutting season.

That's it!

Marcie reached forward, grabbed each by an opposite ear and slammed the two obnoxious tourists' heads together with a satisfying crack. Then she reached down with her left hand, unlatched the door and shoved the stunned individuals outside in the dust where the hyenas could have them.

At least, that's what she had done in her mind's eye. What she did instead was say, "You two should have some respect. Cheetahs are one of the most beautiful animals in the world, and we are privileged to even catch a *glimpse* of one. To see it out in the open the way we have is incredible. Our guide has done a wonderful job of finding animals for us. You two have been acting like idiots ever since the safari started. You should be grateful that this gentleman is willing to put up with your crap. You could learn something from him. I suggest you start thinking about the very large tip you're going to give him when we stop."

The bimbo's eyes had widened and her face had flushed a deep scarlet. New Jersey had stammered unintelligibly, but eventually fell silent and patted the bimbo's knee to silence her. His eyes had dropped to the floor, and Marcie had thought maybe the boorish behaviour was just an act to reduce himself to the level of the clueless and classless friend he had chosen as a traveling companion. Marcie had shaken her head and resolved to tip their tour guide extra herself just for having to put up with these two. As she sat back in her seat, her eyes had shifted to the rear view mirror where the top half of the driver's face was visible. Their glances had met briefly and a wink reflected back at her just before his shoulders had started shaking in a silent laugh.

The remainder of the ride had been quiet. Thank God for silence, Marcie thought as they approached the outskirts of Arusha. *I should have said more three days ago.*

But a more troubling thought shoved the two boors out of her head as Marcie focused now on something that had occurred before she joined New Jersey and his bimbo on the trip. Marcie's generous donations to an international aid agency had helped build a dormitory in Dar es Salaam for some young female students. Silently, she thanked her ex-husband basketball player whom she often referred to as He Who Shall Not Be Named, for the generous settlement he had reluctantly coughed up at their divorce. She also thanked her lawyers who were probably even more deserving of her gratitude.

Marcie thought about the two pretty young girls who had acted as her guides when she visited the dormitory. The girls had been wearing the same uniform as the other female students in the school: black shoes, white socks, a blue skirt with a white stripe and a darker blue v-neck sweater over a white blouse. All of the girls had worn their hair cropped nearly to the scalp. Marcie had been told by the head teacher that individuality was restricted at the school to reduce bullying.

The girls had introduced themselves as Shoni Batanga and Irene Sembaza. Shoni was the taller of the two and certainly the most gregarious. Marcie thought individuality wasn't being completely eliminated when she observed the two girls. In what could have been construed as a minor rebellion, Shoni was wearing a blue men's tie with a large Windsor knot holding it in place just below her open collar.

Shoni and Irene had excitedly pointed out the various features of their new quarters. The long narrow walkways between beds, the spacious kitchen, and the teachers' quarters were a huge sense of pride. The girls had tried to act mature, but their whispered asides and giggles had betrayed their teenage years. As they walked, Irene had favored one leg.

Before leaving the dormitory to plant a tree with the help of some of the boys, Marcie had asked the two girls if she could take a picture. They laughingly obliged with each confidently resting an arm on one of Marcie's shoulders for the shot. Naturally, the new dormitory building formed the backdrop for the photo. As they had said their goodbyes, however, everything changed for Marcie. The girl named Shoni had asked Marcie where she was from and when told she was from America, she had immediately and eagerly begun asking questions. The girl had seemed genuinely interested, so Marcie had told her about living near a large city in Florida called Tampa. The girl seemed to have many more questions to ask, but time was running out. As they walked to the location of the tree planting ceremony, Shoni had asked one final question that stopped Marcie in her tracks and that had bothered her ever since.

So when are you taking me to America?

It was a strange, unexpected request, and Marcie had been alarmed by the girl's question. She had the distinct impression that if given the opportunity, the pretty young girl would accept it in a heartbeat. And that, Marcie knew, could be a recipe for disaster. If the girls asked the wrong person and followed up on a positive response, their very safety could be in jeopardy. Marcie had left the school grounds unsettled and upset by what she had heard.

She didn't know how right she was.

Chapter 4

As the safari truck rolled to a stop in front of Marcie's hotel, she was satisfied with her decision. On the drive back, she had decided to express her concerns to the head teacher. She climbed the stairs to her fourth floor room, tossed her backpack on the bed and headed for the bathroom. A long shower ridded her of the day's dirt and grime, reminding her it was the last day of the safari. Toweled and dressed, Marcie fidgeted as she sat in a chair beside the bed, fighting a feeling of restlessness. She got up and looked out the window to see the never-ending ebb and flow of humanity. She turned and examined the room she had been away from for three days, marveling at how well appointed and modern it was with its king-sized bed and other conveniences.

There was no mosquito netting around the bed like the rooms she'd had on the escarpment during the safari. The electricity and hot water didn't function sporadically as they did in the Serengeti and Ngorongoro Crater. Marcie felt she could have been in a hotel in any major city in the U.S. She sat down in the chair again and reached for the remote, clicking on the television set to a British version of a non-stop talk news station. The fear-mongering newscast delivered by a breathless broadcaster describing impending worldwide doom only caused more weight to descend upon her. She often wondered who was better at terrorizing people: actual terrorists or the all-news stations that cover it 24 hours a day.

Absently, Marcie picked up a book, but the words rolled by without meaning. *Maybe a beer would help relax me.*

Returning to the lounge on the first floor, she sat at a table facing the front door. The popular local pale lager she ordered arrived in a frosted, dimpled mug. The first sip of the Kibo Gold felt cool and refreshing in her throat. She was grateful for the dish of peanuts that sat before her on the table. She took a handful and popped them one at a time into her mouth, enjoying the relaxed atmosphere of the lounge – until her calm was shattered by a familiar raucous laugh erupting from one corner of the room. She hadn't bothered to inventory her surroundings when she walked in. She certainly wasn't expecting to know anyone there, but she grimaced as she recognized the laugh. It belonged to New Jersey. She shrank in her seat with her legs straight out in front of her, her hands folded in her lap and her shoulders hunched, trying to make herself invisible.

Her ruse clearly failed. Marcie heard her name, or some form of it, echoing loudly across the room. It was an ill wind minutes before a Category 5 storm. "Mahcie! MAHCIE!"

Damn! It was impossible to ignore it. Marcie drew herself up and looked over her left shoulder, expecting to see New Jersey and the bimbo. What she saw instead widened her eyes. Sitting together around an empty glass-laden table were the most unlikely pair that she would ever expect to see – New Jersey and the driver. The bimbo was nowhere to be seen.

Marcie saw that the driver was still in his dark grey t-shirt and khaki pants while New Jersey had changed into something more respectable – for him. He was sporting a pale yellow shirt with tan pants. Still, there was not quite enough material in either to bring them together at the waist. Seeing Marcie turn around, the corners of New Jersey's mouth reached for the ceiling, interrupting something he was pontificating about. A wave of a beefy hand beckoned her to join them.

Marcie would have preferred to remain alone, but she was pleased that the driver and New Jersey were sharing a drink and a laugh. *Maybe there is some hope for the human race after all.* She raised her mug in a salute, her head dipping in a nod, but he waved her over again. Deciding to be polite, she left her beer and the half-eaten dish of nuts on the table to claim her territorial rights and sauntered over, hands buried deeply in her pockets.

New Jersey boomed, "Hey, how ah ya?"

It was the same use of the English language that had caused Marcie to shudder every time she heard it for the duration of the safari. He eliminated the "r" from the alphabet and tortured the remaining letters.

He continued, "I'm happy to see you again. I just wanted to say you were right sayin' what you did about our behavior. I don't know what gets into me around that woman. I thought I owed our driver here an apology and a drink for puttin' up with us. My name's Mike, by the way, in case you forgot. Join us?"

Marcie declined, saying she was tired and just wanting to finish her drink and go back to her room. To avoid upsetting them, she took her right hand out of her pocket and summoned the waitress. "Could you please deliver another round of whatever these two gentlemen are having and add it to my tab?" New Jersey's smile widened and he raised his glass in a salute to Marcie. "I wanted to apologize to you, too. I'm sorry if we ruined the safari. You're all right in my book, Mahcie."

"You didn't ruin the safari, but I have to admit I wanted to feed you two to the hyenas a couple of times." Marcie laughed. "Where is the bim . . . uh, I mean your friend, anyway?"

"Who? Tracey? She's upstairs taking a long bath. We enjoy each other's company, you know?" His eyebrows rose up and down several times, accompanied by an innuendo-oozing wink.

Marcie grimaced. Maybe he enjoys *her* company, she thought to herself, but she probably enjoys *his* money. But all she said aloud was, "Well, I hope you enjoy your drinks and the rest of your vacation." To the driver, she said, "Thank you again for the wonderful safari. "Kuwa Vizuri. Be well."

Back at her own table, she sipped her beer, shut out the bar's noise, and turned her thoughts to what had brought her here to Africa and the situation with the girls. She could feel the tension easing out of her shoulders and neck as she took another sip of the cool alcoholic liquid. A ring of water appeared on the table when she lifted the cold glass. She erased it with her finger, leaving irregular watery lines where the ring had been.

A few minutes later, Marcie's brooding contemplation was interrupted by the sight of the driver leading New Jersey Mike to the elevator. New Jersey was weaving slightly and she suspected he had consumed most of the drinks on the table as well as the two she had ordered for them. He waved and slurred, "Take care, Mahcie."

Marcie raised her hand, waved, and returned to her thoughts.

Chapter 5

Marcie wasn't sure how much beer she had consumed but she had decided an hour earlier that if she tried to sleep, the nightmares that had plagued her since the incident two years ago might come back. They hadn't been as prevalent lately but the thought of the two girls could trigger them again, so one drink had turned into a few more than usual. She passed the time with her thoughts and contemplating the African motifs adorning the walls. There were masks, carvings and paintings of Masaai villages, animals and of course, the majestic Mount Kilimanjaro.

The bar had suddenly come alive around her. Conversations in German, Afrikaans and other languages ricocheted crazily off the walls, colliding with each other right above Marcie's table and raining fragments down upon her. Glasses clinked and laughter filled the room. Occasionally, snippets of English spoken by animated people returning from safaris and other adventures rose above the tumult.

Marcie sat quietly. She rubbed her shoulder absent-mindedly as her troubling memories came flooding back. She remembered the incident like it was yesterday even though it had happened two years earlier. Her best friend, Sami, had walked away from her husband in an ill-advised attempt to solve some issues from her past. Helping Sami's husband, Mason, find Sami and get her back from her deadly captors had placed Marcie right in the middle of a gunfight that left two bullet wounds in her shoulder. It still throbbed from time to time and the doctors told her it always would. At least she was still alive and Sami was fine, although both were still recovering psychologically from the ordeal. In Marcie's case, that meant recurring nightmares.

If it hadn't been for Marcie's ex insisting she learn how to shoot, she probably wouldn't be around at all. Because of the ability she learned on the firing range, she was able to wound their foe with a well-placed shot of her own. That slowed him down enough that the situation could be ended. Once she recovered from her wounds, Marcie had enrolled in some self-defense courses at a martial arts training facility and continued her gun training. It gave her a feeling of personal power and security in a world that seemed to be going crazier by the minute.

An extra-loud conversation snapped Marcie out of her reverie and she decided it was time to summon the waitress for her bill and risk another long night and another nightmare. She tilted the glass towards her mouth to drain the remnants and looked towards the bar for her server when something else caught her attention. Joshua, the driver of the safari truck was standing just inside the door. Marcie saw him survey the room before his eyes settled on her. His lips parted in a grin and he waved his hand in recognition. Marcie felt embarrassment fill her cheeks with warmth. He would probably think she was quite the loser sitting in the same seat she'd been in when he was at the bar earlier. He sauntered confidently to her table and asked if he could join her. Marcie used the opportunity to put off going back to her room.

"I wondered if you might still be here. The hotel lets me wash the truck in their parking lot, so I thought I would come in for a drink before going home. I'm glad to see you again. You seemed very, uh, what's the word, distant earlier. I know Mike and his girlfriend were difficult but I hope you enjoyed the safari, anyway. Mind if I sit?"

Marcie smiled. "Of course not. It must be pretty difficult to get all the mud and dust off. I enjoyed the safari very much. I loved seeing the animals, and you were amazing as a tour guide. I didn't mean to seem distant, but I just have some things that I need to deal with, that's all." Marcie thought her words sounded a bit defensive.

Joshua held two fingers in the air for the waitress. Marcie surmised one of the drinks he was summoning was for her, and the waitress obviously knew Joshua's preference. She said, "I'm not sure I should be having another one. I think I passed my limit awhile ago. I'm catching a flight to Dar es Salaam tomorrow." She was sure her speech was slightly slurred.

Joshua slid the chair opposite Marcie away from the table and plunked himself down. "Well, I prefer not to drink alone, so I hope you will stay for at least one. What brings you to Tanzania? Did you just come for the safari?"

Marcie hesitated. She was happy that Joshua had joined her, and since she would probably never see him again, she decided it wouldn't hurt to stay a little longer and even share some of her background. "Well, I came mainly to visit a girl's dormitory that I helped to fund. I have a very strong interest in the school, and I really wanted to see what I'd help build through my contributions." She hesitated before adding, "I decided since I was coming here, anyway, I might as well add some vacation time, so I booked the safari. I originally planned to go to Zanzibar, but today I changed my mind. I'm going back to the school instead."

Joshua was listening intently, so Marcie continued. "I want to become a youth development professional. My dream is to be able to counsel young girls who might be vulnerable to being led astray or to being forced to follow the wrong path. The visit to the dormitory fits right in with my work."

The drinks arrived. Marcie lifted her glass and toasted Joshua's tour guide skills. "What about you? Will you continue in the tour guide business?"

He smiled back at her warmly, obviously pleased at being asked the question. "Actually, I enjoy being a guide, but I'm always looking for something better. I enjoy meeting people like you and learning about how others live. It's noble of you to try to help young people. We need this very badly in my country. I know I'm lucky to have employment. How do you become a . . . what is it . . . a youth development professional?"

Marcie realized she'd had enough beer as she downed the first half of the one that had just arrived. "There's nothing wrong with being a tour guide and you're so good at it. Something pretty serious happened in my life two years ago that caused me to change my whole focus. After that, I was accepted at a local college back home. I completed the final term for my degree, but I knew I needed more. Now that this holiday's over, I'll be continuing my education so I can get an associate degree and be accredited as a youth development professional." Ultimately, I'm aiming for a Bachelor's Degree. I'm required to take in-house training, so I volunteer for various youth-oriented organizations. It's really rewarding, and the best part is knowing that I'm helping others in some small way."

Joshua nodded as if he understood, and smiled. "That's great. You are lucky to have been able to pay for a new dormitory. You Americans are all rich. I would like to move to America some day and be rich like you."

Marcie laughed. She realized her words were coming out louder than they should, but still she continued, thinking, apparently, *I needed someone to talk to.* "Contrary to popular belief, not all Americans are rich. In fact, very few are. We have some very poor areas that are similar to yours in Africa. Honestly, I owe being able to help fund the dormitory to my ex-husband. He gave me a generous settlement when we got divorced, and that's what's made it possible for me to help support the dormitory at the school." She smiled at Joshua dryly. "I guess you could say that's about the only thing I'm grateful for from our marriage."

Popping another peanut in her mouth, Marcie reflected on the early years of her relationship. She tried to subtly dislodge a stubborn nut stuck between her teeth before adding, "He was a professional basketball player. We met after a game in my hometown in North Carolina, when his team was in town. I was working at a bar when he walked in. He was tall, good looking and athletic, and I guess he saw something in me. I grew up in a bad area of town so it was an opportunity for me to find something better. We stayed in touch by phone and through emails and seeing each other whenever he was in town, and eventually we married and I moved to Florida to be with him."

Marcie sighed. "But then when my husband's career was winding down 10 years ago, everything fell apart."

Marcie shook her head and giggled. "You don't want to hear this stuff. Now you know more about me than pretty well anybody on the planet. Tell me about you."

As Joshua talked, Marcie thought how the alcohol had loosened her tongue. Now he knew her life story and that she was single. She looked at the young man sitting in front of her and decided the beer was making him more attractive and she had better get a tighter grasp on her inhibitions. She knew she was tough, but had to admit she felt lonely sometimes. That was something she kept to herself. Even her best friends thought she was unbreakable. She had dated a few times since the divorce and had even had a couple of long-term relationships that were sexually satisfying. But Marcie recognized that in all likelihood, her painful divorce had elevated her standards in a man to near stratospheric, pretty much impossible to attain, levels.

Joshua had cocked his head and raised his eyebrows at the mention of professional basketball. The subject of sports was obviously one he enjoyed. They chatted a little longer and Marcie answered Joshua's questions about basketball and whether she knew Michael Jordan. Sometimes he touched his ears, indicating that he was having trouble hearing her in the crowded room, and he'd moved his chair nearer to hers. As he shared his own hopes and dreams, Joshua leaned in toward her in an obvious move to draw her closer.

Savoring the final few drops of her beer, Marcie continued to listen but her mind drifted back to the two girls she had met at the dormitory. She tried to maintain a level of interest while Joshua chattered away across the table from her. He was clearly trying to be charming and hold her attention – so much so Marcie suddenly realized that his dreams for this night included more than just conversation.

Marcie held up her hand and abruptly stopped Joshua in mid-sentence. "Sorry, but I need to go to the bathroom and I think I will head up to my room after that. But you know what? I've really enjoyed getting to know you tonight. I have an early morning flight tomorrow. Thank you for joining me and for listening. I really do appreciate it. You are a wonderful guy, and I wish you the very best in everything you do."

Joshua's disappointment was apparent by his downturned mouth. He tried to encourage her to have one more drink but he was coming to an understanding that his investment of time to accompany a rich American woman back to her room had yielded zero payback. Marcie assumed he was wishing he hadn't wasted so much time with her instead of pursuing other attractive women in the bar. She wasn't sorry that their conversation had briefly taken her mind off two girls she barely knew in a country she didn't fully understand. But now, unavoidably, thoughts came flooding back.

I can't just walk away. I have to do what I can, at least to warn the teacher about what the girls were contemplating.

Marcie touched Joshua's arm as she thanked him again, paid her bill and turned towards the stairs back to her room.

Chapter 6

Marcie had awakened early in the morning with tiny hammers beating a rhythmic pattern in her head. The drone of the aircraft hadn't helped. The flight from Arusha had managed to make it to Dar es Salaam on schedule, something that was not necessarily guaranteed. Flights, like everything else in Tanzania, tended to run on African time. At least she had been spared the nightmare dreams she had been worried about. Her sleep had been dreamless. Thank God for alcohol.

Marcie checked into her hotel, freshened up and now sat in front of an inexpensive wooden desk in Mrs. Adimu's sparse office. The head teacher's large frame spilled over her chair. Brass earrings dangled from each ear, accenting her brightly-colored print African dress and head scarf. The dress was known as a khanga. Marcie thought the woman's attire was beautiful, but she could feel Mrs. Adimu's obvious distaste for this unexpected interruption to her daily routine.

A phone call after she left a disappointed Joshua in the restaurant bar had led her back to the school. She had called the International Development Agency to advise them she wanted to return to the school to tell the head teacher of Shoni's intentions. She was surprised she had reached anyone at that time of night, but they were still working. The Agency representative assured her they would develop an education program for the students and especially the young girls about leaving the school with strangers – but right now they had other tasks occupying them. They were stretched to the limit. They appreciated Marcie's concern and were happy that she was going back to the school, but they couldn't afford transportation or a translator for a second visit.

Marcie had found a taxi and negotiated a fare that was satisfactory to her and the driver. The Agency did arrange for a translator at Marcie's expense and he was standing to one side in front of the desk. Marcie was thankful Ignace could join her. It worked for both of them. It cost Marcie a little over 46,000 Tanzanian shillings, or about $25.

Marcie brushed a drop of sweat from her forehead and pulled her clinging blouse away from her back. It must be 100 degrees in here, she thought, of the sweltering conditions in the tiny space. *This is what a piece of pottery must feel like in a kiln.* She sat on the only visitor chair in the utilitarian office.

The head teacher stared impassively, unbothered by the heat. Her pencil tapped impatiently on the desk as they sat opposite each other. Their eyes locked.

Marcie tried to hide the irritation from her voice as she attempted to draw information from the teacher. "I don't understand. What do you mean she ran away?"

Ignace listened closely to Mrs. Adimu and translated for Marcie. "They discovered Shoni and another girl, Irene Sembaza, ran away several nights ago. The girls made up their beds to look like they were still there, and when Mrs. Adimu made her rounds, she thought everyone was accounted for."

Marcie froze. *Am I too late?* "Shoni seemed quite eager to leave the dormitory when she talked to me. Too eager. She asked when I would take her to America. Is it possible someone agreed to meet Shoni and Irene?"

"Naam. Yes," Ignace said after listening to the teacher. "It is possible. The girls sometimes sneaked out to meet boyfriends. Because of that, the teachers now lock the door to prevent any possibility of this happening in the future. Head teacher is not sure how they got out, but the girls must have found a way to pick the lock. The door is locked from the inside to prevent men from picking the lock from the outside. The teachers never thought the girls could pick the lock to get *out*."

The teacher reached into the top of her dress and pulled out the chain with the key attached. The chain dangled from her hand as she looked at Marcie and said a few words in Swahili. Although Marcie couldn't understand the language, the intention was clear and confirmed by the translator. "She assures us they take every precaution to ensure the students' safety."

Marcie watched the teacher put the chain back in the top of her dress. She knew the only reason the woman was talking to her at all was because of Marcie's status as a fundraiser. "I'm sure they do. So, there wasn't any visitor that stood out to you? No one that drew your attention?"

The teacher's eyes cast downward. She stiffened visibly. "Of course not. I would have looked into it further if that were the case." She spoke the words in English. There was an undercurrent of defensiveness. And her reaction was just a little too quick for Marcie not to notice.

Marcie glanced at Ignace and saw that he picked up on it as well. A flurry of Swahili followed, after which Ignace turned back to Marcie, his face clouded with frustration, "She says there was a Muzungu here two days after you, and the man acted strangely. He said his name was Smith. She says he whispered something to Shoni and then Mrs Adimu thinks he lied to her about what he had said."

Marcie knew Muzungu was roughly translated into 'white man.' Her eyes met the teacher's. "What did you do?"

The teacher's shoulders lifted and dropped and with upturned hands, she managed some words in broken English, "What can I do? He provides shillings to help build our house for the girls. We must not anger him." Then to Ignace who translated, "They searched the grounds and talked to the other students about the two girls, but no one seemed to know anything."

"Did you call the police?" Marcie's stomach fluttered.

Mrs. Adimu said, "No. They would not help." Ignace added on his own, "You have to understand, Ms. Marcie, young girls disappear all the time in Dar es Salaam. The police have their hands full. They will do what they can when the time is right, and if they are paid well to do it. I think the girls will come back when they have had their fun."

If they are paid well to do it. Corruption. So much for the Swahili phrase I learned for "call the police" – mwite polisi. Marcie said, "You didn't hear anything during the night?"

The teacher sat back, her arms folded across her ample bosom. Her comments were translated as, "I thought I might have heard a car, but cars sometimes go by during the night. There aren't many. We usually travel by walking or by bicycle, but I think there might have been a car. It might have been nothing. We will do everything we can to find the girls. We have over 900 students here. Some walk away. Boys and girls. We can't watch each and every one. You should go home, Ms. Marcie. It's not your concern. There's nothing you can do."

Marcie's stomach churned with anxiety and a feeling of helplessness. The teacher's attitude was too defensive for Marcie's liking. She asked more forcefully, "And what usually becomes of the young girls that disappear?"

Ignace repeated the teacher's words in English. "Sometimes they come back but sadly, sometimes they wind up dead. They are enticed away by men from the city, and some have been kidnapped. They are used until they are of no use, and then they are discarded. Some are forced into labor in mining or agriculture or into domestic servitude." Then he added, "Life in Africa is hard, Ms. Marcie. Less than 25% of girls have the benefit of secondary school. Now, the teacher says she must go. Her lecture starts in a few minutes. She says to thank you for your concern but to put this out of your mind. Just go on with your life, and they will go on with theirs."

Marcie asked one final question. "Can you describe this man? This Mr. Smith?"

The teacher's face soured in distaste as she spoke. Ignace's translation of her description was, "He was tall and dressed very expensively. He had a small beard." He motioned around his mouth and chin and then listened to the teacher. "He was nothing special, a normal muzungu, except his eyes. They pierced the flesh like steel rods."

Marcie frowned at the description. She rose from the chair and grasped the woman's hand. "Assante sana. Thank you. Thank you for all you do." The woman smiled tightly and with a curt nod, she hurried out the door. Marcie tilted her head back, hunched her shoulders and a prolonged sigh escaped her lips.

As she and Ignace stood outside saying their goodbyes, she asked, "Why do less than 25% of girls go to secondary school?"

Ignace's shoulders shrugged. "There are many reasons. Girls who get pregnant are expelled. It's always considered to be the girl's fault. Girls are not expected or taught to be assertive. They do the domestic chores, including gathering water, and they often must miss school to complete their duties at home. Even though education is free now, quite often families can't afford school supplies for all their children; so money is spent on the boys' education. As you can see, there are many, many issues."

Marcie nodded glumly, sighed again, thanked Ignace and asked him to summon a taxi for her. She and the translator parted ways so he could go to his home in the opposite direction. Marcie thought of the girls as she waited at the gate for the taxi, and she recounted the conversation with Mrs. Adimu. Maybe the head teacher was right, she thought. *I might as well continue with my vacation and go to Zanzibar for a couple of days. What else can I do? I didn't know these girls. I'm not part of their lives here. I don't know Dar es Salaam, and the girls could be anywhere.*

She resolved to renew her arrangements to visit the many islands of Zanzibar as soon as she got back to the hotel.

Chapter 7

The old rusty blue car was making a grand entrance as it rolled along the bumpy road toward Marcie, a thick cloud of black smoke contaminating the atmosphere behind it. Its brakes squealed in protest as it ground to a halt beside her. The driver, a jovial individual of indeterminable age, shouted "Hello" in Swahili through the open passenger window. "Jambo! How are you, pretty lady? You are Madame Kane, yes?"

He was somewhere between 60 and 100, Marcie judged. The crevices of his face bore patches of stubble. Marcie recognized the New York Yankees symbol on the cap pulled down over his eyes. Threads dangled from the peak, indicating that the owner of the hat had made good use of it over a number of years.

He was her driver and this was to be her ride. Stale tobacco smoke mingled with other odors from previous passengers nestled heavily on Marcie when she got in the car. She tried to avoid a stain on the seat as she slid across. The scent of strong familiar cologne fought to overpower the other odors as she settled into her seat. It had been a long time since she smelled that particular brand, she thought. Now, she just wanted to get back to her hotel, have a shower and some dinner, and ready herself for the rest of her vacation. As the driver ground the shift to pop the car into gear, Marcie just hoped that this vehicle would make it to her hotel. The hesitation before lurching forward did little to relieve her apprehension.

Marcie stared through her window at the small shacks and mud huts that somehow accommodated large African families. Shockingly thin cattle and goats wandered aimlessly around the yards, raising puffs of dust when they moved, or lazily swatting away bugs with their tails. School-age children dressed in rags shooed other animals to some destination with sticks. There were always people on the move – bicycles laden with bananas or bamboo, business people on their way to or from work. A brightly dressed woman with an enormous jug on her head deftly weaved through the humanity with the adeptness of a running back heading for daylight through a hole in a defensive line. Marcie preferred not to look out the front window as she had observed drivers in Tanzania missing the pedestrians and cyclists by inches. Her mind at the moment was occupied with how she could help this poor community.

Then from the front seat, the driver interrupted her thoughts in decent English, "Something bothers you, pretty lady?"

"No, it has just been a tough day. I'll be fine. Thank you for asking. Oh, and you can call me Marcie."

"It seems like you need a friend, Ms. Marcie. In Tanzania, we say, 'To be without a friend is to be poor indeed.'"

The driver and Marcie bounced on their seats as the car hit a particularly deep rut.

Marcie pushed herself back on the seat and smiled at the driver's advice. "Oh yes. It's always good to have friends."

"Ah, we should all have the temperament of the young. They have no worries. But they are not wise. We have a saying. 'Instruction in youth is like engraving in stone.' There must be instruction. But we have another saying, 'Knowledge without wisdom is like water in the sand.' It is only with longer life that we become wise. But what comes with wisdom? We worry too much. I think you are worrying too much. Do you not agree?"

Marcie loved the old man's use of proverbs to emphasize his point, but she was only half listening, distracted by the events of the day. The reference to the young registered somewhere in Marcie's preoccupied brain. *It's funny he's talking about youth when I was thinking about the two girls.* She murmured, "What makes you say that?" She wasn't sure she cared if he answered. She was lost in the maze of her thoughts.

The driver chuckled. "I think you are troubled by something, and I was just thinking of the difference between you who has some years of experience and the wisdom that goes with it and the two girls I picked up at this very spot two nights ago. They were young and carefree and becoming educated, but they do not have wisdom yet. Rain was falling and the girls' wet clothing was dripping on the floor of my car. They were excited and laughing and having a gay old time, even though they were wet and cold and it was four o'clock in the morning. We should all forget our troubles and enjoy life, right, pretty lady?"

Marcie was only half listening. But as his statement began to crystallize in her mind, she bolted upright as if struck by 10,000 volts.

"*What did you say?*"

Marcie's attention was on high alert now and she focused on the driver as he repeated what he had said. Barely waiting for him to finish, she blurted out, "Where did you take them?"

The driver's heavy shoulders shrugged as his eyes met Marcie's in the mirror. "Oh, they are destined for some trouble, I think. A stray chick is a target for a bird of prey. They are not wise. I was told to deliver them to a house near the bus station. It is a very bad area of Dar es Salaam, pretty lady. They insisted on going to wherever the Muzungu told me to take them. I have taken other girls there at the man's request. He pays me a month's earnings each time I do it."

"What!? Other girls? What did the girls you picked up look like?"

The description provided by the driver was detailed and fit the two girls she had met.

"So you are saying that the girls you gave a ride to are not the first that have gone to this house? Why are they taken there?"

"I don't know for sure what happens after I drop them off, but I think they are sold for domestic service. It's not such a bad life, Ms. Marcie. They live in nice places and they are employed. It's hard to find employment in Tanzania, especially for young girls."

Marcie doubted that domestic servitude was always a good thing. "Okay, what's the name of the man who paid you and what does he look like?"

Hesitant now. "You can't say anything to anyone about this. I have said more than I should already." But he continued to unburden himself. "The Muzungu's name is Mr. Smith. He is always well dressed. He has a tiny beard like a British aristocrat and he has the darkest eyes. They are black daggers that thrust deep into your soul, pretty lady. He is scary and angers quickly. The girls are the first for me from this school. I have taken other girls to the house from other schools. We do what we can to make money here. We have to feed our families. You understand?"

Mr. Smith. It sounds like he's recruiting young girls, but for what?

"Can you take me to the house? I would like to talk to the girls to make sure they are all right. I will match whatever the white man paid you."

In the rear-view mirror, Marcie noticed the wrinkles in the driver's weathered face swallow his eyes as he peered at the rutted road through the dust and dead bugs on the windshield. The car rocked from side to side as the tires rode in and out of the ruts. He blared the horn at a pedestrian who had ventured too far onto the road and into the path of the rickety vehicle before saying, "Oh, I only told you about the happy girls to cheer you up. You seemed so sad. Why do you want to go there? There is nothing there for someone such as you."

Both hands were off the wheel now, emphasizing his point as the car veered towards a cyclist. He must have felt Marcie's hand on his arm as he jerked the wheel back at the last second, missing the man by inches. "It is far too dangerous. It will only lead to trouble for you. I can tell you are a tourist by the way you are dressed and the way you speak. Just enjoy your time in Tanzania and go back home. You must stay away from areas such as the one near the bus station and don't walk about at night. If you do, be very careful. Dar is pretty safe in most places, but a lady such as you has to be extra careful. If something happens, the police will not be helpful unless you pay them. You are best to walk away."

She ignored the reference to paying the police. "I will double what the man paid you. Take me to my hotel first and wait until I come out. Then take me to the house and wait for me."

The driver hesitated, his shoulders heaving, and he blew a deep breath through his lips. Resignedly, he said, "Okay, but I warn you to rethink this matter when you are in your room. If you still want to go, I will do as you ask. I need the money for my family. I have 11 children."

Marcie said, "Assante sana."

She settled back in her seat as thoughts swirled through her head, bumping into each other and slowly giving rise to another headache. *People will do anything for their family. 11 children? How can they look after that many children? What hap-pens to these girls he is delivering to the house? How many other girls? What will I find when I get there? Am I getting in over my head? Everyone tells me the police are of no help."*

Marcie leaned forward again and said, "What's your name?"

"Godfrey, madame."

"May I ask a question, Godfrey? You don't have to answer if you would rather not."

Happy that the subject seemed to be changing, he replied, "Ask anything, pretty lady."

"Your English is so good. Where did you learn English?"

"Thank you, pretty lady. We learn English in school, and I have had many English-speaking people in my car to practice on. Some of my friends do not speak English so well because they don't have the same opportunities to practice." A raspy chuckle came from his throat.

"That makes sense," Marcie replied, "but I'm curious about something else. Why do Africans have so many children? It seems difficult to educate them all."

The driver glanced into the back seat from the mirror. He seemed surprised by the question. "Of course it is a matter of respect, pretty lady. The more children in a family, the more respect the family achieves. Besides, who else will look after the parents when they become elderly?"

Marcie repeated her question. "And education?"

"The boys are generally educated. It is up to the girls to carry the water. We make choices on which boys get educated because we can't afford to send them all to school. You understand?"

Echoing what the translator had said, Marcie commented, "Life must be hard."

"Yes, but pretty lady, one who bathes willingly in cold water doesn't feel the cold."

With a smile and another thank you, Marcie once again sat back in her seat. There was some logic in the man's simple response. But she believed everyone needed to be educated. That is the key and where the most help is needed. Her thoughts slowed along with the old taxi as it chugged up to the hotel entrance.

As usual, young men hung around in front of the door under the watchful eyes of armed security guards who Marcie presumed were assigned to protect the tourists if too many liberties were taken. She wondered what it would take for the security guards to take action, since the actions of the aggressive young men usually just elicited smiles among them. She was familiar with the routine. One of the young men would reach for the door handle while another looked for a bag that he could carry. Each would have their free hand extended, expecting a few shillings for their acts of kindness.

Marcie emerged from the taxi but before doing so, she gently nudged the driver with a hand draped over the front seat. He palmed the money she was handing him as a down payment for the rest of the trip but he turned around, his rheumy eyes searching hers, imploring her to rethink this madness. The deeply lined, weathered face that had seen too much simultaneously betrayed sadness and an apology. She squeezed the old man's shoulder and said, "I do understand, Godfrey. I do. You have to do it for your family."

Chapter 8

The driver was right, of course. Marcie's reflection in the mirror screamed back at her: *TOURIST*! Her white shorts and indigo blouse were not designer labels but definitely of Western quality. Various clothing items from her suitcase lay spread across the bed. The selection was sparse as she was traveling light.

Her decision made, she put on a plain white t-shirt, the kind with no logo that she favored, and a pair of old jeans that she wore for lounging when she was vacationing. They hugged her a little more than she would have preferred under the circumstances, but they were probably the least touristy she had. A pair of worn, weather-beaten hiking shoes with an aggressive tread on the hard sole was exchanged for the sandals she had been wearing. The ensemble was complete. The little makeup she wore was removed with a Kleenex. Another look in the mirror. *This will have to do.* She removed enough money from her wallet to pay the driver and left the rest, along with her watch and jewelry, in the room safe.

She descended the stairs back to the lobby. The taxi was still there, parked a few car lengths from the front door. Although she couldn't see into the taxi from her angle, a cloud of tobacco smoke billowing from the driver's side window confirmed that Godfrey was waiting inside and adding to the ambience of the vehicle. She darted into a souvenir shop to her left to see if she could add to her outfit, but all she could find were baseball caps with the caption, I "heart" Tanzania. *That's no help.*

Continuing through the lobby, she remembered the live potted plants she had admired earlier. Adjusting her angle to the exit, she walked deliberately towards one of the plants and hurriedly scooped up some dirt from the pot. She had to be careful as two stern security staff with rifles stood at the lobby doorway.

"I'm ready," Marcie told the driver who silently shook his head again and ground the car into gear. The last of his cigarette was tossed out the window. As the old car lurched forward, spewing a cloud of black smoke into the humid air, she removed her t-shirt, revealing her white bra. She was pretty certain that, out of habit, Godfrey had checked the mirror to see why she was moving about in the back seat but quickly averted his eyes. She rolled the shirt into a ball, smeared the dirt into it and worked it back and forth for a few minutes. She unravelled the formerly clean shirt and held it up for examination. After smudging the dirt a little more in a clean spot on the back, it was now wrinkled and soiled, not something any self-respecting tourist would wear. She wiped her dirty hands on her jeans. Better, she thought.

My inability to speak Swahili will immediately give away that I'm not a local, but at least the soiled clothes might keep me from getting accosted before I get inside the house.

Marcie put her t-shirt back on, slid back in the seat and wondered what she was getting herself into. As she stared out the window, a swirling congestion of sights and sounds unfolded in front of her. People everywhere. Marcie marveled at the splashes of color from the beautiful garments the women wore, in spite of the heat, humidity and dust of the streets. Many of them were wrapped in the traditional brightly colored khangas, which Marcie knew bore an inspirational message in Swahili along their borders. Some of the women even ingeniously wrapped their babies in the material at the front.

Many men also wore long, comfortable khanga-type garments, but some were impeccably dressed in expensive business suits with shoes polished to a mirror-like finish that somehow successfully avoided the inevitable African dust that rose with each step. Most of the people traveled by foot, rarely making eye contact and yet somehow narrowly avoiding each other or being flattened by a vehicle or cyclist. To Marcie's eye, there was a grudging pecking order among the vehicles, cyclists and pedestrians, and each was resentful of giving way to the other. Horns constantly blared. Pieces of wood, sugar cane or baskets weighed down the bicycles, making them even more uncontrollable and more likely to veer into the path of an onrushing vehicle. The vendors added to the colorful fabric of Dar es Salaam. Marcie could see various open shops where owners of all ages hawked everything from fruit and grains to woven baskets and bracelets.

The Western-style hotel Marcie was staying in seemed incongruous among the other buildings in the area and even more so as they made their way towards the bus terminal. Shacks were constructed of whatever materials could be scrounged, including Coca Cola signs, rusted corrugated metal and pieces of weathered plywood. Wires stretched from a satellite dish on one structure to several other houses in the neighborhood. Marcie thought that surely it was a case of misplaced priorities when a satellite dish requiring a monthly fee was attached to the roof while an outdoor toilet sat behind the house. As they passed the bus depot, a dizzying variety of buses vied for space with the passengers who clambered to find their correct one. The Tanzania Law School campus sat just a few streets away to one side of the bus terminal, attracting the best and the brightest students, but other streets in the neighborhood attracted a far less desirable class of people.

Marcie became aware that the second area was where Godfrey was taking her. As the old car moved along at a snail's pace through the melee of traffic, the population was becoming even denser. Suddenly, there were few cars on the streets. It was as if they had all dropped off the face of the earth. The houses appeared to be drawing closer as if being pushed from behind by a tsunami. The sun was obliterated by the roofs hanging into the streets, and an eerie darkness enveloped the area. People sat on chairs in the doorways, and gangs of youths with their pants hanging at half mast loitered along the route. A toot from the old car caused them to grudgingly shuffle out of the way, but not before hurling an obscenity at the driver. Cat whistles followed when they caught sight of Marcie in the back seat.

Marcie jumped as a leering youth rushed forward and banged on the window, grabbing his crotch and rolling his tongue. As he did so, his shirttail pulled aside, revealing a handgun weighing down the top of his torn jeans. Other youths took turns pounding on the car and gesturing with both hands for Marcie to join them. Godfrey forged ahead, blowing his horn. Finally, the young men seemed to be satisfied that they had terrified the passenger enough and they fell away from the car. That prompted raucous laughter and high-fives all around as they sauntered back to resume their vigil. The one with the gun swaggered back with the rest, the middle finger of his left hand held high.

Marcie knew how it was in the underprivileged areas. They were streets of despair. There was a feeling of frustration, nothing to do, lack of guidance, jealousy of those who had more. It was a complex subject for which there was no easy answer.

Marcie felt confident that she could handle herself – but a jolt of apprehension still shot through her. *I don't know this country. I can't speak the language. Why am I doing this? What am I going to find when I go into that house?*

The answer quickly overcame the negative thoughts. *I just have to find out what happened to those girls. I can't fix everything but maybe I can help girls at home who lose their way if I understand better how things work here.* A hundred more yards down the road and the driver stopped. "The house you seek is down this street. Turn left at the corner and continue to the next side street. It is the second house in. But I must ask you again, please don't do this."

"I have to, Godfrey. I have to go in. Just wait for me here."

As Marcie got out of the car, the motor shuddered and died and the driver's side door squealed as it opened.

The old man was spry for his age. He quickly rounded the corner of the vehicle and said, "Okay then, I'm coming with you. You need a translator." His voice wasn't as firm and confident when he said it, betraying a nervousness that was unsettling.

Marcie smiled and put her hand on his arm. She was grateful for his willingness to help. "Thank you, Godfrey. You are a true gentleman. We will just go in and ask what happened to the girls and leave. It will only take a few minutes."

Godfrey nodded solemnly. He didn't seem convinced.

Chapter 9

Marcie walked with Godfrey back down the street past the vendors and occupants of the shacks. The hustle and bustle of the city core was nowhere to be seen. People were scattered up and down the streets, but it was chillingly subdued. No laughter. Vacant eyes stared from heavily-hooded lids as the unusual pair passed by. The men lounged and smoked or played dominoes. Some of the women busied themselves hanging laundry or pouring dirty water in the street where Marcie thought it would inevitably mix with the water used for drinking. There was an overwhelming stench in the neighborhood and garbage from overflowing piles blew along the narrow street. Vendors quietly held out their wares trying to scrape together a living, touching the interlopers, begging them to buy. Not the lively and enchanting chaos and discord of the markets downtown.

Children played soccer with a ball of twine in the dusty street – the only sign of real life. They laughed and challenged each other as kids anywhere would. Marcie hoped they would somehow be given the opportunity to grow up to fulfill their dreams and not follow in the footsteps of the young men who had harassed them in the taxi earlier. Unfortunately, those young men would be the role models and the cycle was likely to continue unless the children somehow found their way out of the area. Their game was interrupted when they spotted the two newcomers and the youngsters stopped playing to surround them, begging for money. Most had bare feet and clothing hung loosely on their bodies, suggesting the garments had originally been worn by older siblings. Godfrey pushed them away, and he and Marcie purposefully continued walking with taunts ringing in their ears.

As they turned the corner towards their destination, the heat became even more oppressive as the walls seemed to advance towards the pair. Marcie had to concentrate to avoid the rocks strewn long the path, but Godfrey skipped over and around them and plunged ahead. Marcie could almost reach out and touch the walls of houses on either side of her. She guessed that each building somehow housed large families. Clotheslines stretching from house to house threatened to decapitate her with each step she took.

They stopped. *This must be the house Godfrey referred to.* A thin rusted metal barrier separated the interior from the narrow street. Godfrey called out in Swahili to the occupants, and a grunt in response was apparently an invitation to enter as he pushed aside the barrier.

As her eyes darted back and forth, Marcie examined the dark and completely bare front room. The only light came from the sun illuminating the floor through a hole in the wall that served as a window and a flickering blue glow in the back room. The sounds of an action movie echoed in the back of the building, providing a deep and abiding contrast to the stark walls in the front. Godfrey ignored it, steadfastly leading the way into the back of the house.

Marcie's eyes widened at the sight over Godfrey's shoulder. A young muscular man in a green t-shirt sat behind a desk, a stack of American money in front of him. His angular face bore a skimpy beard. His bulging biceps nudged the bottom of his short sleeves up towards his shoulders. A gun rested on the table. Marcie thought she recognized it as being similar to one she shot at the range. Lines of a white substance and a straw lay on the table beside the gun. The movie sounds boomed from large speakers connected to what had to be a 65-inch television set. Marcie judged the man, who was of African descent, to be in his late twenties. He was busy entering something into an expensive laptop computer and had yet to look up. His furrowed brow and the slow tapping with one finger on the keyboard indicated that the work was a challenge for him. He seemed to be oblivious to them being in the same room.

Godfrey waited for the man to say something. Finally, a few words spilled out in Swahili. Godfrey responded. When the man finally looked up, his lips barely moved as he uttered in perfect but slurred English, "And who's she? Why'd you bring her here?"

Marcie could see the man's pupils were dilated, likely from the narcotic on the table. She put her hand on Godfrey's arm to quiet him and replied calmly, "My name is Marcie Kane. I was visiting a school dormitory and met two young ladies who may have come here. If they are here, I would like to talk to them."

More slurring. "Two young girls? Do you see them, Marcie Kane? Maybe they are under my desk, yes? Or under the floor? I can tell you are American. My house is not like yours in America with its many rooms. It's pretty obvious there are no girls here."

Marcie continued in an even voice, "Are you Mr. Smith? I understand a man by that name suggested the girls be brought to this location. I would just like to know where they are or where they went from here. Then we will leave." She felt Godfrey tense beside her.

The reaction was so sudden that Marcie stumbled back towards the door, her eyes wide. The chair flew backwards, crashing against the wall behind the desk as the man leapt to his feet. The laptop jumped on the table and money fluttered to the floor. Some of the white substance drifted into the air. With the finality of the flick of a switch, the man's calm demeanor disappeared, eyes narrowing, his nostrils flared like a wild stallion. Whatever he was on seemed to enhance his reflexes and his anger level as in one motion he swept the gun from the table and pressed it into Godfrey's throat before the old man could move.

The man was screaming now, his face only a few inches from Godfrey's. "WHY DID YOU BRING HER HERE, OLD MAN? WHY DOES SHE KNOW ABOUT MR. SMITH? DO YOU HAVE A DEATH WISH?"

Marcie's hands shot up in a pleading gesture. The gun barrel pressing into the soft flesh in Godfrey's throat created an indentation. Her voice was not as steady as she would have liked. "Please, don't hurt him. He was just trying to help me. It's obvious we have made a mistake. We will just leave and forget we were ever here."

The man's head slowly turned towards Marcie, his eyes slowly undressing her as they roved up and down her tight jeans and dirty shirt. His lips curled in a sneer. A sudden bloom of cold swept across Marcie's body.

He shouted, "Suleiman, get in here." He was unsteady on his feet. The gun now wandered shakily between Marcie and Godfrey.

Marcie endeavored to control her trembling. *What did I get us into? I will never forgive myself if Godfrey gets hurt.*

Her apprehension ratcheted up a notch when she saw the young man who came into the room. He must have been just outside the front door waiting because his arrival took only seconds. It was the leering young man from the street with the gun tucked into his jeans. He had a smirk on his face.

She couldn't understand the language but the implication was clear from the fear reflected in Godfrey's eyes. Something bad was going to happen.

Suleiman withdrew the gun from the waist band of his pants and grabbed Godfrey by the shirt, nearly pulling him off his feet. Godfrey struggled, but the younger man's grip was too strong. The older man was silently pleading, his eyes wavering back and forth between Marcie and the muscular man who now had his gun leveled at her chest. His pulse was visible in a vein bulging in his neck.

Sulieman dragged the stumbling Godfrey through the door and outside to follow his boss' orders. Marcie watched them go silently, her eyes a mixture of confusion and fear. *What is he going to do with me?* Her answer wasn't long in coming. The man traced the gun barrel down between her breasts and across her flat stomach.

Marcie said shakily, "We made a mistake coming here. I understand that now. Please don't let Sulieman hurt Godfrey. This was all my idea. Is it money you want? I can arrange that."

The man stopped outlining her body with his gun and moved it from his right to his left hand. His heavy eyes sought out Marcie's and a dry chuckle rose from his throat. Marcie forced her eyes to remain trained on his.

He sneered, "You think I need money, Marcie Kane? Where will you get this money?" He gestured towards her with the gun. "You can't even afford a clean shirt." Saliva hit Marcie as he snorted. "Look around you. The stack of money on the table is mine. The big-ass television set is mine. I can get more money any time I want, and all I have to do is process girls like the ones you seek."

The gun started following its path again moving up and down her thighs. Marcie felt her stomach muscles contract at the thought of what the man had in mind.

She tried one more time. "What . . . what do you mean by 'process'?"

His response was a sneer as he moved behind her. His gun barrel wandered across her buttocks and between her legs as he leaned forward with his mouth against her ear. He whispered, "I give them a new identity, buy them airline tickets to a new life and send them on their way. I never see them again. I do what Mr. Smith tells me to do and for that I'm paid very well."

Marcie's heart nearly stopped beating. She asked in a quivering voice, "Where did you send Shoni Batanga and Irene Sembaza?" She thought if she could keep him talking, it would buy her some time. For what she wasn't quite sure.

But the man's mood swings were impossible to anticipate. He whirled around to face Marcie once again. "That's enough talk, Marcie Kane. Now we have a little fun."

Marcie turned to run and the man quickly shot forward and grabbed her by the back of her t-shirt, ripping it at the neck. His reaction time was incredible. He spun her around and slapped her hard with an open hand, snapping Marcie's head back. She cried out at the blow and her face stung as if she had run into a swarm of angry bees. Her eyes watered and her ears roared. Her hand immediately went to the spot where it felt like her face was about to crumble into a thousand pieces.

The man once again spun her around and violently shoved her head forward. She had to put her hands out to prevent herself from landing face first on the table. Her elbow landed painfully on the white powder, grinding it into the hard surface. The computer crashed to the floor as the table rocked forward from her weight. The man's left hand was under her shirt, roughly fumbling with her breast. Squeezing. Pinching. His right hand still holding the gun was on her back, pushing her head forward and down.

Marcie struggled in his grasp just enough to make the man feel that she was trying to resist his unwanted advance. He was so strong that he could easily overpower her and to resist was futile. Marcie grimaced and her stomach churned with revulsion, but a new emotion was slowly bubbling to the surface. Rage was taking over. All-encompassing, overwhelming rage. Her face still hurt but that was fueling the fire that was building within. So did the fact that this monster was helping lead young girls into a life of who-knows-what. The blurred table that was right in front of her face was coming into focus as her eyes that had been watering from the blow slowly cleared. She blinked rapidly. Her hands clenched and unclenched. She knew she would have one chance. And it was coming.

The man was panting hard. He muttered incoherently as he tore at her. Marcie could feel his arousal against her buttocks. He removed his hand from her breast and his groping moved to her sides, his thumbs inside the waistband of her jeans, yanking at them to get them down over her hips. In his haste, he hadn't bothered to undo the top button and the jeans resisted. The action meant that the gun was pointing harmlessly towards the ceiling and his full concentration was on removing the obstacle that was preventing him from completing the violation.

Now!

Marcie raised her right leg and drove the solid heel of her hiking boot as hard as she could into his knee, scraping it all the way down the shin to land with as much force as she could muster onto his instep. She could hear the whoosh of air along with a curse in Swahili escape from the man's lips as she connected with the nerves and small bones at the top of his sandaled foot. She then brought her leg forward and drove it back in an attempt to connect with his groin, but his leg was in the air after the assault and her attack was thwarted. The movement caused him to bend forward as he concentrated on the pain in his leg. The taller man's face was now within striking distance, and Marcie's head shot back towards its target. It was a direct hit, driving his nose back into his face. The man roared with pain and when she spun around, both his hands held his shattered nose, trying to stop the flow of blood. The gun was again pointing towards the ceiling.

While the drugs may have sharpened his reflexes, the man's thought process was slowed. While he was concentrating on his nose, Marcie aimed another kick at his other knee and connected. She drove her boot into the joint with as much force as she could, and he toppled like a giant oak felled by a chainsaw, howling in pain. The gun clattered to the floor but didn't leave his grasp. She grabbed at the gun but it simply caused him to tighten his grip. Marcie sprinted for the door but incredibly, he ignored the pain and rolled over, swinging his free hand and catching her foot just above the ankle. Marcie sprawled hard on the concrete floor. She could feel the skin on her knees open as they scraped on the abrasive surface.

From the corner of her eye, she caught a glimpse of the man trying desperately to struggle to his feet on his ruined knee. She scrambled to regain her own balance and half running, half crawling and fueled by fear, she stumbled towards the opening leading to the outside. Luckily, the metal barrier had been left aside.

As awkward as it felt, being off-balance saved her life. As she staggered through the doorway, the retort of the pistol reverberated around the concrete interior and a bullet shaved shards of concrete from the cinder block where her head would have been if she had been upright. A few small pieces struck her cheek and above her eye, opening cuts as easily as sharp scissors cut through tissue paper.

Marcie swiped the blood from her eye and ran through the opening, tracing her steps back to where Godfrey had parked the car. Her ears hissed from the gun blast in the enclosed space. She carefully ducked under the clothes lines and avoided the rocks. The car wasn't there. *What happened to Godfrey? What had Suleiman done to him? Where's the damn car?* She crept back to the corner and peered around to see her silent questions partially answered. Suleiman was running in her direction with his gun drawn. The muscular man was limping behind, bellowing with each step.

There was no time to waste. Marcie ran again. As she looked over her shoulder, she tripped on a rock and sprawled in the mud that a recent rain, or perhaps sewer water, had created. Gathering herself, she thought *I can outrun them but to go where? This isn't my turf. I don't know where I'm going.* It was a rabbit warren of houses tightly woven together like a carpet. Some of the paths separating the houses were merely that, wide enough for foot traffic. Others allowed just enough room for a single car to pass. She could easily get lost and turn right into the arms of her pursuers. She had to get out of there. She turned a corner immediately and there was Suleiman at the other end of the street. Their eyes met. The gun rose and a shot sent the few people who hadn't already retreated into their homes or scurrying to the nearest cover they could find. Some simply dove for the ground or hid behind any object that might provide protection. Marcie had no idea where the shot went, but she wasn't about to stick around to find out.

She turned back in the direction she had come and ducked down an alleyway, nearly knocking over a wide-eyed little girl whose head came to Marcie's thighs. She judged the girl to be about five years old. Marcie put her index finger to her lips in the universal gesture for the little girl to stay quiet. The girl seemed to understand immediately. She looked at Marcie and then at a pile of trash sitting a few feet in front of a shack. Her eyes shifted back and forth between Marcie and the pile of trash until Marcie realized the girl was trying to tell her something.

Marcie nodded to the girl and hurried to the pile, kneeling down behind it. A badly torn canvas tarp lay partially concealed by the trash. It was made of a heavy brown material that had been badly stained during its useful life. Marcie had no time to contemplate what the stains might be. In spite of the abuse the tarp had been given, she knew it would not remain with the garbage for long as someone would claim it to use for bedding or protection from the elements in their house. The stench emanating from the pile assaulted her nostrils and tears glistened at the corners of her eyes. Marcie held her breath and did a quick check for her pursuers. Sulieman and the muscular man stood at the head of the alleyway, conferring. The little girl watched the two gunmen wordlessly. After much arm waving and with an elevated voice, the muscular man sent Sulieman in the opposite direction and limped towards the little girl

Marcie moved further into the shadows of the garbage and did the only thing she could. She sucked in her breath and clambered under the tarp. With a little shuffling, she was able to arrange one of the small openings in the cloth so that she could observe the little girl. Bile shot into her throat, partly from fear but more from her proximity to the smell of something rotting in the sun, buried in the pile that lay directly in front of her.

The girl, who was barefoot and wore a cheap dress that hung loosely like it was two sizes too big for her, stood with her eyes locked on the big man as he approached. As he drew closer, she averted her eyes, fidgeted and kicked at the dirt. The man was close enough to the pint size girl now that Marcie could hear his labored breathing, undoubtedly caused by his swollen nose and damaged instep and knee. Marcie stopped her own breath and waited.

Please, please don't tell him I'm here.

The big man knelt down in front of the little girl, placing his enormous hand on her chin and roughly jerked her face up to look at his. Marcie couldn't understand what he was saying but the intention was clear. He was asking about her in a nasal tone. The little girl's hands trembled visibly but her gaze was unwavering. She was frightened but trying desperately not to show it. Her large, round dark eyes stared at the big man in front of her. There was an interminable silence and finally she raised her tiny hand. This is it, Marcie thought. *She's going to point at me. I have to be ready to fight . . . or run for my life.* Marcie's fingers worked towards the edge of the tarp. She was prepared to throw it off and make a run for it.

The little girl straightened her shoulders as she seemed to gain confidence. Her hand was rising ever so slowly, and she jerked her chin from the man's grasp at the same time. She slowly turned away from the pile of garbage hiding Marcie's location, dragging the big man's eyes with her movement as if connected by a rope. She was finally facing the opposite direction away from Marcie, pointing directly down the alley towards the street. She murmured something in a voice barely above a whisper that Marcie could scarcely hear from her vantage point.

Marcie put her hand over her mouth to stifle a gasp as the big man growled and rather than going around the little girl, pushed her backwards hard enough that she fell hard in the dirt. Hotness spread through Marcie's cheeks at the scene she had just witnessed. She breathed out as she watched the despicable man hobble down the street away from her hiding spot.

In spite of her anger, Marcie didn't move. She observed the little girl who watched the awkward gait of the wounded man walking towards the end of the street. The little girl got up, dusted off her dress as best she could and with her hands on her hips, she put every ounce of her tiny being into sticking her tongue out at the man's back. Marcie stifled a smile as the little girl approached her hiding spot. Throwing back the tarp, she emerged to grasp the little hand that was outstretched towards her. As Marcie rose from her kneeling position, she noted that the street that had so little activity minutes before was now completely deserted. An eerie quiet had settled over the community. She took in long deep refreshing breaths. Marcie felt herself being tugged along by the tiny person who was apparently trying to protect her. She had no idea where they were going but she had a feeling that the little girl, who seemed to be street-smart way beyond her years, had a destination in mind.

Maybe, just maybe, this tiny girl was going to be her savior.

Chapter 10

The little girl's feet slipped in the loose gravel as she tugged Marcie by the hand to an entrance three houses down and dragged her inside. As they entered, she wordlessly pointed through an opening. She waved her hand, signifying that Marcie should exit through the window. Marcie couldn't believe someone so young understood the situation and was actually trying to save her.

In a gesture similar to the one used by the man the little girl had just betrayed, Marcie rested her hands on the girl's shoulders. It was a much gentler action. She pointed to herself. "Marcie," she said quietly. With her eyebrows raised and mouthing the word, "You?' she pointed at the little girl. She motioned in similar fashion twice, and the little girl finally pointed her finger at herself and said with her head bowed, swinging her tiny shoulders and trying to dig a hole in the concrete floor with her shoe, "Malaika." Marcie bent down and gave the little girl a kiss on the top of her head. The dark eyes widened even more and her face creased into a big smile. Her arms wrapped around Marcie in a warm hug. Marcie's limited Swahili vocabulary had forsaken her, but she mouthed the words in English to the little girl. "What a pretty name. Thank you, Malaika."

Marcie climbed through the opening and after three steps, she stopped to look back. The little girl's head and shoulders extended through the opening and she was pointing. Marcie blew a kiss to the girl and ran in the direction she was being directed. She turned a corner and could see a crowd gathered around something on the street. Apparently accustomed to gunshots on the streets, they had re-emerged from their hiding spots. There was such a crowd that she couldn't make out any details, but the hair stood to attention on her arms and the back of her neck. She plunged into the crowd, clearing the onlookers out of her way.

Expressionless faces stared as she pushed on. The chatter quieted. As she got past the final row, it was apparent they were peering inside Godfrey's car.

She dreaded what she would find. *What was everyone staring at?* One older man stood between her and the driver's door, and she grabbed him by the arm and wrenched him aside. His body tensed at the sudden interruption as his fist rose, ready to lash out at his attacker. But he saw Marcie and stepped away.

Marcie's mouth went dry and she clutched her hands to her chest. Godfrey sat slumped over the steering wheel. *Oh my God! What had they done to him?* His face was a mass of welts and his shirt was changing colour as blood from his nose pooled on his chest. His eyes were swollen shut. Marcie's body heaved in a shudder and bile raced up her throat at the speed of a bullet train. Guilt aimed its knife directly at her heart and scored a direct hit. I am responsible for this, she thought, shaking violently. *Is . . . is he dead?*

Suddenly Godfrey coughed, and his chest rose and fell in a slow, uneven rhythm. At least he was still alive! Marcie yanked on the driver's side door and it protested, not wanting to yield. She pulled harder, nearly hitting the man she had shoved aside who was now peering in the front window. The door's hinges shrieked as the rust yielded to her efforts. She tried to push Godfrey towards the passenger side, but she was unable to budge the weight of his unconscious body. A soft moan escaped from his swollen lips.

The man who had been in Marcie's way ran to the passenger side of the car and pulled the door open. He reached across the seat and dragged Godfrey to the passenger side. Marcie slammed the driver's side door as she climbed behind the wheel.

As she turned the key to start the car, the man who had gone from nearly hitting Marcie to helping her move Godfrey so she could get in the car, pulled open the back door. He jumped in. As Marcie turned the key in the ignition and the car's engine tried unsuccessfully to start, she turned to examine him. He appeared to be younger than Godfrey, but there was a distinct similarity. Thousands of hours in the unforgiving African sun had formed deep creases in his dried skin. He wore the traditional white ankle-length tunic, which Marcie understood to be a kanzu, and a colorful flat cap on his head, which she recognized as a kofia.

As the words sprang into Marcie's mouth to tell him to leave, the stranger pointed to the unconscious man slouched in the front seat and said, "Godfrey. Brother." He then pointed to himself and said, "Francis." Marcie didn't know whether they were brothers by blood or by association, but she wasn't about to quiz the man in a language she surmised he wouldn't understand anyway. At the same time, she recognized an angry sound, like a bull bellowing in the pasture. The crowd around the car scattered, leaving her staring out the front window at a frightening apparition she recognized only too well moving toward her from the far end of the street. She knew the muscular man would have his gun aimed at her. Marcie frantically stomped the gas and turned the key again and again, but the car only grumbled. "COME ON!" she admonished, wildly pumping the gas pedal, trying to will the old car to kick into life. She saw the man narrowing the distance between them as he raised his gun, taking direct aim at the front windshield.

Marcie saw the gun kick and the windshield shattered, spraying Marcie and Godfrey with jagged shards of glass. The bullet slammed into the seat between them just as the car finally responded. Marcie jammed it hard into reverse and it lurched backwards, almost unwilling to make the effort to move. She turned the steering wheel at the same time as she heard more retorts from the gun and saw out of the corner of her eye one of the bystanders who had been surrounding the car slump to the ground, obviously hit. *This is becoming a war zone. We've got to get out!*

The car's nose spun through the dust and pebbles thrown up by the sliding tires. Marcie stomped on the brake and felt it touch the floor. At the last second, the brakes engaged and the car slid to a rocking stop on suspension that had long ago deteriorated to the point of non existence. A grunt came from the back seat as Francis was flung from one side of the car to the other. Marcie's breathing thickened as the dust seeping through the shattered front window clogged her throat.

A thick brown and blue fog hung in the street. There was no breeze to disperse the mixture of dust and smoke in the humid African air. A strong smell of burned oil left behind by the sliding car penetrated Marcie's nostrils. The gear shift nearly broke in her hand as she rammed it into drive. The old car heaved forward with the tires spraying a shower of pebbles towards the shacks on the narrow street. Marcie hoped she was aiming the vehicle in the right direction.

As the old car charged through the cloud, Marcie could see Suleiman a few feet ahead. He must have switched direction and come from the opposite end of the street. He had the gun pointed in the classic two-handed firing position, but there wasn't enough time for him to get off a shot. As she aimed the car straight for him, the only thing occupying Marcie's mind was the horrific beating Godfrey had received. With the car bearing down on him, Sulieman leapt aside seconds before becoming a hood ornament on the old vehicle.

Marcie marveled at how the car was responding, as if it had wakened from a deep coma and was now prepared to give her everything it could muster. It was like it knew its owner needed help and it was working to its dying breath to save the man. She kept one hand on the wheel and the other on the horn, trying to avoid the people who had come to see what was going on. They were quick to leap out of the way of the mad woman driving the car.

"Hang on, Godfrey," she pleaded as she drove.

Marcie was so focused on everything happening around her that she jumped when Francis spoke from the back, his voice quivering slightly.

"Hospitali. Ilala."

After Francis repeated it, Marcie finally interpreted Ilala to be the name of the street where the hospital was situated. Godfrey was gasping for air through his swollen lips in the front seat beside her, while Francis leaned forward speaking words of encouragement to him in Swahili and directing Marcie with wild gestures. Marcie feared they were losing the old man and she herded the ancient vehicle as fast as she dared through the narrow turns of the decrepit community. The old car responded as only the aged can when required, even managing to fishtail around some of the tighter corners, spraying the residents with stones and gravel. Marcie pushed on. All she could think of was, this is all my fault. *Godfrey was only trying to protect me, and look what had happened. I don't want to be responsible for the death of the father of 11 children, especially after everything he has done for me.*

With Francis' medley of Swahili, hand gestures and a few English words, they finally escaped the broken community and found themselves back in the hustle and bustle of vibrant downtown Dar es Salaam. It was a straight drive along some of the main thoroughfares to the hospital. Marcie was concerned they would be stopped by the police for the trail of blue smoke the car was leaving behind, but then she realized other cars were doing the same. She kept the accelerator to the floor. With Francis leaning over the front seat gesturing and the old car reluctantly giving its all, it took a total of 18 minutes, although it seemed like an eternity. Marcie prayed it was not too much time for Godfrey.

Marcie skidded to a stop at the front entrance of the white building where the car promptly gasped and died. The driver's door once again squealed indignantly at being forced open, and it ricocheted back at Marcie after she flung it wide in frustration. Marcie nearly lost her balance as she charged around the front of the car and rushed through the entrance of the hospital, motioning wildly towards the car and the occupant in the front seat. Her voice echoed in the hallway as patients and hospital staff alike stared in shocked silence.

A young woman in the green uniform of a hospital attendant approached Marcie, gesturing for her to be quiet and sternly pointing at a vacant chair. Simultaneously, the attendant dabbed at Marcie's face with a white cloth. Marcie pushed the nurse away, vigorously shook her head and pointed again at the vehicle sitting outside. *Not me, him!* The nurse finally understood and turned away, but Marcie was shocked to see red stains on the cloth the nurse had used to wipe her face. She had completely forgotten about the shards of concrete that had torn her skin.

The nurse summoned help and four attendants pushed a gurney to the car. They gently nudged Francis aside and lifted Godfrey onto the cart. A nurse intermittently compressed the old man's chest as he was wheeled back into the hospital and disappeared around a corner into the bowels of the building. Francis was stopped at the door to the corridor where Godfrey had been taken. Marcie could see wetness around his closed eyes and his silently moving lips indicated that he was saying a prayer.

Marcie had never felt more frustrated and distraught. She couldn't speak the language. She didn't know how badly Godfrey was hurt or if he would even survive. She had been beaten and shot at for simply asking questions about two girls she knew very little about. She was obviously in real danger. What if the two men were even now pursuing her to finish what they'd started? They wouldn't have much trouble finding her, and she had no one to protect her.

Marcie sought out a chair in the waiting room beside Francis. Her body was shaking uncontrollably and she bit her lip to hold back the torrent of hot tears that threatened to drown her.

I can't believe everything that just happened, she thought. *What have I done?*

Marcie took one, two, three long, deep breaths to still her body's shaking and repositioned herself in the chair so that she could see Francis more clearly. He was bent forward as if from stomach cramps. His hands rested by his side and his eyes stared unseeing between his knees. Marcie put her hand gently on his arm and said softly, "Francis, do you speak English?"

Francis turned towards Marcie and the look in his sad eyes was replaced by confusion. A shake of his head was accompanied by a shrug. Marcie tried to ask the same question in Francis' native tongue using the Swahili she had committed to memory from the travel book she had purchased before leaving home.

She said haltingly, "Je unajua kuzungumza kiingereza?"

Francis' eyes flickered but the response was still negative as indicated by another shake of his head.

Marcie nodded. She raised her hand, pointed to her chest and then to the front door of the hospital. She aimed her index and second finger downward and wiggled them back and forth in a walking motion. She said simply, "Polisi."

Francis nodded again and his mouth formed an "O." From everything Marcie had heard, she could only interpret his look to mean, "Good luck with the police, lady." She rose from the chair, once again giving the old man a reassuring pat on the shoulder. She wanted to ask a nurse about Godfrey's condition before she left, but there was no one in sight. She couldn't wait. She needed to get to the police station as quickly as possible. There was nothing she could do here right now. As she turned towards the door, the same nurse who had applied the cloth to her face burst through the entrance of the corridor where Godfrey had been taken.

"How is he?" Marcie asked, immediately.

Her query was met with a wave of the hand, indicating not so well. "You next," the nurse said as she looked at Marcie's bloodstained face. She started to take Marcie by the elbow and steer her towards the corridor.

"Oh no, I'm not," Marcie said, firmly removing her arm from the nurse's grasp and turning towards the counter. Before the nurse could react, Marcie reached over the counter to find a pen and paper and scribbled a note to Godfrey. Writing quickly, she wished Godfrey well and told him she would be back soon. She thanked him for everything he had done, signed the note and pressed the folded paper into the nurse's hands. Marcie pointed at Godfrey's name and repeated it out loud.

The nurse nodded her head in understanding, but at the same time the muscles in her face tightened and her jaw set. She picked up a handheld mirror and held it out with her other hand placed firmly on her hip. Marcie took the mirror and looked with some trepidation. A large cut over her left eye lay open exposing the bone underneath and leaking a trail of blood down the side of her face. A series of smaller cuts formed a roadmap below her left eye. The right side of her face was swollen from the blow she had received at the house, and her eye was partially closed. Her hair that she had recently allowed to grow out was plastered to her forehead as if glued in place.

Whoa! Marcie hadn't realized the extent of her injuries, and they left her shocked. *I look like I've been through a war,* she thought. And in some ways, clearly she had. She handed the mirror back to the nurse and said, "Well, all right, I guess I need a couple of stitches. I hope it won't take long."

Chapter 11

Marcie stared at her face in the hotel room. The ragged stitches in her forehead weren't pretty but they would suffice until she could get home to her own doctor. The other scrapes, cuts and bruises were minor by comparison, but together they told an ugly story that could, and probably would be interpreted a hundred different ways by anyone noticing her. She had already felt the eyes upon her when she walked through the hotel lobby. Now she could see why. She made a mental note to buy a pair of extra large sunglasses for the trip home.

Marcie contemplated changing out of her bloodied and ripped t-shirt and dirty torn blue jeans, but then thought better of it. The taxi was waiting on the street to take her to the police station, and undoubtedly her disheveled appearance would make her story more convincing. She knew she would need all the help she could muster. She'd been told repeatedly that slipping enough money into the right hands could produce immediate results when nothing else would. She determined to do whatever was necessary to make the police pay attention. She had decided to stop at the hotel to retrieve some monetary lubricant to loosen any screws that may have been tightened by corruption and greed.

Marcie knew before she left for her trip that policing in Tanzania was a problem, but she had never thought it would affect her. Why would *she* need to come in contact with Tanzanian law enforcement officials? The guide books had told her that the police are hindered by a lack of resources, low salaries, not enough vehicles and lack of proper training. She had read that sometimes they wouldn't respond to complaints at all; or, if they did, that a report may be taken but there would be no follow-up investigation. In fact, the guidebook said, a national poll had determined that the populace believed the police and judiciary to be the most corrupt institutions in the country. Not very encouraging news. Only now she was about to find out for herself whether this was true.

The taxi ride to the police station was short and quiet as Marcie pondered how she was going to approach the situation. She tried not to listen to a small nagging voice in the back of her mind that wondered if she was a magnet for trouble. First the bullet wounds in her shoulder from two years ago and now this. *It seems that without meaning to, I'm attracting danger. Worse than that, people keep shooting at me.* She didn't think she went looking for trouble, but there was no doubt that it was finding her with no problem.

The police station was a large, flat building located near the western style hotels in downtown Dar es Salaam. Marcie entered and was greeted by an attractive woman in civilian clothes at the reception desk. She was polite and easily switched to English as soon as Marcie started to speak. Marcie was surprised that no comment was forthcoming about her appearance, but she supposed the receptionist had seen everything in her job. The woman punched a code into a lock that opened a door into a large open concept room with cubicles in parallel rows down the center and along the sides. Uniformed officers and plain-clothed workers occupied some of the cubicles, but many sat empty. As Marcie walked along the corridor, she could hear groups of people talking quietly among themselves. Fingers tapped on the few computers in the room, and a printer whirred to life in a central location at the end of the corridor. A large computer screen on one wall was attracting the attention of people gathered around it.

Marcie was responding to the receptionist's question about how she was doing when a tall man wearing a blue bomber jacket, an open-necked pale yellow shirt and dark well-pressed pants approached. His gaze fell first on the receptionist and then drifted to Marcie. An easy smile revealed sparkling white teeth, and he nodded to Marcie as they turned sideways to squeeze past each other in the narrow corridor between the two center rows of cubicles. Marcie judged him to be in his early forties and definitely worthy of a second glance. As he turned, one side of his jacket caught on his arm and the butt end of a gun peeked out at the two women from its shoulder holster.

Marcie started to ask about the man, but they had arrived at their destination and she was directed into a small cubicle in the corner of the room. It contained an inexpensive desk and two old wheeled chairs. A battered filing cabinet, its paint peeling, took up valuable space in one corner of the cubicle. It appeared to be sagging miserably from the pile of papers and files hanging off the edges. Marcie was directed towards the chair at the end of the desk, as the other was occupied by a stern-faced African man in a khaki uniform with dark brown high-cut boots. A red cap sat jauntily on his head. It was the only thing jaunty about him. He appeared exhausted to Marcie, and his dour expression and the way he slouched in his chair implied that he would rather be anywhere else than talking to her. The thought of the alert good-looking man in the jacket was but a fleeting memory.

Here we go, thought Marcie as she made eye contact with the foreboding countenance across the desk from her. His eyes drifted down long enough to take in her torn, bloodied shirt and dirty jeans before returning to her face. Marcie thought it's like staring at Mount Rushmore and expecting one of the presidents to speak. Nothing. Their stony staring match seemed to last forever as Marcie waited for some indication that he was going to take her report. The desk was littered with piles of paper. Marcie glanced at a blank notepad and pen, which sat prominently on top of the mess but which the officer made no effort to pick up. Was she supposed to give money to this statue before they even started?

Finally, he leaned forward, cocked an eyebrow and turned his hands upwards as if to say, "Well?" Marcie started to speak, "My name is Marcie Kane. I want to report an incident that took place a few hours ago. I was beaten and shot at, and my friend is in the hospital after he was also beaten. I was trying to find two girls who ran away from their school, and there was this man with a gun who . . . " The words poured out of her until the officer held up his hand like a traffic cop and shook his head rapidly from side to side.

Marcie sighed heavily and she rubbed the back of her neck. She was on the verge of tears. Nearly coming up out of her seat, she leaned over the desk toward the officer and in a voice she barely recognized, cried, "What is it? Is it money you want?" She dug in her purse. "Will *that* help you understand?" The shock of everything that had happened to her in the past 24 hours combined with this man sitting so smugly in front of her was just too much. She was ready to curl up in a corner and scream.

Marcie felt a hand on her shoulder, and a soothing voice said in perfect English, "Maybe I can help you." It was the tall, attractive man she had passed earlier in the corridor. Walking around in front of her, he continued, "The officer here doesn't speak English very well, but he does understand some. His name is Inspector Choyo. There is no need to get out your money, Miss . . .?" His voice trailed off but he waited expectantly.

Marcie looked up into his dark eyes, and tried not to react to his unusually handsome features. "Thank you," she said gratefully, adding, "I'm Marcie Kane from St Petersburg, Florida in the U.S. "Glancing down at her bloodied, torn clothing, she continued more calmly, "I want to report a very serious incident that happened to me a few hours ago, but I don't seem to be getting anywhere." She nodded towards the officer. "This man doesn't seem interested in taking my report."

"Well, that may be a little judgmental, Ms. Kane. He wasn't suggesting you give him money. Inspector Choyo here saw me coming and was just suggesting you wait until I got here. We're working on a case together, so when I heard you speaking English to the receptionist, I thought I might be able to help. At least I can take your report, have it translated and make sure that the police here deal with it. I will be leaving the country in a couple of days, but these gentlemen have been helpful to me, so I would like to return the favor. Besides that, I have some free time. Now, it appears you've had a rough time recently. How would it be if we move to a quieter room and start from the beginning?" He held his hand out to Marcie. "My name is Nathan Harris. I'm with the FBI. Would you like some coffee?"

Chapter 12

Marcie tried to process the information she had just heard as she followed Nathan Harris and Inspector Choyo to a small enclosed room, which was furnished in the same minimalistic fashion as the cubicles. The only difference was that there was a little more room to move around. Her mind raced. *He said he's with the FBI! The FBI? Why in Africa?* She could still feel his strong hand shaking hers only a minute or two before.

The coffee that Harris had ordered arrived along with a sugar bowl. Marcie was so tired that the nice strong coffee and jolt of sugar would surely be just what she needed to revive her spirits. After a few sips, she knew she'd feel ready to tell her story. She reached for the sugar bowl but then drew her spoon back quickly with a small exclamation as she discovered she wasn't the only one who would be enjoying the sweet granules. She looked again before deciding to let the parade of ants running around in the sugar bowl enjoy someone else's coffee.

Nathan Harris had a bemused look on his face. "Local protein," he said with a chuckle as he watched her hesitancy. He lifted a notepad and pen from the desk and his tone changed into something more businesslike. "Now, tell us how we can be of help to you, Ms. Kane." With a sweep of his eyes, he professionally took in her stained, ripped clothing and her bruised and cut face. "You have obviously had a difficult time today. Let's keep it informal, shall we? You can call me Nathan or Nate if I can call you Marcie."

Marcie's eyes widened and she nodded her head slowly as she lifted the mug of sugarless coffee with both hands and took a long sip of the hot, black liquid. She winced at the bitter taste. Still, it was desperately needed to help her through this ordeal. She looked squarely at the FBI man. She judged him once again to be about her age. Her peripheral vision brought into view Inspector Choyo who was sitting stoically in the corner, his tired eyes seemingly never blinking.

Harris took down her basic contact information on the first page of the yellow pad, flipped over to the second, and asked her to relate the events as best she could recall them.

Marcie sat back in her chair, relieved to be able to unload the weight of the day's unexpected events. "Well, as I said, I'm from St Petersburg, Florida. I donated some money to an international aid agency, and they used it to build a dormitory for children who desperately need it. I've come to Tanzania to visit the dormitory." Marcie described the location of the dormitory and the tour she had been given.

"When I was visiting, two young girls by the name of Shoni Batanga and Irene Sembaza showed me around. At the end of the tour, one of them, Shoni, asked when I was going to take her to America. It was an unusual question, but the more I thought about it, the more I was convinced that if someone did offer the opportunity to leave, they would."

Marcie paused to take another sip of her coffee and looked at Nathan Harris over the cup. He finished writing in his notepad and held the pen poised in the air as he looked up with his eyebrows arched, waiting for her to carry on with her story.

Marcie continued, "I contacted the aid agency and let them know there could be a problem, and I suggested that the students should be educated about the perils of asking strangers to take them away. The agency staff said they would follow up, but they also said it could take a while because they were so busy."

Harris interrupted. "When did you do this, Marcie? Was it the day after you visited the school?"

"No, I had a three-day safari booked from Arusha, so I followed through with that and then came back here to Dar to contact them. I was pretty distracted while I was on the safari, to be honest. I couldn't stop thinking of those girls and what might happen to them if they left on their own."

Marcie didn't quite understand the look on Nathan Harris' face, but she could tell he was listening closely. "Okay, then what did you do?"

Marcie recounted going to the school and her frustrating meeting with Mrs. Adimu. She said, "The head teacher wasn't much help. I know she's doing her best. Her job is to teach and she has so many students. I just felt something needed to be done. I was about to give up. I had booked a trip to Zanzibar, and I planned to go. But when I got in the taxi to go back to the hotel, the driver started talking about two young girls he had picked up at the school. It was too much of a coincidence. I knew it was them."

Marcie crossed her legs and held the cup with both hands on her lap. The pain and soreness from her cuts and bruises were starting to throb.

She continued, "When I quizzed the driver about the girls and he described them, I realized it had to be Shoni and Irene. He said he was paid to take them to a certain house and that he had taken other girls there as well."

Harris stopped writing and looked up. Choyo moved for the first time, leaning forward in his chair and clasping his hands in his lap. It was clear to Marcie that there was more interest here than she expected.

Harris said, "Before we go further, Marcie, I know people visiting the schools like to take pictures. Would you happen to have a picture of the girls?"

Marcie reached into her purse, extracted her phone and swiped the icons with her thumb across the screen until she found the photo gallery app. She tapped one of the thumbnails and the picture of her with Shoni and Irene appeared on the screen. She turned the phone around so that the two police officers could see it.

She leaned forward and tilted the screen sideways so she could see it, too. She pointed to the girl on her left in the photo. "That's Shoni." Then she pointed to the other girl. "That's Irene." The two girls beamed, their bright smiles lighting up the photo. They casually leaned on Marcie as if they had known her forever.

"May I?" Harris took the phone from Marcie's hand, tapped the screen a few times quickly, and handed the phone back. "I connected your phone to our printer temporarily and printed a copy for us to hold onto. I hope you don't mind."

"Of course not. Anything that will help."

"Please continue, Marcie."

Marcie sensed from the body language that the interest level in the room was rising with each new detail she shared. The two men were alert now, sitting forward, waiting for what was to come next. She was taken aback that her story was getting so much attention after everything she had heard and read about the police department.

Her body was stiffening more and the cuts and bruises buzzed, but she needed to finish this. She explained how she'd convinced Godfrey to show her the house where he'd taken the girls even though he was reluctant to go there. She described going to the house with Godfrey and being assaulted by the muscular man. She also told them about the beating Godfrey took, being shot at and their escape. The last thing she mentioned was that Godfrey was in the hospital.

Nathan stopped taking notes and sat back in his chair.

"Why are these girls so important to you that you would go back to the school or worse yet, go into a poor area of Dar es Salaam in search of them?"

"I just wanted to tell the teachers about the questions Shoni was asking and the inherent dangers. The girls are too young to have good judgment, and they seemed to be looking for anything that they think will improve their lot in life. I just thought they would go if they got the opportunity. It was obvious that the development agency wasn't going to be able to do anything quickly, so I wanted the teachers to do something to warn the children against going away with strangers."

"Ok, but why would you go into an area you know nothing about, not even being able to speak the language? Do you know how dangerous that could be?"

"I thought I would be able to talk some sense into the girls if I could find them. I didn't dream it was going to get so ugly. I guess I was naive to think I could do something. I seemed to make a connection, especially with Shoni, and I thought I might be able to use my experience to tell her about the dangers and convince her to go back to school."

"And what experience is that?"

"I grew up in a rough area in North Carolina, and I know how dangerous street life can be for teens and especially girls. It's a formative time in their young lives and things can go either way. I saw a little of myself in those girls, I guess, and I wanted to make sure they had some advice from someone who has some experience. The teachers don't have time to spend with them individually. I thought maybe I could answer some of their questions and get them back to the school to finish their studies. Their situation is much worse than mine was, but there are some parallels."

"Did you get any names of these men?"

"The only names I heard were Mr. Smith and Suleiman. Godfrey said it was Mr. Smith who paid him to take the girls to the house. He paid him a few times to drop girls off. I thought maybe that's who we were meeting, but it turned out to be someone else. Suleiman was the name of the young man who took Godfrey away and I think he and his buddies probably beat Godfrey up. I know for sure he shot at us and so did the muscular man." A thought occurred to Marcie. Her words rang in her ears. "I'm sure Godfrey is an innocent bystander in all this. He's a taxi driver, and he was just doing a job for which he was paid. He said he has 11 kids and needed the money. I believe him. But he really didn't want me to go to the house and he kept trying to tell me not to go. He's not involved in this."

Nathan nodded. "We will have to talk to Godfrey, anyway. Can you describe Mr. Smith?"

"I never saw him. I was told he's a Muzungu and had piercing eyes." She shook her head slightly when she realized she had used the Swahili term and corrected herself. "I mean he's white. Everyone describes his eyes so they must be notable. They said he has facial hair. It sounds like a goatee the way everyone describes it. I think Mrs. Adimu and Godfrey can describe him for you."

"Okay. I guess I don't have to tell you how lucky you are to be sitting here."

The depressing events of the day descended on Marcie, pressing her into her chair. She said dejectedly, "I understand that. I just wish I could have seen the girls and talked to them. I don't know where they are. The thug that assaulted me told me they are shipped out of the country, but I'm pretty sure he was high on something. I don't know if he knew what he was talking about. I'm lucky that he *was* high. *That's* the reason I'm here."

Marcie felt Harris' eyes assessing her. She sensed he was looking into her soul, assuring himself that she was being truthful. Finally, he said, "Look, Marcie, I know you're tired, but I would like you to do something for me before you leave. Can you do that?"

Marcie sighed and mumbled, "Sure."

Nathan got up from his desk and disappeared into the maze of cubicles. He returned carrying a large book full of photos. He said, "Please take a look at these pictures and see if you can spot the men who shot at you."

Marcie flipped the pages. Each had plastic sleeves holding pictures of people it would be best to avoid. The men glared at the camera, their lips tight. The photos looked blurry to her tired eyes, and there seemed to be an endless number of them. Her swollen right eye made it especially difficult to focus. To Marcie, it felt as if small bits of glass had found their way into her eyes but the nurse had assured her that was not the case. She knew it was just her body telling her she needed sleep. She tried harder to concentrate. She rubbed her eyes and winced as she made contact with the cuts and bruises on her face.

The photos were all head shots. She flipped through page after page until suddenly, about three quarters of the way in, she came across one that startled her and caused her to tremble, even though she had been half expecting to find him in this rogue's gallery. Her eyes narrowed as she examined the photo in front of her. She pointed.

"That's the man that assaulted me and shot at us!"

"Are you sure?"

"I'm positive. I'll never forget that face. There was so much anger. And whatever he was on just made him even more unstable, if he wasn't before."

"Ok, his name is David Deop. We're aware of him. Keep going, please." Nathan made a note on his pad of paper.

A few more pages and the young man whom she assumed was responsible for Godfrey's beating stared back at her. "That's the other man. That's Suleiman."

Nathan nodded, opened the drawer and pulled out some enlarged photos that were poorly focused and badly framed. They showed the two men together and individually in various poses on the street. The graininess of the photos and the distance from which they were taken suggested they had been taken covertly and were possibly screen shots from a video, but they were clear enough for Marcie to identify the subjects.

"That's definitely them." She pointed to one photo that caught several young men loitering in a street. "And those are some of the others that were with Suleiman."

"Okay, one more question." Nathan removed a map from the drawer, unfolded it and placed it on the table. "Can you pinpoint exactly the location of the house where all this took place?"

Trying to be as precise as possible, Marcie pointed to an area near the bus depot, but she added, "Godfrey or his friend Francis would be able to describe it better than me. I'm sure they are both still at the hospital." She took two deep breaths and ran her fingers through her hair. "That is, if Godfrey's still alive."

"Who's Francis?" You didn't mention a Francis."

Marcie hadn't realized she had held her last breath. She let it out slowly. "Oh, sorry. Francis helped me find the hospital. He helped by pushing Godfrey out of the driver's seat so I could get in. I didn't know who he was, but he climbed in the back seat. He said he is Godfrey's brother, but I didn't know if he meant it literally. He doesn't speak English, but I think he will be at the hospital waiting for Godfrey. They certainly have some affection for each other, if nothing else." She set her empty cup on the desk.

"Okay, we need to talk to them right away, Marcie, so if you have nothing further to tell us, we will get to it." A scraping noise filled the room as Nathan and Choyo both pushed their chairs back. Nathan came around the desk, helped Marcie to her feet and said with a warm smile, "Thank you very much, Marcie. You've been a big help." He handed her his card. "If you think of anything else, please call me, either here or in the U.S. There is a toll-free number on the card that goes directly to my cell phone. Feel free to use it. I will have one of the officers here escort you to your hotel."

Choyo also shook Marcie's hand with a small smile on his face. "Assante, Ms. Marcie." Marcie numbly stuck Harris' card in her pocket and allowed herself to be propelled to the door by a female officer. She had done all the thinking she was about to do today and compliantly climbed into the back seat of the police car.

Night had descended while Marcie was in the station, and she was thankful to be escorted to her hotel. She must have nodded off on the drive to the hotel, because she heard the officer calling her name and telling her they had arrived.

The female officer accompanied her all the way to the door of her room. Marcie mumbled her thanks and struggled clumsily with the lock on the door, overcome by exhaustion. The police woman gently removed the key from Marcie's hand and unlocked the door. Responding to the police woman's query, Marcie waved a weak acknowledgment that she could take it from here. She wobbled to the bed on legs that would barely support her weight and allowed herself to fall limply backwards on the soft mattress.

She heard the officer click the door shut behind her as she left, and Marcie's last thought before darkness overcame her was that she should get undressed.

Chapter 13

Marcie's dreams were not pleasant.

She hadn't been able to lose the big man behind her. She could hear his footsteps crunching in the gravel as they matched hers step for step. His steps were uneven because of a limp. That was all that was keeping him behind her – but just barely. He was only 30 feet back and gaining. Marcie ran to her left in the dark, hoping to evade capture. A huge implement shed lay dead ahead, and she sprinted for the open door that yawned in the moonlight. She didn't know why but she had the overwhelming feeling she would be safe inside the structure if she could only make the opening. And something else was drawing her to the doorway. She sensed the girls and her friend were in there. She had to get inside that shed.

When she glanced furtively over her shoulder, the moonlight glinted on the large gun the man was carrying. I have to make that door, she thought. *I have to stay alive to help Shoni and Irene and my best friend Sami. They're all in there, and I'm their only hope.* The opening loomed larger, but the man was so close behind her, she could hear him breathing. She sensed his hot labored breath on her neck. She knew he could have easily shot her by now, so obviously he wanted something else. He wanted to enjoy her before killing her. So many emotions pummeled her as she ran. The need to save the three women was weighing on her, slowing her down. Her legs burned. At the same time, saving her own life so that she could protect the people inside who meant so much to her gave her strength to push on.

She made it! Marcie stumbled across the entrance into the doorway of the shed, casting another look over her shoulder. As she crossed the threshold, the man behind her suddenly disappeared – just evaporated – as if he had not been there at all. She stopped running. Her hands rested on her knees as she beckoned for breath that wouldn't come. She was grabbing at the air with her mouth and nostrils, trying to stave off nausea – trying not to collapse in a heap on the floor of the shed. Finally, cherished life-giving air filled her lungs, first slowly and then more rapidly.

Gradually Marcie straightened up and looked around. Motes of dust floated in the air, illuminated by the moonlight filtering through cracks in the walls of the old structure. There, standing 10 feet ahead, stood FBI special agent Nathan Harris. His face was gentle, creased only by a tiny smile that curled his lips. He was holding his arms out to her, as if to welcome her into the darkness of the shed. But then he dropped his arms and stepped aside. With a flourish, he bowed and gestured for her to proceed behind him to join a group of people standing with their arms wrapped around each other as if protecting themselves from some unseen menace.

She instantly recognized her friend Sami, as well as the two young African girls and Godfrey. Marcie's shoulders relaxed. *But why did they look so frightened? Special Agent Harris is here. He will protect us.* She clasped her hands together at the sight of them. She started forward to greet the group. She could see their lips moving, but she could hear nothing. She stopped, hesitating to continue. Fear and confusion shot through her as she read their lips. They were pleading to her. She leaned back away from the group when understanding swept over her. They were saying in unison, "Please help us."

She had to help. She started towards them, but Nathan Harris blocked her path. Even in the dark shadows, she was close enough to make out the details of his face. Something was happening. It wasn't the calm face of the FBI special agent anymore. His face was changing right in front of her eyes. It was morphing into something else. A mask was being lifted and a new face was taking the place of the old one. As the mask peeled off the figure's face, dark orbs stared from the eye sockets. More of the mask fell away and Marcie's hand shot to her mouth as she recognized the new person in front of her. She tried to scream, "Run!" to the group but her voice was silent. She screamed again, but nothing came out. The man standing in front of her was Greg Johnson, aka The Force – the same man who had tried to kill her two years ago.

It was Greg Johnson, all right, but this time his eyes were different. They were dilated and lacked emotion. They froze her in place and sent shock waves through her body. They were fixated on her, interrogating her, terrifying her. Marcie's brain was telling her that this couldn't be. Greg Johnson was dead. But she was seeing him standing there right in front of her. Johnson continued to stare through her, but then his countenance changed. He smirked savagely at Marcie as he put his hand inside his jacket. He turned around slowly, withdrew a weapon and fired. The shots rang out in the stillness, and the four people who were so important to Marcie sank in a heap to the floor as if every bone had been removed from their bodies. Blood pooled everywhere around them.

Marcie fell to her knees. The dead eyes of the people she had so desperately tried to protect stared unseeingly back at her. She had failed. Only their blank lifeless stares were visible in the dark. The laughter of the terrifying Harris/Johnson figure rang in her ears. The sound wouldn't stop. She tore her eyes away from the awful sight to look at the murderer. His head was thrown back, his mouth open, his laughter hysterical. Abruptly, he stopped. Marcie could hear only her own breathing in the silence of the shed. She looked up to see the gun swing in a wide arc towards her until it was aimed right between her eyes. The next sound she heard was her own screaming. She had found her voice. She knew the only thing that would stop her from screaming was the bullet that was about to penetrate her brain.

The gun fired.

Marcie sat bolt upright. *Where am I?* Her eyes wide, she frantically looked around trying to recognize her surroundings. She was shaking uncontrollably. Beads of sweat formed a pearl necklace around her throat. She could smell dried blood. *Was it the blood of the group that had been murdered in the shed? Or her own?* She felt her body for wounds, but there was no stickiness of fresh blood. Her face throbbed. She could barely make out the lines in her hand as she held it in front of her face. It was so dark. What had happened to the Harris/Johnson figure? And where were the bodies of the people who had been executed?

Marcie's heart rate slowed just as the fog controlling her thoughts lifted. Her trembling eased as she started to realize where she was. She reached over to turn on the lamp. Light flooded the room. She peeked at the clock, squinting through the fingers of her hand over her face, taking deep breaths to settle her nerves. It was 3:12 a.m. and she was sitting fully clothed on a bed in Tanzania, Africa. There was no large muscular man with a limp chasing her, no Nathan Harris, no Greg Johnson. Sami was safely back in St. Petersburg, and Shoni and Irene were – well, God-knew-where. She prayed Godfrey was recovering and gaining his strength back in the hospital. Yet with everything that had befallen her, Marcie realized she had still never met the elusive Mr. Smith, the man with the piercing eyes that Godfrey and Mrs. Adimu had talked about. Her mind had simply conjured up the eyes in her nightmare from the descriptions she had been given. The dried blood that she smelled was on her crusty t-shirt. And her face still hurt like hell.

Her nightmare was a recurring one that she had experienced many times before. Except now it had intensified even more. Her psychologist had told Marcie that her dreams were her brain's attempt to pull together various fragments of her previous experiences. Her psyche was struggling to turn them into one cohesive puzzle. The muscular man with the limp, Nathan Harris, the two African girls, the man with the dark eyes, and Godfrey had now been added to the mix, allowing her mind's blender to concoct a truly terrifying mess. She had been prescribed Prazosin after her experience helping Mason Seaforth rescue his wife Sami, and she had taken the pills a few times, but the nearly full bottle still sat in her purse. The doctor had told her that the nightmares would eventually subside. And the frequency definitely had slowed down – until now.

Marcie sighed, got up and went to the bathroom. Her muscles were wound tight from her ordeal the previous day and from the nightmare she'd just experienced. With her hands on the sink, she leaned forward, staring at her bloodshot eyes in the mirror. She took deep breaths to settle her nerves. Now it was pangs of hunger stabbing through her stomach. *When was the last time I ate?* She carefully washed her face around the scrapes and bruises. As she undressed and struggled into her pajamas, her arms felt as if lead weights were attached. The thought of traveling even a few short steps to the small fridge in the room to get some fruit was overwhelming to her. One basic human need was about to win out over another. Food would have to wait on sleep.

For the second time that night, Marcie fell into a restless sleep.

Chapter 14

The next time Marcie looked at the clock, it registered 11 a.m. The air conditioner pouring cool air into the room was not enough to keep her pajamas from clinging to her, and her hair was plastered against her head. She lay in bed, gathering her thoughts. She felt better – not completely rested but at least ready to start fresh. She recalled snippets of the nightmare that had terrified her during the night. The scenario was definitely the same, only multiplied exponentially by the new developments of yesterday.

The thought of the smiling faces of the two girls, Shoni Batanga and Irene Sembaza, shoved aside the night terrors. She was still anxious about their fate, but realistically, she realized there wasn't much else she could do. She was just ready to go home. There must be programs back in the States to help young girls like Shoni and Irene with proper means to warn them of the dangers of trusting strangers. Maybe she could work with the aid agency to develop something for Africa. There were avenues she could pursue, once safely back in St. Petersburg.

Which meant it was time to think about her situation. She would be leaving the country soon. She grimaced as she rolled out of bed. Her body was incredibly stiff and sore from the ordeal she'd been through, but she couldn't afford to stay in bed. There was too much ahead that had to be done. To lie there was, unfortunately, not an option.

The first order of business was to fire up the room coffee maker. With caffeine, she could function. Wincing in pain as the water ran over her bruises, Marcie showered and applied some make-up to camouflage the bruises on her face. The swelling around her eye had gone down, and she could see more clearly. Growling in her stomach reminded Marcie again that she hadn't eaten in

24 hours, so that was next on the agenda. The rolled-up, ripped and bloodied clothing she had worn the day before landed with a thud in the trash.

Marcie remembered the typically light breakfasts in Tanzania and knew that wasn't going to cut it. Besides, the thought of Ugali wasn't appealing at the moment. She needed something other than the porridge-like substance that was a staple during the safari. Lunches usually didn't happen until around 1 o'clock. It was getting close to that, so she took a chance at the restaurant in the hotel. The waiter glanced at her battered face but said nothing. He just quietly took her order of prawn curry with tomatoes and rice cooked in coconut milk.

Feeling better after getting something into her stomach, Marcie hailed a taxi and asked to be taken to the hospital where she had left Godfrey and Francis the night before. She wanted to check in on the old man and satisfy herself that he was okay before she left for home. Besides, she owed him money. As the taxi pulled up to the hospital entrance, the old car was just where she had left it. Only now the hood was up and legs protruded from the engine compartment.

Marcie paid her driver, got out and approached the vehicle. She recognized Francis' profile as he leaned deep into the front of the car, wrench in hand and muttering softly. He was tapping on some part of the engine with the tool, apparently resorting to verbal threats and violence to get it going. Marcie didn't want to startle him, so she waited for him to turn around. When he did a few minutes later, the road map of crevices in his leathery face deepened with a huge grin.

"Ms. Kane," was all he said in acknowledgement as he motioned with his grease-stained hand and wrench towards the hospital entrance. His chin also pointed to the front of the building, urging Marcie to go inside. Marcie squeezed his arm with both hands, captured his eyes with hers and said, "Thank you."

A response to her inquiry about Godfrey at the desk directed her to Room 212. As Marcie walked down the hall to the stairs, she thought of other times she had visited hospitals, not knowing what to expect when she turned the corner into the room. She knew it was often not good. Too often, the strong person you had seen last was not the same one who was laden with tubes and surrounded by machines in an antiseptic room.

But fortunately this time was different. The Godfrey she had last seen was covered in blood, his eyes swollen shut and his breathing labored. The Godfrey she saw now was sitting upright with a bandage on his head, shoveling Ugali into his mouth as if it were his last meal. His face was still puffy and bruised from the beating, but his spoon stopped in midair when Marcie turned the corner, his eyes widened in surprise and his swollen lips spread wide in a big smile.

He gently dabbed the corner of his mouth with a napkin, but his mouth was still full when he sputtered, "Ah, pretty lady, s'nice to see you. How are you? Alright? Francis told me he was in love with you for all you did."

"I'm doing good, Godfrey. It's nice to see you as well. The question is, how are *you* doing? We were worried we were going to lose you yesterday."

"I'm a tough old bird, pretty lady. I've taken bigger beatings from stronger men than that before. Given a few, too." He chuckled. "I'm just waiting for Francis to get my car fixed so I can get out of here."

"Are you sure you're ready to go? You should probably stay another day or two to make sure you're okay. You got beaten up pretty badly."

"I have 11 mouths to feed, pretty lady. They say I only have a minor concussion. I will be fine. Oh, I had two visitors – woke me up early this morning. Said they had talked to you. They wanted to know everything I knew about what happened. Thoughts were a little fuzzy, but I tol' them what I remembered."

"Was it Inspector Choyo and an FBI special agent named Nathan Harris?"

Godfrey nodded. "Yup, never thought I would get a visit from the FBI. Good-looking man, too. You should check into that." His chuckle broke off into a cough. Wiping his mouth on his sleeve, he continued, "Must be somethin' special to bring the FBI here. Anyway, I told 'em exactly where they could find those men. My days driving the girls there are over, no question, and I'm happy about that. I was never, how do you say it – easy with taking them there, but the money was good and I needed it for my family. In Tanzania we say, 'Make some money but don't let money make you.' Maybe I was letting the money make me, but I hope you understand."

Marcie looked at him sympathetically. "I do understand, Godfrey. Listen, there's something I would like you to do. Not right away, but when it's safer to go back into the neighborhood." She handed him two envelopes containing some

Tanzanian shillings. "The first envelope is for you. It's the money I owe you for taking me to the house. I feel I owe you so much more for what you went through."

"I'm grateful to you, pretty lady, and I'm sorry for what happened to you."

Marcie shook her head, "I'm fine. But there's a little girl there who helped me escape. Her name is Malaika. Without her, I don't think either you or I would be here. Could you please give the second envelope to her?" Marcie described the little girl and watched as Godfrey's eyes brightened.

"I will do that for you, pretty lady. It's the least I can do. I will search her out and give her your gift. She was just helping someone in need in the African way, but I'm sure she will be grateful for your thoughtfulness."

They chatted for a few more minutes, and Marcie asked him to write down his address before she went on her way. She gave the old man a big hug and a kiss on the forehead and left with a feeling of sadness in her heart for the kind old man and his large family and the many others just like them who had so little. But they were happy with what they had, and she knew she would never forget the old man and his African proverbs.

Marcie was pleased to see the nurse who had stitched her in the front hall. She walked over to thank her and asked how much the bill would be for Godfrey's hospital stay. After paying the bill, she strode out of the hospital into the bright African sunshine that would have been unbearable had it not been for the cool breeze blowing inland from the Indian Ocean. She bade farewell to Francis and climbed in the taxi to take her back to the hotel to prepare for the long journey home.

Looking out the windows from the back seat of the taxi, Marcie reflected on her time in Africa. She thought about Nathan Harris. *Not bad-looking for an FBI special agent. Who am I kidding? That's based on a sample size of one since he's the only FBI agent I know. He's not bad-looking, period. Oh well, it's not like I will ever see him again.* Then she thought of the wonderful Tanzanian people she had met. The friendly, smiling girls at the dormitory, the generous and happy Godfrey, the tolerant and amorous tour bus driver . . . *They have so little and they expect even less of people they meet. Yet they have all these great qualities that people back home who have everything sometimes lack. Most of all, they are so resilient.*

Marcie just hoped the same could be said for Shoni and Irene.

Chapter 15

After spending the day shopping and enjoying the sights and sounds of Dar es Salaam, Marcie boarded the overnight flight bound for Amsterdam. She was proud of her purchases. She pulled the shopping bag from her carry-on bag beneath the seat in front of her and examined the piece of tanzanite, a beautiful blue/violet gemstone that Sami could ask a jeweler to make into earrings or a necklace. Mason would be getting a brightly colored African shirt. He will probably only wear it in the backyard, she thought of her conservative accountant friend.

The flight was uneventful, but included a stop in Nairobi, making it that much longer. Thankfully, the plane wasn't full so Marcie was able to stretch out across her seat and the two vacant ones beside her for some much needed rest. A movie and food occupied the rest of her time. For the trip home, she had chosen a blue linen short sleeve shirt that she left untucked over white cargo pants. Her go-to print travel jacket hid the wrinkles that would inevitably manifest themselves en route. Her bruises would heal soon and she absent-mindedly rubbed the itching on her face indicating that the cuts were already starting to mend. Once again, face makeup limited the number of stares she received, although the sunglasses she wore on the night flight may have increased the number of glances she attracted. She decided to call it a draw between the makeup and the sunglasses.

As the plane made its descent into Amsterdam, she was deciding what to do. She had a six-hour layover before continuing to Tampa, so she had time to look around. Maybe catch a tour bus and see some of the downtown area. She had seen the Schiphol airport on the way to Tanzania and knew there were many retail stores and restaurants to occupy the traveler's time, but she had done that.

She wanted to see the rest of Amsterdam. A tour would be great – she might even see the much talked-about red light district.

Marcie cleared customs and found a seat in the common waiting area where she rummaged through her handbag so she could store her passport in a secure section. Her concentration was fully on the task at hand when a gentle male voice interrupted her thoughts.

"Well, you certainly look different than you did when I saw you last."

Her eyes shifted from the depths of her handbag to a pair of tan suede desert boots and then wandered up the blue jeans to a red golf shirt that highlighted a set of broad chest muscles. A tan leather jacket was slung over one shoulder of the man who was addressing her, and a leather bag hung casually over the other. He held a large coffee in a paper cup. Marcie looked into the soft dark eyes of Nathan Harris, the one FBI special agent she knew and thought she would never see again. She felt her heart lurch and her face broke into a smile.

Huh! Not bad, Marcie thought. "Well, Mr. FBI man, are you following me?" With a flourish, she removed the sunglasses, revealing her swollen eye. "Are you *sure* I look better?"

Nathan Harris chuckled, "Um . . . okay, maybe not as much as I first thought. You know it's an FBI agent's job to follow people, right? Actually, I just arrived. My flight was delayed in Dar. You know what they say. It's better to be on the ground wishing you were in the air than to be in the air wishing you were on the ground. Now, I'm just waiting for my next flight back home to Atlanta. How was your flight?"

Marcie propped the sunglasses back on her face and chuckled at the old air travel adage. "I managed to stretch out on the seats and got some rest. The flight was uneventful, which is just the way I like it. I have six horrible hours to kill here, though. How about you?"

Nathan sat down beside Marcie, shifting his bag to the floor and draping his jacket over his knees. He sipped his coffee. "I still have a few hours here before my next flight. There's nothing worse than killing time at an airport, is there?"

Marcie nodded her head in agreement. "That's for sure. I was thinking of finding a short tour of Amsterdam after I get some breakfast. The meal on the plane was the usual cardboard eggs and dry toast. Do you know if there are tours from the airport?"

Harris nodded. "There are. I did that once when I was here on a long layover. It's a great way to use up some time." He pulled the jacket from his knees and stood up. "I'm a bit famished myself. If you don't mind, I'll join you for breakfast and point you in the direction of the tour booth after."

Marcie was thankful that she would have some company for at least part of her layover. And she couldn't help feeling her heart racing just a little faster whenever she was near him. Besides that, she had some questions for the special agent. This would be an opportunity.

"Sure, let's go."

They walked by a myriad of stores boasting electronics, clothing, lingerie and liquor, finally settling on a café with a section of tables stretching out into the mall walkway. Marcie looked at the menu. "I'm looking forward to a good cup of coffee. Some of my friends seem to think I'm a coffee snob."

Nathan's lips closed slightly in a half-smile and he raised an eyebrow. Leaning forward toward her, he whispered, "Well, if you insist on having ants with your sugar, you're going to have to place a special order, and it will cost you extra. The staff has to go outside and capture them off the sidewalk with tweezers, and you know the cost of labor these days. The ants don't come cheap."

Marcie threw her head back and clapped her hands together at the reminder of the first time they met. Any fatigue the two were feeling was quickly flushed away by the laugh they shared.

After placing their order, Marcie said, "So, you have to tell me what brings an FBI special agent to Africa. Or is it so secret that if you tell me, you'll have to kill me?"

Nathan chuckled. "No, it's not much of a secret, and whether you know it or not, you helped the case I'm working on, so I don't mind telling you a bit about it."

Marcie frowned, surprised that she had been helpful to his case. She rested her forearms on the table and leaned forward. "So, let's have it. How was I helpful?"

He began his explanation. "Maybe a bit of background would help first. Do you know much about the FBI?"

"Well, I see people on television with those jackets with 'FBI' in huge letters on the back. They always manage to solve the crime within an hour. All I know is that's quite the standard to live up to."

Harris nodded slightly. It seemed as if that's all most people knew. "Our job at the FBI is to protect the United States from any number of threats, including terrorist activities, fraud, espionage, cyber crimes, you name it. We focus on any threat that might affect national security and safety. When there's a threat, special agents are assigned to look into it and deal with it. Africa has become a hotbed of such activities because of its economic situation. The internet and ease of travel has made it much simpler for certain individuals to turn their hand to highly-profitable but definitely-illegal enterprises. It's our job to investigate anything in that realm that may hurt us back home."

Marcie listened intently. She knew Harris was being serious, but she said half-jokingly, "So, you might be able to do something about those emails I get from Nigeria telling me if I just send my credit card information, I'll receive a billion dollars from some long-lost relative?"

The playfulness of her question was lost on Harris as he was now in full FBI mode. He nodded. "Actually, that's one of the things we *are* working on." He shrugged. "The trouble is, every time we shut one down, two more pop up. There are people every day who fall for it. Especially elderly people, unfortunately. It's just too lucrative a business for young, computer-savvy Nigerians to ignore. They're called 'Yahoo boys' in Nigeria and believe me, the Nigerian community is not proud of them. The scams are all web-based, and the FBI is doing our best. But actually, no, my assignment is different from that."

Their meals came, and they both dug in hungrily, commenting about the lack of good food served on planes these days. While she ate, Marcie could hardly wait to hear more about what Nathan Harris was involved in and how it somehow was tied in with her own experience. She took a sip of her coffee, smiled and said encouragingly, "So you weren't in Tanzania because of an internet scam, then? "She sat back with her legs crossed and listened intently.

Harris dabbed at his mouth with his napkin, laid it down beside his plate, and picked up where he'd left off. "Well, one of our roles is to investigate document fraud. As you can imagine, fraudulent documents can enable all kinds of illegals to enter the country, including terrorists, and it can also lead to human trafficking – bringing people into the U.S. to work illegally. It can include sexual slavery, forced labor or commercial sexual exploitation. The FBI found out that there is a major illegal trafficking ring originating in Tanzania, so I was sent over to investigate and assist the local law enforcement officials there to do their work." Harris stopped to gauge Marcie's reaction.

Marcie felt a tingle run through her body. *Sexual slavery? Could he be referring to Shoni and Irene?* She asked quietly, "And how did my information help?"

"I can't talk about the case too much, but we've had our eye on the big guy you pointed out – David Deop. He's no bit player. The photos you looked at – not the head shots but the other ones – were from some surveillance pictures we took a couple of weeks ago. He disappeared from the location where the pictures were taken, and we'd lost track of him. When we talked to Godfrey after speaking with you, he and Francis were able to describe exactly where he took you. We sent some people in to arrest Deop and Suleiman. They're both cooling their heels in the local jail, along with some other guys who were with Suleiman."

"What do you think happened to the girls?"

"I'm not sure you want to hear this, Marcie, but it's possible they were processed and taken to another country."

There's that word "process" again. "Deop referred to 'processing' the girls. What do you mean by "'processed'"? Marcie really wasn't sure she *was* ready to hear his answer.

"Girls are kidnapped or convinced to go with a recruiter and are given stolen passports or ones which have been purchased and modified, along with other documentation so they can travel. Sometimes the passports are completely bogus – they're forged. The people that do that kind of work are in high demand, and it's very lucrative. In the espionage world, they're called cobblers. There's another way to obtain a fake passport, and that's to bribe an official in a passport office who will create one for you. The most valuable ones are from countries that have

visa-free agreements with the United States. It reduces the required paperwork."
Then shrugging his shoulders, Harris said, "It's hard to say what may have happened to the girls, though. Investigator Choyo and his colleagues are interrogating Deop and Sulieman, probably as we speak. Hopefully, they will get some answers."

"So why are you going home? Shouldn't you be there to help?" Marcie grimaced inwardly. It came out a little more direct than she intended.

"My job in Tanzania has ended for now. There is a trail of human trafficking from there to the United States. In fact, some of the trails have led to your area – Tampa. That reminds me, you are now considered to be a potential witness, so you might have to testify against Deop and Suleiman. But the way things move in Africa, it won't be any time soon. It might be a long time before it ever comes to trial."

"So I may get an all expense paid trip back to Tanzania?" Marcie smiled thinly, her mind still on the girls.

Nathan grinned back at her. "I have a feeling it will be a written affidavit or by Skype, but you can always hope. I have a question for you, though. You said there was a laptop on the table. Did you see Deop use it?"

Marcie tilted her head. It seemed like an odd question, but she responded, "He was working at it when we walked in, but he could barely type. He was using the old hunt-and-peck method."

Nathan nodded distractedly and Marcie could see there would be nothing more coming from *that* conversation.

She had another thought. "You said there's a trail that leads to the United States? Is there a chance the girls are in the U.S. – maybe even Tampa?"

"There's always a chance. They could be in Europe, or anywhere else in the world."

Marcie was growing more worried by the second now. "Tell me more about what happens to girls like them."

"It's not pretty. Women and children who are trafficked are often promised work in the domestic or service industry, so they can earn money for an education. However, when they arrive in their new country, their passports and identification papers are taken from them. They can be locked up, beaten or forced to take drugs; and they can only repay their debts by working in some menial-level service industry or even at brothels, strip joints or massage parlors."

Nathan sipped the last of his coffee, and Marcie took the opportunity to ask, "Who's behind these things? What sort of person would do this?'

"It's a hugely lucrative business for everyone involved, Marcie. Except for the girls, that is. It's an industry estimated to be worth about $32 billion worldwide. That's billion with a 'b.' The only illegal business that generates more revenue is the drug trade. The victims are generally anywhere from 12 to 25 years old. As for who would do it, it could be motorcycle gangs, Chinese Triads, Russian mob, organized crime, just businessmen . . . The problem is that we don't exactly know how the girls get out of Tanzania yet. If girls end up in the U.S., they could use the documentation I mentioned to fly directly from Dar to the U.S. They could be taken to Libya or Morocco and forced to travel in a boat full of migrants across the Mediterranean to Italy or Spain first. That's always a worry because I'm sure you've read about boats full of migrant workers capsizing. Or, the girls may be flown to Mexico with false passports and cross into the U.S. by truck or walk in through a tunnel. The traffickers use different methods to avoid patterns. No matter how they travel, it wouldn't be a pleasant trip. When they get to their destination, there's a good chance it will be even less pleasant. Are you starting to see the extent of the problem?"

Marcie felt a wave of nausea flow through her. She was wondering if she was going to be able to hold her breakfast down. Her shoulders slumped as she wrapped her arms around her chest and leaned forward with her elbows on the table. "Don't they ever try to escape when they find out what has really happened?"

"Some do, but often they just become hardened and continue to do what they're doing because it's a job to them. Sometimes their new life, as hard as it is, is easier than the one they left behind. If they do try to escape, they are often caught and beaten or even killed. By all accounts, the life of the girls that you met wasn't the most pleasant – at least until they moved into the dormitory. They lived on their own. Their siblings had moved out. Most of the girls who become victimized by human trafficking rings are looking for the promised land." Harris looked steadily at her. "You're looking a little nauseous. I'm just trying to point out to you that finding the two girls you are so focused on is going to be next to impossible. Maybe I can give you some friendly advice, Marcie. Remember the great time you had in Africa and remember the girls, but try to forget about what may have happened to them."

Harris paused, aware of Marcie's distraught appearance. "Now, why don't I show you that booth where you can catch the tour bus around Amsterdam?"

Marcie nodded, but her mind had not left the girls yet. "I'm fine, really. It's just so sad that girls can be taken advantage of, and it's even worse that there are people willing to do it. I think that people who have less just need a good opportunity. I believe we're all born with certain skills, only some people never get the opportunity to use them." She paused, then continued, wondering what this good-looking FBI agent would think of her next words. "I think that's where those of us who have more come in. We can provide opportunities for people like this by offering education. I appreciate you telling me about the dark side, though. It saddens me and as you say, we just can't let ourselves be overwhelmed."

Her countenance brightened. "Maybe we should have another coffee and dessert before I go find the tour. What do you think?"

Harris smiled and immediately waved his hand to the waitress. His haste to order suggested that he might have been debating about proposing the same thing. He looked at Marcie. "Can I suggest a Stroopwafel? It's a Dutch delicacy that originated in Gouda here in the Netherlands. You should try it. It's a very decadent dessert, and there's a neat trick that goes along with it."

Marcie felt that the agent had dropped his official FBI cloak for the moment, and was letting his real personality show through. She was intrigued and nodded her agreement. When the smiling waitress delivered the two thin layers of batter with a sticky syrupy substance in the middle, Marcie waited for the trick Harris had promised.

The cookie was about the size of the top of their coffee cups and Harris laid his on the top of the steaming liquid. With a lift of his eyebrows, a crooked smile and a flourish of his hand, he said, "Behold – the cookie is softening and the syrup is melting. It's an amazing treat. But remember this – it isn't just every magician who is willing to divulge the secrets of his tricks."

"I'm impressed," Marcie said, clapping her hands. She did the same with the delicacy as Nathan had and took a photo with her cell phone before biting into the delicious cookie. She dabbed at her mouth to remove any drips of syrup that might have escaped. "Mmm . . . this is amazing. But I'm beginning to understand. You're really David Copperfield here undercover. You FBI guys think of everything." She laughed as she took another bite. So how did you come up with the idea of putting the cookie on the coffee cup?"

"I would like to take credit for it, but it's something the Dutch have been doing for years. I happened to notice people doing it last time I sat here on a layover. I never tried it before, to be honest." He laughed. "It works well, though."

Marcie agreed. The combination of the cookie and hot coffee together were a delight. Then she asked, "What about that Mr. Smith that the head teacher and Godfrey referred to? The guy with the piercing eyes everyone comments on. Is he the head of the snake?"

She immediately regretted her question as in a flash, Harris' stony FBI countenance re-emerged. "Hard to say. He might be just a recruiter," Harris said between bites. "We will be trying to find and interrogate him. He would have valuable information on which schools they are targeting and hopefully, on which girls have been recruited. We have a long list of girls that have disappeared in Tanzania. He's definitely a person of interest."

They talked more about the issue of human trafficking until Nathan switched subjects. "That's enough about me and what I do. Tell me about Marcie Kane."

Marcie surprised herself when she said, "Well, I can tell you I dreamt about you after I met you at the police station."

Harris' eyebrow rose. "Oh? A pleasant dream, I hope."

Marcie grimaced and shrugged sheepishly. "Nope, not really, it was more of a nightmare."

Harris' mouth turned down and his eyebrows knitted together in a frown, but before he could protest, she proceeded to tell him about the menacing Harris/ Johnson figure and waking up in a cold sweat, not knowing where she was.

Harris was listening intently. When she finished, she shifted uncomfortably in her chair. She avoided eye contact by picking at an imaginary piece of lint on her sleeve. But Harris was completely sympathetic. He said, "I'm aware of the situation you were in two years ago. That must have been horrible for you, but at least the ending turned out all right. Your friends and their daughter are safe, and it's over. The bad guys are behind bars or dead and can't get to you.

"You know, when I started this job, I thought I could save everyone. I thought I could change the world. It didn't take long for me to realize it just isn't realistic. I lost a young hostage in a shootout when the person holding him chose to shoot the hostage and himself before my team and I could stop him. The hostage was 10 years old. I was having nightmares like you. I went to a psychologist. I thought of quitting the FBI. I even thought of suicide.

"But the one thing that prevented me from having more nightmares and allowed me to get back to doing my job to the best of my abilities was when I began to realize that I can only do what I can do. No more. But no less. Marcie, you seem to be the type of person who has to do everything you can, so you owe yourself that, but that is all you can do. You can't allow yourself to be overwhelmed by the depths to which humanity will go to hurt others for their own personal gain. If you help a person or two along the way, you have accomplished something. If more people did that, there would be a lot of people helped."

Marcie's eyes met his. She saw a genuine sincerity behind the tough outward appearance she hadn't seen in a long time. It was like they were kindred spirits. Warmth spread through her, ending up in her cheeks. She averted her eyes and then said, "Okay, how is it you know about my experience? Am I under investigation?"

Harris chuckled, "Well, I have to admit I was curious about your story. You managed to escape some pretty tough people and do some damage at the same time. It isn't everyone who would bother to change their vacation plans to try to help two girls they barely know. And then to go into the part of town that you did was just asking for trouble. You are either very brave or very naïve. Besides that, it's my job to be curious."

Marcie thought that with the access to the kind of sophisticated equipment the FBI has, he probably knew more about her than she did. But all she said was,

"I think it was just a matter of seeing a potential problem and wanting to do something about it."

Harris' mouth widened in a smile. "Now that I know you a bit better, I think I can understand that. I do have one question, though. The news articles specifically referred to the incident you were involved in two years ago as a shootout. A shootout implies that both parties know how to shoot. So, I'm just curious where you learned to handle a gun."

Marcie looked amused. "One thing my ex did for me was to make sure I knew how to use a gun. He took me to a range that you probably don't want to know about where I learned how to fire a weapon accurately. I enjoyed it, and it came pretty easily to me. I'm pretty good with my Smith and Wesson at home, and I don't mind carrying it when it needs to be carried. With the laws we have in Florida, it gives me the option of protecting myself and don't kid yourself – I will in a heartbeat."

"You know what? I believe you. And your martial arts skills?"

Marcie shook her head. "I wouldn't call them skills. I took some courses and learned how to defend myself with a few techniques. I never expected to have to use them. I got lucky, thank God! I was scared to death. I just happened to hit the right spots."

"Well, you certainly did that. Deop's leg was in pretty bad shape, and his nose didn't look too good either when we picked him up. He wasn't prepared to tell us he had been beaten up by a woman, but we assumed you had done the damage. I don't think I'd want to get on your bad side." Harris shook his head. "You're a delightfully complex woman, Marcie Kane."

They continued talking about their lives. Marcie discovered he was born in Philadelphia to an African American mother and white father. He was married to his job and felt because of his travels and the dangers of his chosen career, it would be unfair to commit to a relationship with a woman. Marcie told him more about her ex and how she had taken to calling him He Who Shall Not Be Named after the divorce. He laughed heartily at the name. She told him of her upbringing in North Carolina.

They chatted easily until a comfortable silence hung between them and their conversation slowed down. Almost simultaneously, they both glanced at their watches. Each cast a second look in surprise. Harris leaned back in his chair and said, "I guess you won't be seeing Amsterdam on this trip. Sorry about that. It's been almost three hours since we sat down, and I'm going to have to head for my gate to check in. No wonder the waitress keeps giving us dirty looks."

Marcie agreed. "I don't know where the time went, but I enjoyed our conversation. No need to apologize. The time has flown by, and I will look forward to seeing Amsterdam another time. Thank you, FBI Special Agent Harris."

"You don't have to be so formal, but thank *you*, Ms. Kane."

Harris paid the bill with an extra tip to their server for tying up her table so long, picked up his bag and jacket, and slung each over the same shoulders as before. Marcie put her sunglasses back on and walked with him to his gate where they said goodbye and shook hands. Marcie took a deep breath as she sensed the presence of his light cologne. Not too strong. Just right. She watched him walk through the security area and waved when he paused at the door to turn around before he disappeared. Slowly she turned towards her own gate.

As she walked, she thought hard about their conversation. She had never told anyone about her nightmares, aside from her psychologist, and yet she had been comfortable spilling everything to a man she had just met – and an FBI agent, no less. And yet he seemed to understand her. She'd also shared things about herself that most people would only get out of her after they had known her for, oh, say a decade. Marcie was puzzled by everything that had happened, but she also felt as if a weight had been removed from her shoulders. He was right that she should try to stop thinking about what may have happened to Shoni and Irene. It made so much sense. For her own sanity, it was best for her to put the two girls out of her mind totally. As Nathan had said, only the authorities would be able to do something about it.

And then against her better judgment, she found herself thinking more about FBI agent Nathan Harris, and hoping that she would see him again.

St Petersburg, Florida, USA

Chapter 16

Marcie awoke to the sound of the ocean lapping against the shoreline. The breeze sifted through the open patio door, filling the room with fresh morning air and causing the vertical window blinds to tap softly against the wall. The smell of freshly brewed coffee from the machine she had preset the night before beckoned to her, urging her to get up to enjoy the day.

She got out of bed and threw her arms back to stretch the night stiffness out of her body. She put on her white Ralph Lauren robe over her purple silk pajamas and wandered to the kitchen. The aroma of fresh coffee permeated the air and she filled the favorite large mug she had acquired on a visit to Disneyland. She splashed a touch of French Vanilla creamer, her morning guilty pleasure, into the steaming liquid and carefully took a sip. On the way back to the balcony, she plugged in a CD and the relaxing R&B sounds of Pharrell Williams filled her condo. Marcie slumped down in a wicker chair with her feet up on a comfortable stool. Folding the side of her robe across her slender legs and sipping her coffee with a satisfied sigh, her gaze fell upon the shimmering water of the Boca Ciega Bay.

Marcie loved the condo she occupied on the Pinellas Bayway in St Petersburg. It was one of many condo buildings along the Bayway, and it was only a short drive to the white sands of St. Pete Beach and everything that area had to offer. Marcie could have afforded something more luxurious than the condo she had purchased but didn't feel the need. The generous divorce settlement with He Who Shall Not Be Named had set her up securely, and she was grateful for the lifestyle she had.

Even on cooler days, a glance through the condo's large front glass wall afforded a spectacular view of the Bay on one side and a panoramic vista of downtown Tampa on the other. Sometimes the waves rose and fell, leaving momentary white mounds as the water lashed horizontally across the sand. Other times like today, the ocean water was mostly calm, and the breeze nudged very small waves, illuminated by dancing diamonds of sunlight, shimmering towards the shore. The sun glinted off the Sunshine Bridge in the distance. White trails remained on the water, left by a zigzagging speedboat whose driver was attempting to dump three bikini-clad young ladies from the inner tube it was towing. Their squeals of delight drifted up to her tenth-floor condo. The aqua fit instructor was preparing for the morning session on the pool deck, where he would soon be delivering his bored encouragement to a group of senior women and a couple of men trying valiantly to stay loose and maybe even shed some extra pounds.

Marcie held her coffee cup with both hands, savoring the flavor with every sip and trying to absorb the fact she was really home. Pharrell Williams was declaring he was "Happy," and she had to agree. It had been three weeks since she'd returned from her trip to Africa, and only small reminders of her wounds remained. The stitches in her face had dissolved. Her doctor had assured her that the small scar that still showed would disappear. The nightmares still persisted, but not as often and they were definitely not as gruesome.

Marcie had fallen into a routine of attending her social work courses and immersing herself in researching everything she could on the subject of human trafficking. It was a fascinating but tragic subject. The fact that men, and sometimes women, were taking advantage of unsuspecting girls was intensely disturbing. But she felt she could accomplish something through the courses she was taking. She filed the smiling faces of Shoni and Irene in the back of her mind, along with other sights and sounds of her trip. She didn't want to forget them, but she couldn't allow herself to be consumed by them, either.

Marcie hadn't heard from Nathan Harris, but she hadn't really expected to. Well, so maybe she had hoped a little bit, but again, it wasn't something to dwell on. Harris was probably busy chasing the bad guys and he'd been very honest and upfront that he didn't see a future in settling down with anyone. So she would need to let that go as well, although it wasn't easy. There had definitely been a chemistry and connection between them. *The few hours we spent together over the warm Stroopwafel was something I won't forget for a long time.* She was happy she'd taken a photo of it as a reminder of the delicacy and her brief time in the airport with Nathan Harris. She only wished that she'd thought to capture him in the photo at the same time.

Marcie shifted her thoughts to the day's activities. She would be going to Sami and Mason Seaforth's house in the late afternoon for a barbecue. She always looked forward to seeing them. She hadn't had the opportunity to tease Mason for awhile, and she always enjoyed that, as well as spending time with Sami. In the meantime, it was shaping up to be a day of cleaning the condo and maybe catching a quick swim in the pool before going to the Seaforths.

Marcie finished her coffee, enjoyed a leisurely brunch and changed into her bathing suit. The cleaning of the condo could wait. She examined her athletic body in the mirror. She loved working out and was proud of the figure she managed to maintain. She was determined to keep it that way through a strict diet and exercise regime. It wasn't something she had to work at; she enjoyed doing it.

A handful of people occupied some of the white plastic lounge chairs on the pool deck, but no one was in the water so she placed her phone, hat and cover-up on an unoccupied lounger and began to swim lengths. The pool was warm and inviting, and her easy front crawl carried her end to end with barely a ripple. Feeling invigorated, she toweled herself off, applied sunscreen and stretched out on the lounge. The sky was clear except for the odd puffy cloud – floating clumps of cotton candy in the sky that looked as if a child had pulled them apart. A bird of prey soared on the currents, searching for a fish that dared to swim a little too close to the surface. The sun's rays warmed Marcie's body, relaxing every muscle one by one. *It's going to be a hot one today.* She put on her hat to shield her eyes.

It would be nice to hear from a certain FBI agent, but I'm happy to be back into my nice relaxing routine. Besides that, it's a beautiful lazy Sunday.

Chapter 17

Detective Albert Baker hated Sundays. Well, this wasn't quite true. He hated being called back into work on Sundays. He actually liked Sundays, but he never felt relaxed because in the back of his mind, he was always waiting for the phone call. Some Sundays were worse than others. Some days his internal radar told him something was going to happen, and usually it did. The phone would ring, and without a protest, he would be back at work, investigating someone's horrible death. Today he had that feeling. It was almost a sixth sense – similar to someone with arthritis who can predict the weather with incredible accuracy, but with deadlier consequences. Over the years, Baker had found, his sixth sense was entirely too accurate.

This particular Sunday had started out as a peaceful, relaxing day. He and his wife had spent a little longer in bed than usual. He had been married to Anna for 25 years, and they had never bothered to have children. Anna was a successful, high-profile lawyer and with Baker's law enforcement career, they just never found the time. However, they both looked forward to the year when they would be able to retire and enjoy a day like today without fear of the phone ringing.

Before going outside, Baker prepared Eggs Benedict for them. He loved to do that on Sundays. As Baker stood at the counter, their white Persian cat Siam wound around his legs, purring softly. Baker checked the cat's dish, which was full of the food his wife had put in it before retreating outside. "Yeah, I don't think so, Mooch. Go get your own food," Baker urged, gently shoving Siam in the direction of her dish with his sandal. The cat responded by casting a withering glance with her golden eyes in Baker's direction, letting him know that he was dead to her for the foreseeable future.

He checked the steaks marinating on the counter in a Pyrex bowl. They would be ready for grilling later. He placed the Eggs Benedict on two plates and took them to the backyard patio where he set one in front of his wife and the other at his place. He sat beside Anna who was dressed in similar Sunday attire to his – shorts and a t-shirt. A soft breeze occasionally sneaked under the colorful umbrella protecting them from the sun's rays.

They were empty nesters, so the day could be their own. Anna said through a bite of her Eggs Benedict, "We need some vegetables, and it's a beautiful day. Why don't we take a ride down to the Farmer's Market? Then later maybe we can go to see the concert in the park that we talked about. We could grab a slice of pizza at the Market and then come home for a nap before we go to the concert." She smiled at him, arching her eyebrows and making air quotation marks to emphasize the word "nap."

Baker smiled. "So you think you can entice me into bed with a slice of pizza? Not only that, but do you really think that form of physical activity will offset the calories?" He liked to tease his slim wife about the perils of fast food even though weight wasn't an issue for her.

Anna responded, "It's not me I'm worried about. That frame you like to call husky seems to be getting huskier before my eyes. I'm only doing this for you. But if you'd rather, I'll eat pizza, you can have a salad. Then we can forego the nap." The air quotation marks appeared again around the last word.

Baker chuckled. He knew they would likely both be eating salad. Anna controlled her weight through diet and exercise, but she did treat herself to a slice of pizza occasionally. For him, the issue was stomach problems that he controlled with an antacid. That, added to a bad back issue he had been experiencing recently, made work that much more stressful. Or maybe, he thought ruefully, it was the other way around. He tried to curb both with over-the-counter medication.

In spite of their yard's relaxing setting, the beautiful day and their shared plans, Baker still felt on edge as he had so often felt on Sundays during his 24-year career. The acute feeling of foreboding was keenly strong today. He shifted in his chair, hoping he was mistaken.

Anna looked across the table at her husband. She could not see his eyes because of the sunglasses they both wore, but she could see his body language.

"Your Eggs Benedict are fabulous again, dear. They just get better every Sunday." She paused. "You have that feeling again, don't you? You're fidgeting."

"Thank you, but am I that obvious?" He said with a chuckle, "We *have* been together too long. You know me too well."

"Well, maybe you're wrong. You've been known to be wrong once or twice before in your life. How's your stomach?"

Baker shrugged. "I hope I'm wrong. My stomach's okay, actually. There aren't any cases right now that are especially bothering me." He laughed, adding, "Remember when our drug of choice was alcohol? Now it seems it's Tums and Aleve."

Anna's face erupted into a broad smile that lit up her whole face. She loved her man's sense of humor.

They sat quietly, enjoying their breakfast and their time together. Baker could feel the sun's rays on his back as he leaned forward for the paper that was rolled up beside him on the glass table top. He always retrieved it from the front doorstep before preparing breakfast. He slipped off the elastic holding the paper together. He would eventually end up with the local news, but the sports section was what interested him the most. He liked to comment on the odd story that appealed to him, and sure enough, he soon found one and mentioned it.

Dead silence. He poked his head around the edge of the paper to see Anna absorbed by her e-book. He often kidded her about how involved she became in her books and movies. He would smile when he saw her head move in unison with the actor's in a movie or when it was difficult to dislodge her from her book. Once he suggested that she would be oblivious to an airplane crashing in the back yard until she finished the chapter she was reading. That comment was met with an initial strong denial, followed by a shrug and a sheepish, "Well, maybe."

Only the sound of a bright red cardinal chirping away happily in the hedges and a lawn mower started by a neighbor somewhere in the distance intruded on their peaceful back yard. At first the sounds were ignored by the couple absorbed in their reading, but too quickly another, much closer and all too familiar sound destroyed their tranquility. It was the first few notes of George Thorogood's "Bad to the Bone" coming from Baker's cell phone. He had not yet figured out how to change the ringtone Anna had downloaded to his phone as a joke, but now it was interrupting their morning – and probably all of their day's plans.

Baker and his wife stared in unison at the phone as it played its tune. It was as if all ambient noise stopped as they zeroed in on the black object that had become as much a part of the anatomy as a right arm. Baker's head tipped back until he was looking straight up at the puffy clouds drifting by in the sky. He brought his head back down and looked at his wife with a frown. His shoulders slumped and she heard him let out an audible sigh.

It was on the third ring when Anna said, "Aren't you going to answer it?"

Baker picked it up reluctantly, his eyes narrowing as he punched the screen to connect harder than intended and said one word. "Baker."

Anna watched her husband as he listened, nodded slowly and said, "Okay. All right. I'll be right there."

He pressed the End button on the phone and turned to look at his wife. "Well, looks like my sixth sense was right again. I guess you'll need to shop for vegetables and go the concert by yourself. Keep that thought about the nap, though." As he rose from the table, Anna heard her husband say almost under his breath, "Why do people have to kill each other on Sundays?"

Chapter 18

The officer on duty had referred to it as a "suspicious" death. The original 911 call had said there was a body lying in a ditch on Interstate 275 and the caller didn't know whether the person was alive or dead. The inconclusiveness of the call meant that all the emergency responders had showed up: police, ambulance, fire trucks. The first officer on the scene had confirmed it was a body. Baker drove his Crown Victoria at close to 80 miles per hour, the emergency red and blue lights on the visor flashing and siren on. There wasn't much traffic leaving Tampa, and the stripes on the interstate rolled by in a blur.

After he got the call, Baker had changed into one of the rumpled suits he normally wore to work. His partner, Tom Finch, sat on the passenger side of the car. Finch had the build of an athlete and his casual blue V-neck t-shirt, khaki pants and Skecher shoes would have been comfortable at a park. An oversized watch with little knobs sticking out in all directions that Baker thought would challenge a NASA scientist sat on his tanned wrist. Finch's eyes were masked by a pair of aviator sunglasses and a Tampa Bay Rays baseball cap sat on his head.

Baker had originally been partnered with Tom Finch to mentor him, but he'd quickly found himself impressed with the younger man's dedication and commitment to his job. The junior detective was careful to listen and observe, and as a result, he had learned quickly. Finch was a great asset to the force, and Baker had grown to like him a lot. He reminded Baker of himself in the early days before stomach problems and a bad back.

The pair didn't speak as they drove. The high-pitch squeal from the air conditioner made communication nearly impossible and reminded Baker that he needed to get it serviced. To turn it off meant humidity from outside would seep in and turn the car into a steam bath. But there had just been too many crimes lately occupying his time, and Baker hadn't been able to leave the car at a service garage. As he drove to the latest atrocity, one thought crept into Baker's head — this city has gone bat shit crazy.

The familiar change in traffic flow was evolving as they drew closer to the crime scene. The interstate into Tampa was absolutely devoid of traffic as vehicles had been diverted around the scene. Meanwhile traffic on the outbound lanes of the interstate had become a writhing mass of metal and plastic gliding along on rubber at a snail-like pace as the occupants craned to catch a glimpse of what was going on across the highway. The whoops and yelps from the siren urged the vehicles out of the way as Baker deftly wove in and out of the lethargic procession.

They crested a hill to the sight of a series of flashing lights on the other side of the interstate announcing the crime scene. There was no mistaking the location. The flashing lights drew attention to it as if it were a Hollywood premiere. A row of emergency vehicles had parked haphazardly along the shoulder on the side of the road going into Tampa, opposite to the side Baker and Finch were on. Some were double parked.

Baker kept going, looking for the emergency vehicle cut-through access to the other side that he knew was about a quarter mile down the road. As he wheeled the big car into a U-turn toward the westbound lane, the tires squealed on the hot pavement until they bit into the gravel on the right hand shoulder, sending pebbles flying. He slid the vehicle to an abrupt screeching stop behind a patrol car parked at a slant with its nose angled towards the ditch.

Baker noted the blue and white tent that had been erected in the middle of the area and glanced at his partner. "Lots of action going on here." Finch nodded as he regarded the yellow police tape establishing the crime scene perimeter and a number of people, including paramedics, patrol officers, the Crime Scene Investigator and his forensics team, and the Medical Examiner performing their various duties. To a layman, it would be a fascinating scene with people carefully milling about in latex gloves inside the perimeter, ensuring there would be no contamination of evidence.

As he opened the car door to step out, Baker noticed that the refreshing breeze he'd enjoyed under the shade of the umbrella in his back yard had somehow disappeared. The suit he was wearing was lightweight, but the blazing sun beating down made it feel like a horse blanket. "It's like a friggin' blast furnace out here," he scowled. "I'm sure these guys enjoy being here on a Sunday as much as I do, and especially a day like today."

Finch wasn't quite so sure. "I don't know, Al. Some of these guys love to be here. They live for overtime checks."

They carefully descended sideways down the steep slope into the ditch, grabbing onto tall stalks of grass for balance as they went. They ducked under the police tape and avoided two sandals that lay in the grass separated from each other by a distance of about six feet.

A patrol officer in his thirties acknowledged Baker and Finch as they drew closer. They identified themselves and noting the officer's name tag, Baker said, "Good morning, Officer Ramone. It looks like you have quite the party going on here."

The Crime Scene Investigator whose job it was to coordinate the forensics team to collect and preserve evidence stood nearby and moved closer when Ramone started. "Yes, we have a deceased young black girl under the tent." He gestured towards the temporary structure. "I arrived here just before the medical people. When I saw the body, I cordoned off the area and called the ME." He nodded towards the Medical Examiner. "I thought we should put up the tent because of the heat. Looks like we could be in for a storm later on, too. I've already recorded the names of everyone here in the Crime Scene Log. The people that called it in are still here. They're waiting in that Volkswagen over there." He pointed to an ancient faded VW van parked at the far end of the row of emergency vehicles. "I isolated them as far away from the scene as I could, but they're a little spooked. I knew someone would soon be along to talk to them."

Baker could see movement behind the glass of the Volkswagen. He knew they would be anxious for someone to tell them they could leave.

The officer checked his notes again and briefed Baker and Finch on everything that had transpired since his arrival. Baker was pleased at his thoroughness and thanked him and exchanged nods with the Crime Scene Investigator.

Baker walked towards the Medical Examiner taking notes beside the tent. The ME's name was Michael Hernandes and he was in his fifties. He was about 5'6" and wore rimless round glasses. A few strands of hair lay pasted to his shining bald head.

"Hey Mike, don't you think you should be wearing a hat?"

"Hi, Albert. It's some hot out here, isn't it? I'm not going to be out here much longer. I've done about all I can do. I need to get this poor girl back to the morgue so I can do an autopsy."

Since protocol put Hernandes in charge of the body, Baker directed his chin and index finger towards the tent. "Mind if we take a look?"

Hernandes shrugged. "Sure, knock yourself out. Just don't take too long. Some nasty weather in the forecast."

"So everyone keeps telling me," Baker mumbled as he pulled on his gloves and sauntered to the tent with Finch by his side. As they entered, they saw a tarp covering a mound. A sheen of moisture immediately popped up on his forehead in the stifling air of the canvas structure. He uttered a small grunt at his protesting back when he leaned down and lifted the heavy cloth. A black girl stared back at him with unseeing eyes. She looked to be in her late teens, and she had once been pretty and full of life. But no more. Her body was bent and twisted, like a doll that had just been tossed into a dumpster. She was fully clothed, but her jeans and white t-shirt were torn. One of her bare feet was tucked awkwardly under her opposite leg. Baker checked her wrist and saw a cheap watch. The plastic face was broken and the watch had not kept on ticking as the ads promised. It had, in fact, stopped at precisely 1:48.

The girl's face indicated she had been beaten. Baker yelled out the tent door, "Hey Mike, can I look at the other side of her head?" A positive response came back and Baker turned the girl's head to one side and observed an indentation in her matted hair where some sort of object had caved in a section of her skull. It wasn't Baker's job to judge, but he surmised that this injury would turn out to be what killed her. The final determination would be up to the Medical Examiner.

Finch knelt beside him. He shook his head, "Such a waste. I'll never figure out why people do these things. Look at her legs. The way one is crumpled under the other like that, it looks to me like someone just tossed her from a car speeding down the highway. Do you think that indentation happened when she landed? Maybe that killed her."

Baker said, "Yeah, it looks like she may have been dumped from a car all right. She probably rolled a few times and ended up here in the ditch. That would explain the sandals lying where they are. I don't see any rocks that she might have hit her head on. Hard to tell if the grass was trampled by anyone other than by the crews that are supposed to be here. We'll take a look at the photos the guys took to see if there are any footprints, but my guess is she was tossed out of a car moving at a pretty high speed. Her body wasn't just placed here, that's for sure. Not the way it's twisted like that. If no one comes forward to say they saw something strange, the perps might have waited until they caught a break in the traffic before they threw her out. The time of death might give us a better idea of when she landed here." Baker uttered another grunt as he stood.

Finch noticed the grimace on Baker's face. "How's your back?"

"Ah, it's nothing compared to what happened to this poor kid. Every time I see something like this, it reminds me that no matter what ailments we have, there's always something worse."

Finch nodded slowly, but made no further comment on Baker's health. He knew it would do no good and would just aggravate his partner.

Baker saw Hernandes waiting for them as they emerged from the tent. At least they could breathe now. "That's some crease in the side of her head. When do you think she died?"

Hernandes shrugged before responding. "Well, based on the state of rigor and the temperature of her body and factoring in the heat, I would say she's been dead for about five hours."

"Five hours? That would put it at around 4 a.m. this morning. Her watch stopped at 1:48."

"Can't explain that one, my perceptive friend. That's what you guys are getting the big bucks for. Now, I'm getting out of this heat and if you're ready to let her go, I'm going to get started on the autopsy."

Baker was satisfied that the scene had been handled properly, but he wished that the established perimeter had been widened. A body thrown from a car, even at 40 miles per hour, would travel a long way before coming to rest, and the perimeter had been established just outside where her sandals had landed. It was possible her sandals hadn't come off immediately after she was tossed. But he congratulated the officer on doing a good job, and asked him to move the tape. The officer acknowledged that he would, adding that he would order a grid search of the larger area to be conducted. Baker said, "Good, just make sure it's done as soon as possible." Then he added with a tight smile, "Apparently, there's a storm coming."

He added, "Okay, let us know as soon as you have something. I want to run anything that distinguishes her through NCIC to try to figure out who she is. If that doesn't work, we'll work with Hernandes to put the information in NamUs. We'll put her fingerprints through AFIS as well."

The technical acronyms spilled out of Baker's mouth like scrabble letters dumped from a container onto his cluttered desk. The ME heard his name mentioned, and he and Finch nodded in unison. For them, the explanation was quite clear. Finch would start with NCIC, the National Crime Investigation Center and the best friend of every law enforcement officer – and he would do it from the computer in the car. It was a database of criminal information available 24-7 to anyone with the right credentials. Information had to be entered by a law enforcement officer who had undergone strict screening, and it was controlled by layers of passwords. There were certain restrictions regarding the type of information that could be entered. A person of any age who is missing under circumstances indicating that that person's physical safety may be in danger could be entered into the system. If details about a young black girl that matched the characteristics of the victim lying in the ditch had already been entered, NCIC would help them identify her and bring them a step closer to finding her killer.

Finch would also enter the girl's fingerprints in the Automated Fingerprint Information System or AFIS, which used algorithms to find matches for prints already in the database for any number of reasons. If the girl's fingerprints had been entered in the system, they would be matched, and that would also help identify her.

If they were still unable to identify the girl, her information – including characteristics such as sex, race, distinguishing body features and even dental information – would then be entered in NamUs or the National Missing and Unidentified Persons System.

Baker motioned to his partner to join him. "Let's go and talk to the people in the van. They're the ones who made the call about the girl's body." As the back of Baker's hand came away damp from wiping it across his brow, he was feeling a little envious of his partner. Finch could have just stepped out of GQ Magazine. His forehead was devoid of perspiration, and the perfectly rounded peak of his baseball cap shaded his eyes. His sunglasses now rested jauntily on his cap.

Finch acknowledged Baker's instruction with a wave of his own, revealing a small wet stain in the armpit.

Baker hauled himself up the slope. *Maybe he isn't perfect, after all.* A close-lipped smile crossed his face as he dug a small cylindrical package out of his pocket and popped an antacid in his mouth.

Chapter 19

As they trudged down the road to the van, Baker noticed the cars still slowing to a crawl on the other side of the highway as occupants craned their necks to catch a glimpse of someone's misfortune, giving them a story they could share over dinner with friends and family. Baker knew the flashing LED lights from the emergency vehicles lining the edge of the highway could be seen for miles in either direction, in spite of the bright sun beating down. They would draw the eyes of the curious like bees zeroing in on honey. The rubberneckers would not be able to see anything from the highway other than door after door of emergency vehicles and one old van as they passed by. Even if they had been able to see past the parked vehicles, the tent and the tall grass growing in the ditch obscured the sight of the body.

Baker was well aware that vehicles would be backed up to Interstate 75 by now, and those who were not in sight of the action would be cursing the idiot who had created this mess. Baker wondered why they just didn't continue on to their destinations at a safe speed to enjoy their Sunday family time.

As Baker approached the old Volkswagen he speculated about whether it had been declared roadworthy recently. Rust had been munching on the wheel wells for some time and daylight was visible through ragged holes in the metal. The plate announced it was from Georgia.

With a practiced flick of his wrist, his wallet unfolded, revealing his credentials for the driver to see. Finch was right behind, looking over Baker's shoulder at the occupants of the vehicle. He copied Baker's action to present his identification. The driver and the woman sitting in the passenger seat appeared to be in their thirties and apparently hoped to capture a former period in history they'd been too young to enjoy when it happened. Both sported tie-dyed shirts and torn jeans. He had long straggly hair and a sparse goatee. A boy of about eight silently slouched in the back seat, his eyes wide and his mouth open as he stared at the activity down the road in the ditch.

Baker started the conversation. "Good morning, sir. Thanks for calling 911. I'm Detective Albert Baker and this is my partner, Tom Finch. We're the lead investigators on this case. Could you please tell us how you discovered the body?"

"Of course," the driver said. His right eye had an occasional tic and Baker wondered if it was always there, or if the driver was unusually nervous, perhaps because of pot in the vehicle. "The dang car overheated right at this very spot, well, across from where the girl was. I pulled over to give it a chance to cool down, and young Travis there wandered off into the ditch to kill some time. It takes about an hour for this old junk heap to cool down enough in this heat to continue on. That's when the boy found the girl's body. He came high-tailing out like he was being chased by a bear. He's pretty shook up."

"Did you approach the girl before you called 911?"

"No, sir. I went to see what the boy was going on about. I saw what he saw and I called for an ambulance."

"Okay, you did the right thing. If it's any consolation, if your vehicle hadn't overheated here, the girl probably wouldn't have been discovered until a mainte-nance crew mowed the grass or somebody looking for beer bottles found her. It's too bad your son had to see her. A victim assistance person will be along shortly to speak to you both and the boy if you like. It won't take them long to get here. To be honest, sometimes counseling is advisable after something like this."

"Thanks for the offer, but I think we'll be okay once we get back home."

Baker looked in the back window at the boy. He wasn't so sure he agreed. "Just be aware that sometimes there is a delayed reaction to what people see. My partner will leave his card in case any of you would like assistance. Mind if we talk to your boy? I'd prefer to do it in our car, if you don't mind."

"No, go ahead. Do what you have to do. We believe in peace and harmony in the world, and to see something like this is just sickening. Anything we can to help catch whoever did this . . ."

Baker nodded his thanks, and he and Finch walked behind the van to Travis' open window and introduced themselves.

"Good morning, Travis. I'm Detective Baker and this is Detective Finch. We would just like to ask you a couple of questions, if that's okay? I know you've had a tough day so we'll let you go soon. How're you doing?"

Travis didn't answer.

The driver spoke up in a louder than normal voice, "Tell him how you are, Travis. Hurry up, boy. We have to get on our way."

So much for peace and harmony, thought Baker. He said to Travis, "Have you ever been in a police car? We'd like to show you our car and just ask a couple of questions. Would that be all right? Then you can be on your way, okay?"

Travis looked at his dad who impatiently waved his hand, urging the youngster to go.

The detectives and the small boy walked over to the police car and got in. Baker pointed to some of the equipment in the vehicle, explaining calmly how each thing worked. As he did so, Finch removed a small recorder from the glove compartment and flicked the switch. Travis listened wide-eyed, but said nothing, and soon returned his gaze to the activity in the ditch.

Finch motioned to Baker to hold off until he changed the batteries to bring the dead recorder back to life. Baker asked Travis about school and his favorite sports, but the questions received only monosyllabic responses.

On Finch's signal, Baker said gently, "We're going to record this, okay, Travis? Now can you please tell us what you saw?"

With an effort, Travis pulled his eyes away from the scene and stared downward in the direction of his running shoes, but his eyes remained unfocused. His voice was barely above a whisper. "I saw the girl lying in the ditch. I thought she was sick, but her body was all twisted. Is she . . .is she . . .dead?"

Baker squeezed the boy's arm. "I'm afraid she is, Travis. You were very brave telling your parents about her so they could try to help. Did you try to wake her up?"

Softly again, his eyes still focused in his shoes. "No, I just came and told my dad. I didn't want to get close to her. I was scared."

"Okay, Travis. Detective Finch and I are proud of you for what you did. You handled yourself like an adult. Thank you." After asking the boy a few more questions to verify the time he'd found the body and to confirm the state it was in, Baker said, "Can you tell us how old you are?"

"I'm eight years old," Travis replied almost inaudibly. Baker and Finch shook the young man's hand and thanked him again. Baker escorted Travis back to the van while Finch walked to the driver's side window to document information about the witnesses and to give them permission to be on their way.

Albert Baker stood at the roadside, gazing down the highway. Trees in the distance by the side of the road shimmered in the oppressive heat rising from the pavement. He loosened his tie and tugged his damp shirt collar away from his sticky neck. He stepped aside as the emergency vehicles pulled away from the roadside, and the officer in charge of diverting traffic would be told to allow them back onto the interstate. Baker thought sadly about the waste of human life. A young person's life snuffed out before it even began, and an even younger person who will be troubled forever by things he saw that he can't ever unsee.

Who was the girl? How did she end up in the ditch? And why? Who would want to do that to her?

With a heave of his shoulders, Baker walked back to join Finch at their car. Just as with every other case he had worked on, he was determined to find answers to his questions. A reporter he knew from other cases intercepted him before he got to his car.

"Any comments, Detective?"

Baker looked away to settle himself before answering. He understood the role of the news and tried to cooperate as much as he could, but even though he had been cleared by the brass to speak to the press, it was a part of his job he didn't much care for. Baker didn't slow his step, but as he brushed by the reporter, he said through clenched teeth, "We have no idea who she is, where she's from or what happened to her. When we have some information, we'll let you know." Before the reporter could say anything more, Baker got inside the car, slammed the door, turned the key and the car and its noisy air conditioner came to life.

Looking at Finch with a sigh, he turned his head back towards the closed window, checked the side mirror, stomped on the gas and sprayed the reporter with dust and loose gravel as he pulled into the traffic.

As he drove back down the interstate towards Tampa, the thunderheads forming in the west and the odd jagged fork of lightning streaking through the darkening sky suggested those grilled steaks would have to wait. *I guess they were right about the storm.* Not much wonder there's something brewing with this heat, thought Baker.

It would be a long time before he got home, anyway.

Chapter 20

The investigative team had been assembled to compare notes as soon as they returned from the crime scene. Priorities were established for the investigation and the case review had taken most of the night. They had finally concluded that there wasn't much more they could do so they all went home for a few precious hours of sleep.

The rain everyone had predicted had been relentless. Baker had only been in bed a few minutes when he awoke with a start and opened one eye to see the clock flashing 4:23 a.m. The clock had apparently stopped sometime after he got home – the electricity interrupted by the storm raging outside. Lightning ripped open the dark clouds and lit up the room through the closed drapes. Thunder crashed immediately after every strike. He got up to go to the bathroom and flicked on the light. Nothing. When he got back to the bed, the clock had gone dark. Next to him, his wife slept peacefully, oblivious to the raging storm outside.

By the time he woke up – a little later than usual without the alarm – the rain had stopped. Baker had dressed quickly and driven to work with the window down, enjoying the air that had been freshened and thankfully, cooled by the overnight deluge. Now he sat in front of his computer ready to start work again on the investigation.

The detective knew he was going to be in trouble with the boss for saying what he did to the reporter. After all, he had admitted that the police had no clues about what had transpired and no leads – and then there was the little thing of spraying the reporter with gravel as he pulled away onto the highway. If the reporter complained, Baker knew he would be receiving a phone call or a summons to the boss' office so the old man could rip him a new one. Those in the department who were trained and had approval to deal with the media were told to cooperate and to put as positive a spin as possible on their quotes. He knew his action had been childish, but the death of the young girl, coupled with the lack of apparent evidence, the suffocating heat, and his own struggles with his bad back and stomach had upset him just enough to unleash his frustrations on the reporter. He regretted his action.

Albert Baker scrolled through the morning news to see what the media had to say about the latest murder in the Tampa area. He knew in the overall scheme of things, it would take much more than that to make the headlines, even though the girl's death would change things forever for her family. An article about aid money not reaching people in Haiti screamed from the headlines of the front page.

Baker scanned the Haiti article and a couple of others before coming to the section titled "News Near You." Sure, he thought, this is where it would be. He quickly scanned local headlines about events around their city until he came across a short article about a young black girl tragically found dead in a ditch alongside I-275. The couple from Georgia were quoted and Travis was mentioned. Baker took a deep breath when he saw that his comments were summarized by the terse words, "There was no official comment from Detective Albert Baker of the Tampa Bay Police Department who is in charge of the investigation."

Baker frowned and turned his attention to the endless paperwork that needed to be filed. The phone call did come from the police chief, but it wasn't the tirade he expected. The old man said the reporter thought the gravel spraying incident was intentional. But Baker's boss had simply chuckled and admitted that he had often wanted to do the same thing but never had the guts. He reminded Baker that next time he should vent his frustration away from the prying ears of the reporters.

Baker thought back for a moment to the time his career started. Back then, it was all paperwork, but now it involved a lot of time sitting at the computer, entering information into a database. He kind of related to the Luddites who protested the advancement of technology at the start of the early 1800s. True, their issues related to advancements like spinning wheels replacing less skilled work, but he thought the exponential growth in technology of today impacted people the same way. He also blamed sitting hunched over at the computer for his bad back.

Grudgingly, he admitted it was nice to have instant access to information.

It was late into the morning when the Medical Examiner called.

"Hi, Albert. It's Mike Hernandes."

"I know, Mike, I can see your name on my phone display. What's up?"

"I'm about to start the autopsy on the girl from the ditch. You wanna come over and observe?"

"Sure, I'll be right there." Baker was always of the opinion that it could save time later if he was actually on hand to observe the autopsy. Even though Hernandes was thorough and quick with his reports, it just seemed more expedient to be there.

The two exchanged greetings when Baker arrived. Baker also acknowledged the Crime Scene Investigator who was on hand to take notes of everything that transpired during the autopsy. Hernandes peered over his round glasses at the detective. "I've already taken photos of her with her clothes on and removed the clothing. Photos and X-rays have been taken of the wounds. She died from blunt force trauma. Somebody whacked her pretty hard. Your weapon will probably turn out to be something round and very hard or maybe even somebody's fist."

That immediately raised all kinds of questions in Baker's mind. A fist? Accident? Intentional? "Okay, let's see what else comes up."

Hernandes performed the rest of his examination, taking pictures and speaking into the microphone around his neck. The whole process was always recorded for future reference. Baker stood back, arms folded, leaning against the wall, saying nothing and waiting for the experienced ME to finish his work. Baker perked up at mentions of a defensive wound on the girl's arm and some broken fingernails. Hernandes had commented into the mike that the girl's left arm was broken, and she had suffered some fractured ribs in her past. Of particular interest to Baker was Hernandes' statement that one of the girl's legs was shorter than the other and that she would have walked with a distinct limp. He also mentioned some kind of illness.

After two hours, the autopsy was done. Hernandes turned to the detective. "You must get tired watching this stuff. I'll write up the report and get the preliminary version to you in the next couple of days."

"Thanks, Mike. Autopsies have always interested me. I don't know how we could determine a victim's identity or the facts surrounding what happened to them without an autopsy." Baker stopped, then added, "Mike, what can you tell me about her wounds and the limp?" Baker braced himself for the forensic pathology lecture he knew was inevitable.

"Well, you know I probably shouldn't speculate, but since it's you . . . The cause of the wounds will be for you to figure out, of course, but if I were to speculate, I would say the broken arm was peri-mortem. You do remember the traumatic time-frame terms 'ante-mortem,' 'peri-mortem' and 'post-mortem,' don't you?"

Baker opened his mouth to say that he did remember the terms from the previous ten lectures but closed it again. This was Hernandes' show and the ME continued. "Ante-mortem is the easiest type of trauma to detect in forensic pathology. It occurs before death, and we can determine that because the healing process to repair the wound has already begun or is even completed. The broken ribs our young Jane Doe suffered came from an old wound that had healed. I wouldn't care to speculate on what caused it, but the injury was definitely ante-mortem.

"With bones, it's all about the elasticity remaining. Breaks after death or post-mortem tend to shatter as the bone dries out. There's no evidence of shattering in the other wounds she has. They're fresher, which makes them peri-mortem. Her broken arm is splintered, indicating that it occurred either close to the time of her death or soon after, possibly from being thrown into the ditch. The recent bruise on her arm and her broken fingernails appear to be defensive wounds from trying to fend off her attacker.

"While I'm at it, I might as well tell you about the head wound. It has to do with coup and contrecoup head injuries."

Baker knew exactly what they were from sitting in on numerous autopsies, but he let Hernandes proceed with his explanation without slowing. To himself,

Baker thought the ME should consider teaching in his spare time.

"By definition, a coup injury occurs when a moving object hits the head. The trauma causes the brain to slam against the skull where the impact occurs. For example, being hit by a fist would do that. A contrecoup occurs when the head hits a stationary object. So if a fist hits someone's head, the force causes the brain to impact that side of the skull and then rebounds over to impact the other side of the skull and voila, you have both coup and contrecoup. Our young lady suffered the injury twice. The first blow may have knocked her down, causing her to strike her head against something. It's hard to tell which killed her, but there was definitely a major impact on both sides. By the shape of the impact on the right, I would say she was struck by someone who is right-handed before she fell against something."

Baker thought that knowing the person they were looking for was right-handed really didn't narrow the search much.

Baker suddenly realized that Hernandes was still talking. "There are two other things that might help you identify her more easily, though, Albert. The first is the limp you mentioned. One of her legs is slightly shorter than the other. There isn't a big difference, but it would be enough to give her a distinct limp. I would say she was born with it. Or it could've been caused by something like malnutrition."

"Well, at least we can enter that information in the system and see if we come up with a match. What's the second thing?"

"The second is that there is some enlargement of her spleen. You probably heard me mention that. There could be a number of reasons, but we'll be able to determine the cause through the blood analysis. I do have a theory that I will definitely follow up on. I will be able to eliminate a few possible causes just by looking at the spleen. For example, it doesn't appear to have become enlarged by trauma."

Hernandes paused. He stared thoughtfully at the spleen which sat in a dish on the table. His head was cocked to one side, and he tugged repeatedly on his right ear. Baker had seen this position many times, so he waited. Finally, the doctor said. "Based on what I'm seeing, there's a possibility, and I repeat, possibility, that she had sickle cell disease."

"What?" "Sickle cell disease? Okay, let's say your speculation is correct. How does that diagnosis help us figure out who she is?"

Hernandes took the stage again. "Sickle cell disease develops when the hemoglobin in the red blood cells becomes rigid and forms a shape that looks something like a sickle. The diseased red blood cells only live about 10-15% as long as normal cells. The dead cells clump together and stick to the walls of the blood vessels so blood flow is restricted. In undeveloped countries, the mortality rate from the disease is pretty high for children up to around five years of age. If a child makes it to five, they have a good chance of living a decent life with the disease *if* they take proper medication.

"Some of the symptoms are pain in the limbs, fatigue, stress . . . stuff like that. The pain can be chronic. Since this young lady's spleen is enlarged, if SCD caused it, it wouldn't have been long before she started having some of the symptoms if she weren't already. She would've needed treatment soon. If a black girl with sickle cell disease turns up in your Missing Persons system, there's a very good chance it will be our girl here.

"The blood tests can determine whether or not that's what it is. Of course, the report will also show her DNA and any other distinguishing I.D. you might be able to enter into that all-knowing computer system of yours. It will take a while. Oh, and based on what I've seen so far, Albert, I would say she was somewhere between 15 and 18 years of age. If she did have sickle cell disease, her life span would have been reduced, depending on the treatment she got. With the right treatment, though, people with the disease can live beyond 50 years of age."

"Yeah, well, her life span shouldn't have been reduced the way it was. She should've been given the opportunity to correct the problem and live a normal healthy life," Baker replied tersely. He sighed. "Okay, well, this certainly helps, Mike. At least it's a start to figuring out who she is." Baker scratched his head momentarily and then asked, "I'm curious, though. What causes sickle cell disease?"

Hernandes had already started cleaning up, so the answer was surprisingly short. "As I mentioned, it's most prevalent in underdeveloped countries. It's passed on at birth. It's not contagious or anything. It's just something that some parents give to their children." He stopped what he was doing long enough to add with a little smile, "It's the gift that keeps on giving."

"Any guesses as to which underdeveloped countries are most likely to produce this disease?" queried Baker as he turned to leave.

"Hard to say," responded Hernandes. He looked over at Baker. "Don't get me wrong, Albert. There are somewhere between 80,000-100,000 people with the disease in the U.S. But it's more widespread in underdeveloped countries. About all I can say is that based on her skin tone, you might want to look first for her birthplace somewhere in Africa."

Baker smiled for the first time this morning. "Well, that narrows the search down to a continent of about a billion. If you're right, of course. Anyway, thanks again for letting me sit in, Mike. Oh, and I should be able to pass the next test on the two coups and the three mortems, thanks to you." Baker grinned, raising his hand in a casual wave. "Take care, my friend."

The two men shook hands and turned away to carry on with their respective duties. Baker waved at the Crime Scene Investigator when he looked up briefly from his note-taking.

On the way back to the office, Baker called Finch's cell phone to let him know about their Jane Doe's limp, the fact that she may have been born in Africa, and about her possible sickle cell disease. He asked his partner to enter the new information into NCIC. He wasn't really expecting much even with the new information. *Africa?* What are the odds we're going to find anything at all?

But Detective Albert Baker would have been surprised to know how wrong he was about to be.

Chapter 21

Detective Baker walked back into the office, poured a cup of the thick black liquid that passed for coffee, and settled back behind his desk as he turned on his computer. He let the coffee cool for a few minutes before taking a sip. He grimaced at the taste as he had countless times in the past, then set the cup down and frowned slightly at the dark ring near the top of the cup where the coffee had been.

His office looked like a hurricane had swept through recently. The bookshelves bulged with various law enforcement books threatening to topple to the floor, the pages Baker deemed important marked by yellow stickers. Files and newspapers lay on the cabinets that occupied the corner of the room, and his desk was littered in paper. Yet Baker's colleagues knew he could immediately place his hands on anything that he needed to. He was just about to check his emails when a tap sounded on the door.

Finch stood leaning against the door frame with his arms crossed and a file dangling from one hand. With a wave, Baker summoned him into the office, and his protégé plunked himself down in the chair on the opposite side of the desk to Baker. Finch slouched with his legs straight out and his feet crossed at the ankle. His lips wound into a smug smile. As usual, he was casually attired in designer jeans and a white golf shirt that emphasized his permanent tan. The file he had been carrying now rested on his lap and he peered at Baker around steepled fingers without saying a word.

Baker finally spoke first. "Did you find a woman that would actually spend some time with you last night or what?

"There were so many to choose from, I decided it was best to disappoint them all. No, I was just wondering if you really thought we'd get anything back on the girl in the ditch from the information we had. Talk about a long shot."

Baker frowned at Finch's demeanor and shook his head. "No, I know it was a long shot. It was worth a try, though. Hernandes thinks she might have been born in Africa. The possible disease Mike mentioned – sickle cell – should help us identify her, eventually. Maybe she was born here in this country, but it's possible her family moved here from somewhere else at some point. Maybe the results from the DNA test will tell us something and we'll put a notice about her on the news to see if anyone comes forward. I probably could have used that reporter for that if I hadn't sprayed him with gravel. Maybe *you* should talk to him."

Finch's face broke into a wide smile. "We may not have to do all that. As you know, I ran the information through the National Crime Information Center when we were still at the scene, but nothing came back. However, when I entered the additional information from the autopsy, we did get some matches. Five, to be precise. One of the matches is pretty interesting. It comes from information that was entered by an FBI Special Agent by the name of Nathan Harris in Atlanta."

Baker's eyebrows rose. "What matched?"

Finch sat up and tossed the file on top of the pile that was perilously close to sliding to the floor. Baker slammed his hand on the pile to prevent the inevitable avalanche. He propped his reading glasses on his nose, opened the file and scanned each of the documents. They were printed versions of Missing Persons Reports filed by law enforcement officials across the country identifying the name, age, sex, race, height and weight, eye and hair color of young people who had disappeared. Baker knew there were over 400,000 missing kids under the age of 18 recorded in NCIC – and more than half were girls. He wasn't sure if he was surprised that only five popped out, or if he was surprised that *any* matching criteria had actually surfaced given the vague information they had available.

The first four sheets bore similar information, but the photos were wrong. The height or weight recorded was also slightly different than the dead girl's. Notes had been made on each entry that the person had a limp. Baker reached the last one and froze in disbelief. The face of the dead girl leaped off the page. He was sure it was the same girl – at least, there was a striking similarity between the victim now lying in the morgue and the girl staring back at him from the page. The image had been cropped from a larger photo. Baker read the description twice, absorbing the information.

As Finch had said, there was an annotation that it had been entered by Nathan Harris in Atlanta and it described a 17 year-old African girl who had disappeared in Tanzania. The entry was made about three weeks previously. The physical characteristics seemed to match the girl in the morgue perfectly. Then he got to a note at the bottom, which read, 'Irene Sembaza has a distinct limp.'"

Baker's chair creaked as he leaned back, weaving his hands together across his stomach. His computer screen flickered as he jarred the desk, and the screen-saver whirred back to life. His eyes stared unfocused at a photo on the wall. *Could it possibly be that easy to identify her? Is this just coincidence? Tanzania? What would she be doing here in the U.S. then?*

Finch broke the silence. "So why do you think an FBI agent in Atlanta would be entering information about a girl missing in Tanzania?"

Baker's eyes swung back to his colleague. "Beats me. Must be related to a case he's working on. Did you get anything from the automated fingerprint system?"

"Nope, no matches in AFIS."

"Okay, I'm going to give this Nathan Harris a call to see if he can shed some light. Stick around. I'll put it on speaker."

Baker dialed the number at the bottom of the sheet and pressed the button to activate the speaker on the phone. He was certain it would be a direct line, and sure enough, it was picked up on the fourth ring.

"Special Agent Harris, this is Detective Albert Baker from Tampa. I'm here with my partner, Tom Finch. We have you on speaker. Hope you don't mind."

"Not at all, Detective Baker. How can I help you?"

"Am I catching you at a good time?"

"Well, you know how it is. The bad guys never sleep."

They both chuckled in shared acknowledgment. "Ain't that the truth? Listen, I'll get right to the point. We have a young girl in a morgue here and we've entered what we know about her in NCIC. We got a handful of matches, but the one that stands out is an entry you made about three weeks ago."

He heard a sharp intake of breath on the other end of the line. Then, "Three weeks ago? You mean the girl in Tanzania? You've got to be kidding. There were two of them – which one are you talking about?" There was a momentary silence on the phone. "Here it is. Their names were Irene Sembaza and Shoni Batanga."

"I wish I were kidding, but I'm not. It looks to be Irene Sembaza," Baker responded. "Everything seems to match, right down to the limp. The picture sure looks like her. The ME here says she was probably born with the limp. He also thinks maybe she had an illness called, uh, just a minute, let me check . . ." Baker shuffled through his notes. "Sickle cell disease."

"I don't know anything about that. I'll tell you why I entered her name, though. I'm working a case on human trafficking, and I was in Tanzania helping the authorities there investigate a local connection. By coincidence, a woman who also happened to be from the Tampa area came to us a couple days before I left. She had stumbled across these young girls during a school tour, and she was concerned by something they said about running away and trying to get to America. It turned out her fears were well founded. Sure enough, the girls did run away from their school, and we think they were caught up in the human trafficking ring I was investigating.

"The woman went looking for the girls and ended up at a house used by a guy named Deop and his buddy Suleiman. Deop's adept at forging documents and arranging false paperwork to get people out of the country. It's funny, but the woman said he was having trouble typing, but she also said he was high on something so that could explain it. He was using the house as a drop for girls to get processed before they're taken to other countries. We also found another house a few doors down full of computer equipment and high-resolution printers. The neighbors weren't shy about pointing them out to us."

Baker asked, "So, you really think the two girls the woman met became part of the human trafficking ring?"

"We don't know for sure, but if Deop got hold of them, there's a good chance. We know that Deop and Suleiman are only the tip of the iceberg. I'm sure the local police will get what they can out of them, and then we'll use the information to try to get to the head of the snake. It's a much bigger issue than just

Deop and Suleiman, that's for sure. I entered the information in NCIC expecting to get a hit from somewhere eventually, but I never actually dreamed the girls, or at least one of them, might end up right there in Tampa of all places."

Harris elaborated more on the case for the two detectives. Then, in response to the unasked question, he said, "I wasn't able to get any fingerprints on the girls. We checked out the dormitory but there are so many girls living there, it would be impossible to isolate anyone's prints. We checked their homes, too, but it's not like they have chrome appliances that will hold prints. There was nothing useable there, either. So it's unlikely you'd find anything in AFIS."

"No, we didn't. Do you have any other information? What about this woman in Tampa? Do you think there's some connection between her and the girl somehow ending up here?"

"She's actually from St. Petersburg. I can't see her being involved, Detective. I think it must be just coincidence. She was lucky to escape alive after meeting with Deop. He tried to kill her and she fought back with everything she had. She also saved the life of the taxi driver who took her there. I will tell you, though, that my boss isn't so sure. He wants me to keep an eye on her to make sure she doesn't have anything to do with it.

"Based on the information I gathered in Africa, the girls were taken to Deop who would've set them up with the paperwork to send them off to various parts of the world. Thanks to the woman, we nabbed him. He hasn't told the African police department much, but he did say the girls were given an escort to travel and were promised jobs or education when they arrived at their destination. He says he didn't know where they were being taken, but of course it would probably mean the sex trade or service industry plus a bunch of debt that they can never pay off. It's debt bondage. You know how it works. We're fighting a business that brings 50,000 girls a year into the U.S. The going rate for Asian girls sold to brothels in the U.S. is around $20,000. An African girl would probably bring at least that much."

They talked more about the case, and Baker shared what little he knew about the girl in the ditch. Finally, Harris said, "The picture I put in NCIC was taken by the woman. I cropped out her and another girl. The other girl, Shoni, is also in the system. Hopefully, you don't find her in some ditch as well. You could always ask the woman to identify the girl in the morgue but it would be kind of hard on her. She was beating herself up over not being able to do something for the two girls. I've been meaning to call her, anyway, to make sure she's okay. I've just been so damn busy. I'll give her a call. If the dead girl turns out to be the one missing from Tanzania, this is going to become an international case and it's over to me, anyway. If we need her to identify the girl, I'll set it up with you."

"Okay, I'll let you know. How do you like working the human trafficking gig?"

"You know what it feels like sometimes? Remember that carnival game where you whack a gopher with a mallet and another immediately pops up? That's a bit what it's like. But we'll keep shutting them down in the hopes that one day there will be an end to it."

"Well, keep fighting the good fight. Thanks, Agent Harris. By the way, just for the record, what's the woman's name?"

"Her name is Marcie Kane."

Baker sat back in his chair, which groaned in response. He knew that name! Baker cast a quick incredulous glance at Finch. He could tell by his partner's expression that he remembered it as well.

"Wait a minute. We know that name," Baker said evenly. "If it's the same person, she was involved in a case about two years ago where a friend disappeared. She and the friend's husband tried to play detective, things got complicated, and she got shot in the process."

"It's the same person, Detective. Our flights coincided at the Amsterdam airport and we spent some time having coffee. I had already done some research on her, but she told me a bit about her experience. I don't think it's one she wants to repeat. Based on my conversation with her, she would have to be an Academy Award worthy actress or have another personality that I didn't get to meet to be involved in this. As I said, she's tough, though. She managed to escape some pretty rough people in Tanzania with a little ingenuity and some martial arts thrown in."

Baker slowly shook his head in Finch's direction. "I'll be damned. This gets weirder and weirder. So how do you want to handle this?"

"I'll send a scan of the photo of the woman and the two girls, but I don't think it will help much. You already have Irene's picture. Let me know if you still think it's our girl. If it turns out to be her, just send me everything you have on it and I'll add it to my files. I'll call Ms. Kane if need be at that point. I need to talk to her again, anyway, as I said. I would like you guys to stay involved, but if everything works out, you might have one less case to worry about, Detective."

"Well, I'm kind of like you, Agent Harris. I'll still be whacking gophers."

They both laughed quietly and after wishing each other good luck, the phones were disconnected.

Detective Baker closed the file and handed the papers from NCIC back to Finch. He marveled at the twists and turns life take sometimes.

In Atlanta, Nathan Harris leaned back in his chair with his fingers linked behind his head. He knew he'd feel bad if the dead girl turned out to be Irene Sembaza. At the same time, it gave him two things he had been hoping for. It might be the break he needed to get his temporarily-stalled human trafficking case going again. The second was that even though he would be imparting bad news in the case, he now had an excuse to call Marcie Kane.

Chapter 22

Marcie welcomed the fresh air drifting through her condo. Opening the patio door to allow the sea breeze in was a rare opportunity during summer days in St. Petersburg, so she planned to take full advantage of it. The humidity had broken sometime overnight. According to the internet news, a wild storm roared through the area and the power had been out in some parts of Tampa. She had had a dreamless sleep and missed all the action, but some small branches with a few leaves still attached lay on the pool deck, attesting to the fact that they hadn't been spared from the storm's wrath.

She felt good. After toasting herself in the sun at the pool yesterday, she had spent an enjoyable afternoon with Mason and Sami Seaforth. It was always a relaxing time with them; and after their harrowing experience together two years previously, they had grown even closer. Marcie had set aside cleaning her condo to be with her friends, but it was worth it. Now she'd just finished doing that task, even straightening the framed prints on the wall and adjusting the hippopotamus and rhinoceros carvings on the sofa table. Her morning workout at the gym had left her invigorated. She wasn't expecting to see anyone, so her knees peeked through the holes in a pair of faded jeans and she wore an oversized but comfortable Tampa Bay Rays shirt. As she put it on, she thought how long it had been since she had gone to a game.

Her early afternoon lunch of a crunchy tuna wrap with celery and red peppers had left Marcie feeling full, and dinner was the furthest thing from her mind. Instead, she was now relaxed and engrossed in a book by one of her favorite authors, stretched out on the lounge on her balcony. When she looked up, she could see the waves beyond her bare feet as if they were inches away. She drew on a straw for a sip of the lemonade she had poured before sitting down. Time for more ice, she thought. But first she set the book down on her lap, laid her head back against the lounge, and closed her eyes. Only for a minute, she thought, as her body melted into the chair.

She didn't know how long she had been asleep. A buzzing sound awoke her and she opened one eye to see her phone dancing crazily on the glass table with each ring. The screen read "unknown number." *No, I don't need my carpets cleaned.* Sure that it was a nuisance call, Marcie reluctantly picked up the phone with a sigh and hit the answer button, ready to blast the person on the line. But as soon as she said hello, her heart leaped. The caller on the other end wasn't a nuisance caller at all. In fact, quite the opposite. The voice in Marcie's ear belonged to Nathan Harris.

Marcie sat bolt upright. Her elbow caught the plastic glass holding the remainder of her lemonade and sent it careening across the glass table top and toppling to the floor. Her attempt to catch the glass caused her chair to tilt precariously forward and she grunted as she caught herself. Despite her efforts, the contents splashed on the area rug covering the balcony floor and the cup landed with a clatter against one of the metal supports holding up the screened wall. Marcie was sure Harris would be able to hear the commotion. Marcie chuckled at her clumsiness and one thing flashed across her mind. Thank God this isn't a video call.

Recovering, she blurted, "Hi Nathan. To what do I owe the pleasure of this call? Are you in town?"

"No, I'm in Atlanta. I wanted to see how you're doing. Are you still having nightmares?"

Marcie dabbed at the carpet with her napkin as she leaned forward with the phone snagged between her ear and shoulder. "I'm doing okay, actually. The nightmares still pop up every once in a while but they aren't nearly as graphic. You haven't starred in one recently." She laughed. "How are you? Still saving America from the bad guys?" Marcie straightened and caught herself looking down at the clothes she was wearing as if Nathan could see her through the phone line. She determined that if he suggested a video call session, she would definitely change clothes first.

"Doing my best, but it's a constant battle," Nathan replied. "Listen, I'm sorry I didn't call earlier. I've been caught up in a couple of cases that are consuming my time. What have you been up to?"

"Oh, you know, sharpening my martial arts techniques, improving my shooting skills, learning how to apply makeup to cover bruises and cuts . . . just preparing myself for my next vacation."

They both laughed at that. They talked comfortably, covering the three weeks since they'd last seen each other in the Amsterdam airport, until Nathan abruptly changed the subject.

"Marcie, I do have another reason for my call. I wanted to see how you're doing, but I'm afraid I have some bad news about one of the girls you met in Africa."

Marcie's shoulder and stomach muscles constricted. Silently, she leaned back in her lounge and pressed the phone closer to her ear to make sure she heard every syllable. His words sounded ominous.

Nathan continued, "A girl fitting the description of Irene Sembaza was found in a ditch on Highway 275 on Sunday. You may have heard it on the news. The body's in a morgue in Tampa. I got a call from a detective in your Tampa Bay police department. He said the girl would have had a limp from one leg being shorter than the other. From the description I was given, it sounds like it could be Irene. The investigators have seen the photo you took, and they sound pretty convinced it's her as well. Marcie, I'm sorry to have to tell you this."

Marcie drew in a sharp breath. She felt a physical stab at her heart, and questions made her head feel as if it was about to explode. *Irene Sembaza was dead? In Tampa? How did she get here? Why was she here? What could have happened to her? And then, most importantly of all, where's Shoni? There must be some horrible mistake.*

She realized she hadn't said a word since Nathan had told her the bad news. "Are you okay, Marcie?"

Marcie's voice was barely above a whisper. She rubbed her forehead with her free hand. "Uh, yes, I'm just trying to process this. I checked the news on the internet this morning, but I didn't see anything about it. I can't believe this. Nathan, what happened to Irene? Was it a car accident?"

There was a long pause before Nathan Harris said quietly, "No, it's worse than that, Marcie. She was murdered."

Marcie held her head in disbelief, trying to shake off what she had just heard. Nathan wasn't making sense. Her voice rose. "Murdered!? No! That can't be right. Why would a young girl like Irene be murdered? Why would Irene even be in Tampa? Of all the places in the world the girls could have been taken, why would they end up here?"

Before Harris could answer, a horrible thought sent a shock through Marcie as if she had been struck by a lightning bolt. "Oh my God, Nathan, they could have been looking for me. I told Shoni I was from a city near Tampa. I thought they could look up Tampa on the internet and learn a little about the U.S. by doing some research. I never dreamed they would actually try to find me." She was frowning with deepening concern. Her entire body was becoming numb.

Nathan said softly, "Marcie, we know for sure now that the girls were given paperwork to be sent somewhere as part of a human trafficking scheme. Deop confirmed that. We aren't certain that it was Irene's body in the ditch, but if it is her, we don't have any idea why they would be in Tampa." Nathan was silent for a few seconds and Marie wondered if he was considering what he should say next.

"It isn't your fault, Marcie. You couldn't know what they planned to do, and you can't blame yourself if something happened to Irene. The people that do this sort of thing will do anything to get these young girls in their clutches. They promise them education, jobs, marriage, wealth, anything to persuade the girls they are doing the right thing. Then when the girls get to their destination – which they don't control, by the way, they have to go where they're sent – they find out they were misled, but by then it's too late. I just wanted you to be aware in case you heard about this on the news and saw the girl's picture."

"What about identification? Did the investigators find anything?"

"They found her wallet with some identification, but it wasn't Irene's name. It's an indication that she was given false documentation before leaving Africa."

"This is awful. What can I do to help? How're you going to make sure it's Irene?" Before Harris could reply, Marcie said quietly, "I met Irene. I didn't spend a lot of time with her, but I'm pretty good with faces and I think I would know her if I saw her. Do you want me to look at the body to see if it's Irene? It's not something I *want* to do but if it would help, I guess I could do it."

"We talked about that, but I didn't want to put you through it with the nightmares you've been having. If the nightmares have disappeared like you said, they could start up again because of this."

"I want to do it, Nathan. It's the least I can do for those girls. Would my verification after I see the body count as official?"

"It's preferable to have a close relative identify a body, but it can be someone that knows her well. I know you only met her once, but if you feel you might be able to positively identify her, it will give us sufficient grounds to try to contact her relatives in Africa."

"All right." Marcie fell quiet for a moment. Then, "You haven't said anything about Shoni."

"No, there's no sign of Shoni. They may have split the girls up. Shoni could be anywhere, I'm afraid. If you're sure you can do this, it would save us some time – but only if you're sure you can handle it. I need to come down to meet with the detectives on the case, so I will go with you. By the way, were you aware of Irene having a blood disease of any kind? Or was she complaining of feeling ill?"

"No, it never came up. All I know about is the limp. I don't think they would have mentioned something like that to me in the time we had together. Why?"

"The detective told me the ME who did the autopsy said her spleen was enlarged and that usually indicates a blood disease. It would've helped identify her if someone confirmed she had the disease. We won't know what the disease is until the blood tests come back. The examiner thought it might be sickle cell disease, in which case Irene would have possibly displayed some symptoms. She would've been unusually tired or perhaps had episodes of pain while you were with her."

"I didn't see evidence of anything," said Marcie, thinking back. "And she didn't say anything. She wouldn't tell *me*, though. I only saw her for a few hours. I'll bet Shoni would know – if she turns up."

"Yes, I agree." Harris' voice took on a much more serious tone. "Marcie. Just so you know, you won't have to actually be in the same room as the body. It will be on a screen, but you'll be able to tell if you think it's Irene. If it is her, then this becomes my case because it will be international, which means it falls into the FBI's jurisdiction. But the detectives that investigated it initially are Albert Baker and Tom Finch. You might recognize the names."

Marcie's brow crinkled. "Baker and Finch! I never thought I'd hear those names again. I never actually met them, but my friends Mason and Sami Seaforth certainly had a lot to do with them."

"Yes, that's what I heard. Okay, I'll make the arrangements for you to view the body. It will likely be later in the week, but I'll keep you posted." Nathan Harris stopped and his tone changed. "It's nice talking to you again, Marcie. I just wish the circumstances were different. If you change your mind about viewing the dead girl's body, please don't hesitate to let me know. No one will blame you if you decide not to do this."

"Thanks, Nathan, but I'm a big girl. I can handle it. Besides, I want to do what I can. It will help me, believe it or not, in spite of the circumstances. Just let me know when the arrangements are set."

Marcie hung up and set her cell phone back on the table. She hated the thought of that poor girl lying in the morgue. She decided she would try to keep herself occupied until the time came to view the body. She would start by clearing up the mess on the floor.

And she knew she wouldn't be able to stop herself from thinking about seeing Nathan Harris again in a few days.

Chapter 23

The sound of Marcie's heels clicking on the concrete floor echoed through the cavernous underground garage as she walked towards her BMW convertible. Nathan had called 24 hours earlier to let her know he was on his way to Tampa and had asked her to meet him at the morgue. She turned the key in the ignition and the voice of Isaac Hayes filled the car. She loved to drive with the top down and listening to the car's powerful sound system at ear-splitting levels. But the events she faced today made Marcie elect to leave the top up this time and the sound turned down low.

She had chosen to wear a modest black dress, which matched her mood, and low heels. As she exited the garage, it became apparent the day wasn't going to brighten her disposition. The pavement was wet, and the leaden sky was threatening to open up at any moment to spill more rain on the city. She quickly rolled up her window to shut out the rising humidity. It was going to be a strange day for sure. She was excited about meeting Nathan again, but apprehensive about seeing the dead girl. She had managed to fill the days leading up to this moment by taking her courses and going to the gym. She had also puttered around the condo, which was cleaner now than the day she moved in.

The drive took about 45 minutes. Traffic was light, and she made good time. The gas pedal was her friend and she used it liberally, changing lanes frequently. She loved the feeling of power under her foot. The windshield wipers intermittently swiped droplets of water thrown up by adjacent cars as she sped along the interstate. Her shoulders tightened as she turned the corner and into the parking lot of the government building that housed the morgue. Three men huddled deep in conversation under the canopy at the entrance to the building. One stood out in his navy suit with a white shirt and striped blue tie.

Marcie felt her pulse quicken as she parked her car and saw Nathan Farris walking over to her door, extending his hand in greeting.

"Marcie, it's great to see you again. Did you have any trouble finding the place?"

"Hi, Nathan, it's great to see you, too. No, no trouble finding it. Mr. GPS seems to know everything."

Marcie felt the strongest urge to lean in to Nathan and give him a hug, but with the other two men standing a few feet away, she decided discretion was in order. Besides, his stiff body language didn't exactly invite any contact other than a firm handshake. As they walked towards the entrance, Nathan said, "So, how are you feeling, Marcie? Are you ready for this?

"I'm as ready as I'll ever be."

"Good." They had reached the two men standing at the entrance. "Marcie, I'd like to introduce you to Detectives Albert Baker and Tom Finch. I don't believe you've met, but you certainly know of each other from previous experience. These two gentlemen investigated the scene where the girl we think is Irene Sembaza was found, and they became aware of my involvement through our automated Missing Persons database. They're here because they were the first investigators assigned to the case. If this is Irene Sembaza, as I told you the case becomes international under FBI jurisdiction, but Albert and Tom will still be involved with the case. I thought you'd like to know that."

Marcie shook the detectives' hands and thanked them profusely for their part in resolving the situation two years ago with the Seaforths. As she did, she watched for any sort of reaction from the pair when Nathan mentioned the possibility of the FBI taking over the case. After all, there was *always* animosity when it happened on TV. She didn't detect any.

Nathan said with a calm, professional tone, "I think the Medical Examiner will be ready for us now. Marcie, his name is Mike Hernandes. Just to reiterate, he will ask you a few questions first to establish the depth of your knowledge of the victim and then you will be shown the body on a monitor. You will not have to be in the same room as the body. An autopsy has been done but she is covered with a sheet up to her face. You will see the right side of her face where there is some bruising, but more damage to the left side will also be visible. This is never easy for anyone, and don't expect it to be any easier just because you aren't a family member or close friend. The ME can recommend a resource for counseling if you feel you'd like it later. Don't hesitate to tell us. Are you okay with this?"

Marcie nodded, but didn't respond.

Nathan put his hand on her back and gently guided her down a hall and into a room. Despite the feeling of his hand on her back, Marcie's legs felt like she had lead weights attached to her feet. She was nervous, yet she knew she had to see if it really was Irene. She was introduced to Mike Hernandes, and it was exactly as Nathan had explained. She was grateful to him for explaining what was going to happen. Hernandes gently went through the same information again, and also mentioned that he could arrange for grief counseling if required. He did everything in his power to reduce her anxiety level, yet she could feel her tension rising with each minute that viewing the body was delayed. She told him what she could remember about Irene, which she admitted wasn't much, and watched as the men reached a silent agreement.

Marcie held her breath as Hernandes switched on a camera. The screen filled with an image of a stark white room with the body lying on a gurney. Marcie was asked by Hernandes if she was ready for a closer look, and after murmuring that she was, she held her breath as the camera zoomed in on the right side of the girl's face. Just as Nathan had said, the right side of the face was bruised but there was swelling partially visible on the left side of her face and head.

The girl lying under the sheet looked so small and oh, so young.

After a few seconds of viewing, Marcie could feel tears welling up. She felt an overwhelming feeling of sadness despite not knowing the victim well. Marcie knew the girl lying there would not have the opportunity to fall in love, to have children, to enjoy a career and retirement – to live a full life. She had been bru-tally robbed of that opportunity, now and forever. It was so unfair, and Marcie felt herself choking back sobs.

"I'm almost certain it's her," Marcie whispered.

Hernandes said, "So just to be sure, you are saying that you are almost certain the girl is Irene Sembaza?"

Marcie nodded.

"No offense, Ms. Kane, but can you tell us how you can be so sure when you only met her briefly one time?"

Marcie's chest felt constricted, and Nathan handed her a tissue from a nearby box. She dabbed at her eyes and said, "I can't be 100% sure, of course, but everything fits. I only spent a short time with Shoni and Irene, but I know you've seen the picture that was taken of me with the girls. The facial features here are identical to those of the girl I remember meeting and in the photo. You mentioned this girl had a limp? Well, I distinctly saw Irene limping. I don't want to believe it, but I'm afraid that the girl is Irene Sembaza." Marcie sniffled and blew her nose softly into the tissue.

Hernandes added, "For the record, were you aware of any disease the girl may have had?"

"No, I didn't hear anything about that. They didn't mention it. She looked fine to me, other than for her limp."

Hernandes reached for the switch on the wall, and the room where the dead girl lay went dark, taking the camera image with it.

Now it was Nathan's turn. "Thank you, Marcie. We appreciate you taking the time to do this. I think we have enough to ask Inspector Choyo in Tanzania to contact Irene's next of kin." He hesitated, then added in a deeper and more serious tone of voice: "Gentlemen, it looks like my human trafficking case has now become a murder investigation."

Nathan asked Marcie to wait for him in the waiting room while he finished with Baker and Finch.

Marcie did so with a heavy heart.

It wasn't long before he rejoined her. He sat in the chair beside Marcie with his body turned towards her. She had been staring at the floor but her eyes, heavy with sadness, looked up and held his as soon as he sat down. He said, "How are you holding up?"

"I'll be fine. "I feel so bad for Irene and her family. I'm sure it's her, Nathan. And now I'm scared to think what's happened to Shoni."

"We were pretty sure it was Irene based on the limp and the photo you gave me, but we needed your opinion since you're the only one who's actually met her. Marcie, thank you so much for doing this. I'm so sorry I had to put you through this." Harris' professional tone changed abruptly. "Listen, I'm staying tonight at the hotel. Do you have time to join me for dinner? It would probably do us both good to lighten the mood a little over drinks and dinner."

Marcie brightened as she tilted her head to the side. Although the weight of viewing Irene's body was trying to push her into the bench like a physical force, she fought it off, drew herself up and attempted to change her mood. "I'd love to," she said with a smile. "And, Mr. FBI man, I assure you that I'll spend the rest of the afternoon canceling *all* my other dinner engagements just so I can make myself available for you. But it's only because you came in from out of town. Did you have some place in mind?"

Nathan's broad smile betrayed his pleasure at having his invitation accepted. "I'm in your 'hood so that puts me at your mercy. What do you suggest?"

"Well, if you don't mind coming down the road to my part of town, we could go for something a little more upscale at the so-called pink hotel, aka the Don Cesar, or we could have something casual on the beach. My favorite is Shady Pete's Seafood. Apparently, the owner, whose name is Pete, called it that because of the shade from the sun you can find inside. Although the local folklore is that it's because Pete spent a bit of time behind bars for a little racketeering. It sounds a little sketchy and it doesn't look the best from the outside – well, okay, it doesn't look the best on the inside, either – but the food is amazing. They've won a bunch of awards for best seafood on the beach."

Nathan glanced out the window. The clouds had been replaced by bright blue sky. "You know what? I'm all about the casual tonight. Let's check out Shady Pete's. It sounds wonderful." Then he asked innocently, "Do I need to bring my gun?"

Marcie laughed good-naturedly. Laughing felt good after what she had just been through.

"Not unless you want to shoot a few elderly tourists. Shall we say 6:30?"

"We have a date. I will see you there."

Nathan accompanied Marcie to her car and they smiled at each other as they parted company. She still felt anguish about the young girl on the gurney. *And what about her family?* Marcie knew that soon her grief would be replaced by anger at the thought that someone would do something like this to that poor girl. And then she thought: What about Shoni? Is she also here somewhere? Is she in danger, too?

Marcie knew she would have to try to find out.

But for now she had dinner with a good-looking man to look forward to. There was no telling what it might lead to, and it sure as hell beat her original plan of a grilled chicken sandwich and fruit cup at home alone.

Chapter 24

The building was little more than a large, low wooden shack on a side street at St. Pete Beach. Expensive cars with a variety of out-of-state license plates filled the gravel-covered parking lot. A rustic teal blue wooden fence separated the parking lot from the building. The color of the fence matched the blue canvas storm awnings, which would serve as walls for the building when the weather called for it or when the evening's activity ended.

Marcie's sandals crunched on the trail of crushed seashells, sending tiny geckos scurrying for cover as Nathan led her from the parking lot to the entrance. A large wooden sign with the name "Shady Pete's" burned into its surface hung over the opening. Patrons in gaudy beach attire laughed and toasted each other at an L-shaped bar. Marcie said, "I bet if this bar was given the ability to talk for one day, it would not have enough time to divulge all its secrets about the politicians and celebrities who have worshipped before it."

One wall sported a fish net laden with brightly-colored seashells. A veritable who's who of the entertainment and political world adorned the other walls in photos hung side by side in cheap frames. Most were signed by the grinning, drink-holding subjects of the photos. The walls were so cluttered that any time a new celebrity's picture was added, a lesser-known celebrity's photo would have to be removed and added to the growing pile behind the bar.

The restaurant wasn't full yet, but Marcie and Nathan chose to sit across from each other outside at one of the tables constructed of planks supported by 6 x 6 timber pilings. Plastic clips secured the inexpensive checkered tablecloths to the edge of the planks. They were both casually dressed – she in a bohemian-style long white sleeveless dress and he in tan pants with an open-necked blue shirt.

Marcie had noticed immediately that for the first time since she had met him, he was wearing glasses.

The patrons at the other tables included an older couple and a young family. The raucous noise from the inside was partially blocked by a strategically-placed bamboo wall, so only the occasional outburst drifted out to the beach. Gulls squawking overhead tried valiantly to disturb the relative quiet of the outdoors and occasionally worked up the courage to land nearby, hoping for a morsel or two to fall to the ground.

Marcie and Nathan each enjoyed a meal of lightly blackened mahi mahi stuffed with crab and covered in a lobster sauce and sipped the locally brewed craft beer for which Shady Pete's was known. The conversation had been relaxed and casual, and in the few quiet moments, they glanced at the sun as it slowly drifted across the cloudless sky on its daily path to meet the ocean at the horizon. Nathan excitedly pointed to a school of dolphins as they swam by, their glistening skins reflecting the sun's rays when they surfaced. Marcie laughed at his excitement and called him a land lubber.

"So, how're your courses going?" Nathan asked.

"Oh, I'm enjoying them. I have one early tomorrow on influencing youth behavior that I especially like. Most of the students don't like the professor because he rarely cracks a smile, but he knows his stuff and that's an area I'm most interested in. The rest of the class is all younger than I am so they don't have the same tolerance level as me, I suppose. I think the instructor's about the same age as I am. I've asked him questions after class a few times and he never drops his serious side, but really, who cares? His course will help me with a career in youth development and that's my ultimate goal – to help girls like Irene and Sheni before it's too late."

"Based on what I've seen, you'd be fantastic at it, Marcie. You have empathy, and that's so important to be able to relate to young people. As for the age thing, in order to do that job, I would think life experience counts for a lot."

"Thank you, Nathan. That means a lot coming from you."

They continued to learn more about each other and their respective hopes and dreams. During a brief lull in the conversation, Nathan looked out across the beach to the ocean and observed, "I wonder how many photograph albums this view has been immortalized in over the years."

Marcie nodded, "It would be interesting to know. I'm sure there are photos from this very spot all around the world. I can't believe how nice the weather is now, considering the humidity earlier. I guess the sea breeze has blown the humidity to Tampa. It's just gorgeous out here." Marcie paused and then said through a flirtatious smile, "By the way, just so you know, this is one of the nicer restaurants I normally go to."

Nathan was momentarily taken aback before he realized she was kidding. "Well, I can't decide whether the décor should be classified as early American kitsch or just plain charming, but I would certainly award five stars for the food. That's the best seafood I've ever had. I think this is just what the doctor ordered. Relaxing, beautiful night, great scenery, wonderful dinner companion – what more could a guy ask for?"

Marcie sat back on the bench, crossed her legs and her lips formed into a pout. "I don't know what more a guy could ask for, but I noticed you put your dinner companion last on the list."

"It was placed last on my list for emphasis," Nathan retorted.

Marcie smiled. "Seriously, I've enjoyed this evening. It's been a long time since I've been out with a man for dinner, let alone someone I actually enjoyed spending time with. Thank you. And just to show you I'm not a complete redneck, let's go down the road for a drink at a slightly more upscale bar. My treat."

Nathan agreed, and they hopped into Marcie's convertible. She put the top down and muted the radio that blared to life as soon as the key was turned, causing a few heads to turn in the parking lot. They drove to a large hotel on Gulf Boulevard and walked out onto the patio where they took seats at a small table that brought them close enough together that their knees nearly touched. Marcie felt warm from the proximity of their bodies. The view was similar to the one they had just left, but the sun was dropping into the ocean, lighting up the horizon and sending splashes of orange and red hues shimmering across the waves. A young couple sauntered hand in hand down the beach, unwittingly in step with the music drifting across the bay from someone's back yard. Subtle lights came on to cast ambient illumination around the patio.

The scent of Nathan's cologne wafted towards Marcie on the breeze. She was sure it was the same one he wore in Amsterdam. It wasn't overpowering – just enough to escalate her already-heightened senses. This felt so much different than the drinks she shared with the amorous tour bus operator in Tanzania. She studied Nathan's features as he talked. His hair was cut short, leaving only a fashionable hint on his scalp. When he smiled, his mouth lit up with bright white teeth and his eyes sparkled. Marcie found herself intrigued with the way his eyebrows knit together when he was deep in thought. The more serious moments also highlighted lines around his eyes that Marcie thought could have been etched by the nature of his work. His glasses were angular with a curved frame highlighted in red that added a little flair. Their classic design suited his face perfectly.

Marcie was very attracted to the way he dressed, the way he smelled, his mannerisms, and the easy confidence he had about him.

Whoa, wait a minute, girl.

She smiled at Nathan and looked down at the table.

Tiny fragments of the napkin she had been picking at lay strewn about in a small pile. There was something she had to get into the open.

She lifted her head to make eye contact again. "Nathan, I can't put my head in the sand and pretend none of this is happening with the girls. I hate to ruin the evening, but do you mind if we talk about it for a few minutes?"

Nathan's face darkened as if a shade had been drawn over it. Marcie could see the FBI persona had been summoned, but he managed to maintain a casual tone. "Of course not. You won't ruin the evening, Marcie. I've been waiting for you to bring it up. How would it be if we talk about it over a Bellini?"

"Bellini? What's that?"

"It varies, but generally it's a cocktail made from peach juice, syrup and a sparkling wine. Sweet, but tasty and refreshing on a summer evening."

"My, aren't you just full of surprises. Sure, let's go for it."

Marcie waited until the drinks arrived and then leaned her head forward towards Nathan so their conversation couldn't be overheard.

She knit her hands together on her lap and said in a hushed tone, "I haven't had much time to process any of this, but I just find it so hard to believe that Irene ended up here and that she's dead. What happened to her is so sad. It's going to take me a while to get over it."

"I know it must be difficult for you. A lot has happened in a short time and frankly, I'm surprised she turned up here as well. I can't explain it, Marcie. All I know is that the FBI will be putting all its efforts into finding her killer. You have to trust me that we'll do everything we can to get to the bottom of it."

"I believe you will, Nathan, but there's a bigger issue for me now. I feel sad for Irene and her family, but I understand there's nothing I can do about it. Her death is unconditional and there's nothing I can do or say that will change any of that. I have to deal with that in my own way and move on. When I start working in the field, I can't get so close to people that I'll be torn apart every time something like this happens. If I do that, I won't last long doing what I want to do.

"But Nathan, I want to help the living. Where do you think *Shoni* is? Shoni and Irene were inseparable, according to the teacher in Tanzania. I think there's a very good chance she's here, too."

"I've been thinking about that. It's possible the smugglers separated them and sent them to different parts of the world. She could be anywhere. We just don't know enough yet, Marcie. When we find Irene's killer, we'll understand better."

"I'm not sure I *can* let it go, Nathan. I know me and this is going to bother me until Shoni turns up. I know I've asked you this before, but what happens to the girls when they get sent to North America?"

"The hard facts are that you likely won't ever see her again, Marcie. I hate to say this, but most are forced into prostitution. Worldwide, there are two million children forced into prostitution every year. About half are in Asia and about 50,000 end up in North America somewhere."

Marcie was stunned by the numbers. When she opened her mouth to speak, nothing came out. She simply shook her head.

Nathan continued. "The lucky ones, if you can call them that, are forced into the service industry as hotel maids or working for a rich person or something like that. It's slave labor. They work for practically nothing trying to pay off the impossible debt they have incurred. That's why Irene's murder is unusual. The girls are an investment to the people who bring them over here, so she must have done something like try to escape, that made her expendable. Even then, the traffickers would typically teach her a lesson with a beating and use it as an example to the other girls. They wouldn't kill her."

Marcie leaned forward. "What about her limp? Would that make her vulnerable?"

Nathan stared into Marcie's eyes and said nothing for seconds. "I suppose anything's possible at this point. It's something I hadn't considered. I don't think most of the guys looking for sex would care if she had a limp or not, but there is the disease. Maybe she was murdered because of that. We just don't know yet, Marcie."

Marcie felt cold in spite of the warm outside air. "What can I do to help, Nathan?"

"You can't do anything, Marcie. Try to push everything aside and let us do our job. If I may be so bold as to suggest, probably the first thing you should do is get some sleep. Didn't you say earlier you had a class tomorrow? This has been a tough day for you. I have an early flight, too. I hate to call it a night, believe me, but sometime while we've been sitting here, the sun went down and the lights came on." He smiled and nodded towards the nearly full moon reflected on the water.

Marcie knew the evening would have to end, but she was disappointed, nonetheless. She looked around the patio and noticed that only a few people remained. She had been vaguely aware of people coming and going, but Nathan had held her attention throughout the evening.

She said reluctantly, "Yes, I guess you're right. But you have to promise to keep me posted when you find out anything."

Nathan assured her he would and after Marcie paid the bill, she drove Nathan back to Shady Pete's parking lot and parked beside his car. The place was still hopping, but the crowd they could see through the open wall had become much younger while they were gone. Marcie walked around her car to join Nathan at the passenger door where he awkwardly shook her hand. Marcie felt Nathan's warmth penetrate her skin, but he quickly drew his hand back.

As Nathan opened his door, he said, "Marcie, thank you for a lovely evening. I promise I'll call you soon."

Marcie watched him pull away in her rear view mirror as she drove onto the street.

I hope you do, Nathan Harris. I really hope you do.

Chapter 25

The glass shower door had become opaque from the steam in the bathroom. The water raining down from the large shower head onto Marcie's skin was as hot as she could stand to wash away the last vestiges of her latest nightmare. She had awakened from the dream, got up and removed her pajamas and tossed them on the bed as she walked to the shower. A groan escaped from her lips as the clock's face defiantly reminded her it was far too early for anyone in their right mind to be up. She had slept well at the beginning of the night, comfortable in the thoughts of her evening with Nathan. But the memory of her visit to the morgue earlier in the day and seeing Irene's lifeless body lying there quickly shoved aside the good thoughts.

Marcie adjusted the shower head from the massage setting to soft rain. Clasping her hands beneath her chin, she turned her body slowly, closed her eyes and tilted her head to indulge in the gently cascading water. She recalled the latest near-death experience she had dreamt about during the night. This one was as vivid as always and left her sitting bolt upright in a cold sweat. Since her psychologist would want the details when she met with him next, she ran through the dream in her mind.

I was walking at night through a wooded area when I came across a clearing. A young black girl's inert body, dressed from head to toe in a white cotton shroud, lay on a picnic table. I could only see the right side of her face but I could tell she was a pretty girl. From about 15 feet away, it became apparent that the left side of the girl's face was badly damaged. I was close enough to realize I knew the girl — it was Irene — and she wasn't moving. I reluctantly pushed forward, but I was struggling to move, as if I was knee deep in mud. I was about 10 feet away, but I just couldn't go any farther. It was like I was wearing lead boots. Try as I might, I just could not lift my feet. I could only stand and stare at the body.

As I stared, I suddenly noticed movement. Without a sound, the girl's head slowly turning towards me. I stopped struggling. I was so afraid and confused. I wondered how that could be. She's dead! When the left side of the girl's face became visible, it was obvious that it had been smashed in. As the head stopped turning, the right eye stared at me. It was steely grey, unblinking, and it sent wave after wave of shock through my body.

I recall turning to run but I was still immobilized. I pulled my right leg with my hands as hard as I could, grunting at the effort. Nothing. As I struggled, I noticed from the corner of my eye that something else was happening. I looked back at the table. The body was fading from view but something new was replacing it. A new girl appeared in place of Irene. Lying in the same position, the new girl started to rise at the waist, simultaneously turning her head in the same slow manner that Irene had.

When the girl was facing me, I knew immediately who she was. It was Shoni. I was so happy to see her. I reached toward the girl and Shoni returned the gesture. Suddenly, my feet came free and I pitched forward. I started to run towards her but as I did, a fissure opened under the table, followed by another and then another. The cracks spread like tentacles in all directions. I tried to dodge around them but Shoni held up her hand, motioning for me to stop. The fissures widened beneath the picnic table and the earth gave away, crumbling in upon itself. As the hole widened, the ground beneath the table collapsed into the yawning gorge, carrying Shoni with it.

I reached forward to grab for Shoni, but it was too late. The table and Shoni's body dropped end over end into nothingness in a mad race to find the bottom. Shoni's screams echoed in my ears, fading as she dropped. When I reached forward, I was brought to the edge of the abyss and the motion left me perilously balancing on the ragged margin of the hole. I flailed my arms to try to prevent myself from following the girl I was unable to save. I was teetering back and forth on the boundary of oblivion. I couldn't maintain my balance. Gravity was winning, and I was about to fall into the crevasse. I was so shocked and afraid. I thought, this is it, this is the way it's going to end. But I didn't want to die this way. I wasn't ready to die. I tried to pull myself back, but the ground was slipping away beneath my feet. I flung myself backwards towards a rock. I wrapped my fingers around the piece of granite, trying to hang on But there were no edges to grasp, and my fingers lost their grip. The ground collapsed beneath me, I slid over the edge and then it was my turn. I began to fall into the bottomless pit ... down ... down ... down ...

Marcie's body felt ice cold despite the steam in the room from the hot shower, and she shook her head as she toweled herself off. Her nightmares were much too vivid. At least it wasn't Nathan Harris who shoved me into the pit, she thought wryly. Things could be worse. Her psychologist had encouraged her to re-imagine a happy ending to her nightmares – one in which she took control of the outcome. It wasn't easy to do. She imagined reaching out and grabbing Shoni before she fell into the pit. She imagined escaping before the hole collapsed and the two of them running hand in hand to safety. But it was a half-hearted effort to change the outcome.

Marcie thought the best way to change things was to find out what had happened to Shoni. She got ready for her class, dressing in caramel colored pants and a yellow blouse, poured a glass of orange juice, and turned on the stereo CD player. She sat on the chair on the balcony and stretched her legs out with her feet on the stool. Marcie had to admit it was a peaceful time of day, even though it was ridiculously early to be up. The ocean was dead calm. The sun's rays peeked around from behind her building, unwrapped the day and cast rose-tinted hues across the water. There was no hint of breeze, but her feet framed an early morning sailboat silently drifting in the distance. The only sound, other than the stereo, was a seagull hovering over the beach and indignantly squawking its displeasure about losing a battle over some tidbit. Marcie closed her eyes to absorb the quiet of the morning and think about everything that had been happening.

It was relaxing. Too relaxing. She woke up with a start and realized she had dozed off. Hurriedly she gathered her belongings and rushed out the door of her condo to get to her courses on time. As she dashed to her car, her phone chimed and she was delighted to see a text from Nathan thanking her for the evening and telling her to have a great day. She responded in kind with the wish for safe travels. The message exchange left her with a feeling of enthusiasm for the day ahead.

Today's course focused on the use of verbal and non-verbal communication skills to influence youth behavior. The lecturer everyone disliked, Braden Maxwell, stood at the front of the room. He was tall and wore well-pressed navy slacks, a white shirt and yellow tie. His hair was brown and perfectly groomed and his expression was disciplined as usual.

According to the brief but impressive bio in his curriculum vitae in the course preamble, Maxwell had the benefit of real-life experience: his primary job was as a well respected counselor for sex trafficking victims. He consulted on developing support systems, building training programs and providing referrals to victims in need. The students appreciated his experience but it still didn't make him more likable to them. He sometimes delivered the course material in a monotone (as subject matter experts often do), and today was no different. Marcie noticed more than one student yawning or staring off into space. Role-playing scenarios to represent discussions between a youth and his or her development officer helped enliven the discussion, but there was an overwhelming indifference among the younger students in the room.

At the end of the class, Marcie walked to the front where Professor Maxwell was standing.

"Excuse me, Professor Maxwell, do you have a minute?"

Maxwell stopped stuffing his notes into his briefcase and looked up. Seeing Marcie, his face maintained its granite-like facade. "I suppose, Ms. Kane. What can I do for you?"

"Actually, it will take more than a minute. I would like your opinion on something that happened with two girls I met in Africa."

There was a hint of interest. "Africa? You were in Africa? I guess I can make some time. I don't start my next class for an hour. Would you like to go to the cafeteria?"

Marcie was wondering if this was a mistake. This guy had all the personality of an Easter Island Head, but she had been impressed by his background and apparent understanding of young people that he was trying to impart to his class, so she decided to take him up on his offer.

The cafeteria was austere like every other college campus eating facility, with inexpensive tables and chairs and an aisle where the food was collected and paid for. At this time of day, they were nearly alone. A couple sat holding hands and staring dreamily into one another's eyes by the window. A single worker remained behind the counter cleaning up the dishes. Marcie and Maxwell ordered coffee and took their cups to a table on the opposite side of the room from the young couple. As they sat, she told him her story about meeting Shoni and Irene at the dormitory in Africa, and then about Irene's subsequent murder.

Maxwell listened closely to everything she was saying, his eyes fixed on hers. He was so attentive that it unnerved Marcie, but she wanted to fill in the background before getting to her real reason for wanting to talk to him. She knew Nathan wasn't going to give her the information she needed, so Maxwell was her best bet.

He asked a few questions about how she had met the girls, and he appeared especially interested when she mentioned the FBI. His expression didn't change when she got to the point of wanting to meet with him. "So here's the reason I wanted to talk to you. You have talked about young girls who get off track one way or another, whether it's of their own choosing or by being trafficked domestically or internationally. As sad as it is, there's nothing that can be done for Irene, except find her killers. The FBI is looking into that. But it seems that the girls might have been caught up in some sort of human trafficking scheme, and Shoni might still be out there. You have a lot of understanding in that area. I was just hoping you could give me some ideas on what might have happened to her or if there's any way I might look for her."

Maxwell's chest actually seemed to puff out at the compliment. Marcie thought because of his personality, compliments were probably rare so pandering to his ego might be a way to get him to open up.

"First, I'm sorry to hear about the young lady who was murdered. The FBI you said? They did some good work in discovering who she was so quickly."

"It was fortunate the way it happened, I suppose. Good fortune for everyone but Irene and her family. I happened to meet an FBI agent in Tanzania and told him about the girls." Marcie went on to explain how she had gone to the morgue to identify Irene.

"It's odd that an FBI agent would be in Tanzania."

Marcie could feel her frustration growing that Maxwell was focusing on that part of her story. "He was there investigating a human trafficking case. Now, getting back to Shoni, do you have any ideas what would happen to her if she came to this area? I think there's a good possibility that she's in the area since Irene was found here. If I'm able to find her, how do I get her out of this mess?"

The answer was not what she was expecting. Maxwell stared impassively at Marcie. His tone was flat. "I don't see how you think you will ever be able to find the girl. The odds of her being in Tampa are astronomical, even though her friend was here. I think you should be focusing on other girls you *can* help, not some girl from Africa who could be anywhere. That's why you're taking these classes – to spend your time trying to help those who can be helped." He got up, turned and tossed his final words over his shoulder. "I have to go to my next class. Thank you for the coffee."

Marcie leaned back in her chair. She frowned as Maxwell strode away with his chin in the air. As she stared at the retreating back of the man whose opinion she had sought, she mumbled under her breath. "She's not *some* girl from Africa. At least have the decency to remember her name. The girl's name is Shoni."

Chapter 26

Marcie sat in front of the television set finishing her dinner. The news was on, but her mind kept wandering. She had settled into a routine the last few days. She had met with the psychologist and he thought she was progressing. He had listened carefully to her description of her latest nightmare and reiterated his position that she should rethink the ending to give it a positive outcome. His advice was to push Shoni out of her mind, which she knew was easier said than done. She continued attending her classes. Braden Maxwell, the pompous ass, acted as if they had never had their conversation. He was the same toward her in class as he had always been, but Marcie was determined to get as much out of his lectures as she could. Even though her level of respect for him as a person had diminished like an extinguished candle flame, she still valued his experience and insight into how to deal with wayward teenagers.

But no matter how Marcie had occupied her time over the last few days, thoughts of what could have happened to Shoni still wiggled their way into her mind. Each of her nightmares recently had involved a teenage girl reaching for her; and each time Marcie failed to rescue her. She understood now that no one was going to help her look for Shoni. She knew that the FBI was doing its best to find her, but she felt she had to at least try on her own.

She and Nathan had exchanged a couple of pleasant text messages over the last few days. He only ever asked how she was doing and kept his tone impersonal, but she always felt warm after their exchanges. She hoped he would tell her if there were positive developments in the case, but Marcie also knew that the FBI wouldn't allow him to share much information with her. After all, she would still be considered a potential witness after what happened to her in Africa. And possibly he *was* trying to protect her. It felt good to know that maybe someone cared enough to *want* to protect her.

Marcie chased a wayward spiral of pasta salad around her plate when something interrupted her thoughts. What was it that the newscaster said? Something about a human trafficking ring? Marcie reached for the TV remote and turned up the volume. It was the final part of the story, but the reporter was saying something about an undercover operation resulting in an arrest of a number of people in the area whose ages ranged from 18 to 68. The banner headline over the onscreen graphic said all were apparently involved in a just-uncovered human trafficking ring in the Tampa area. Could this be what she was looking for?

The newscaster was now on to another story so Marcie hurried into the room she had converted to an office and turned on the laptop. She quickly scanned the news items for Tampa and found the article. It involved a five-day undercover investigation of a domestic trafficking ring in a county in the Tampa area. The article included a number of photos of those arrested for prostitution. Although young women were included in the photos, Shoni wasn't among them. Marcie thought that would make sense since the newscaster had referred to the case as "domestic," which she understood to mean trafficking within the U.S.

Marcie sat staring at the computer screen. She reread the article a few more times. She glanced at her night stand beside her bed. As if on autopilot, she wandered over and slowly opened the drawer. There in its resting place was her Smith & Wesson 442 handgun. Marcie picked it up and sat on the side of the bed.

Her gun was always in the drawer by her bedside when it wasn't in an ankle holster or tucked into the waist band at the back of her jeans. She was grateful to He Who Shall Not Be Named for insisting that she learn how to use it. She checked it as she had been taught. She always told anyone who would listen that she would defend herself if need be. Florida's gun laws allowed residents to carry concealed weapons after obtaining a state-issued license, and Marcie was on the side that argued that it was a right. She had had many outspoken arguments with her friend Mason Seaforth about the law. They agreed to disagree. There was no question in Marcie's mind that she definitely felt safer carrying a weapon when she thought it might be needed.

Marcie liked the way the gun felt in her hand. It wasn't much larger than a cell phone and weighed only 15 ounces. Everyone at the shooting range where she practiced marveled at her accuracy, but they all recommended that she should carry something bigger with a longer range. She countered that the wadcutter ammo she used would do just fine in any situation she might find herself in. If anything ever did happen, it was likely to be someone trying to steal her purse, so it would be close range.

She looked across the room at the computer screen again. It was difficult to make out the words from a distance, but by now she had read the article enough to remember precisely what it said. *There was a human trafficking ring right here in Tampa. Is it possible that Shoni's involved?* Without hesitation, Marcie made up her mind. She couldn't just sit and wonder, perpetuating the nightmares that interrupted her sleep every night. Funny how time works, she though grimly. Right now, it felt like time for Shoni was running out. That thought was a weight on Marcie, battering her, and she knew she wouldn't rest until she did something. When you're waiting for something exciting like a vacation or Christmas – or when you're lying in bed recovering from an illness – time seems to move at a snail's pace. Yet at other times, like now, time races by so quickly you wonder how you'll keep up. If she didn't make a move now, time might rush past, and without help, time might run out forever for Shoni.

Even though it was a long shot, at least she had to make an effort to find out what had happened to Shoni. It was the only way she could live with herself. Marcie walked purposefully to her closet and pulled a rich brown leather shoulder bag off the shelf. It would pass for any bag on the street with one exception – it had a cleverly-concealed "carry pocket" with a universal holster into which she slid her handgun.

Next, Marcie went to her computer and opened a JPG file of the photo of her with Shoni and Irene. With the help of editing software, she quickly cropped the photo so that only Shoni's image remained. Then she added a text box at the bottom with her contact information. With a few more key strokes, a handful of sheets emerged from the printer with six copies of the newly-created image per page. Deftly she cut them into individual handouts with her paper trimmer. Satisfied with her handiwork and her decision, Marcie put the photos into her bag, tossed the strap over her shoulder and strode out of the condo.

Chapter 27

Blaring music filled the car as its tires hummed along I-275 towards Tampa. A full moon led the way to Marcie's destination. She wasn't sure what she was trying to accomplish. Hopefully, just taking action would at least temporarily put her mind at ease. As much as she didn't want to believe it, the news item she had heard on television, along with the discussion she'd had with Nathan, helped her understand why Shoni might be in North America. It was far from a pretty thought. And to think Shoni could end up the same as Irene, murdered and tossed out into a ditch. A cold chill ran through her body when Marcie thought of Irene's murder. It didn't make sense to her since, as Nathan said, the traffickers would have considered the girls to be a lucrative investment. So why kill her?

In spite of the usual lane reductions from construction and a semi that slowly wandered across three lanes of traffic as if the driver thought he was the only one on the road, Marcie reached the general area of her destination in less than an hour. It soon became apparent that she had found exactly what she was looking for. She stopped for a red light at an intersection, looking sideways at the street to her right where a flat building loomed in the dark. A street light lit up the building just enough to make out multiple windows with shades drawn. Two of the windows were boarded with plywood which some aspiring artist had adopted as his personal canvas. The name on the front of the building was highlighted by bright floodlights.

It was an office building of some sort.

Exhaust rose from a car in the lane at the front of the building, and a woman with a short skirt exposing her bare backside leaned into the car on the driver's side. It was clear from the woman's appearance and the animated discussion that a negotiation was taking place.

The street Marcie was driving on had been identified in the news item as the "corridor for prostitution," and Marcie began to see why. She drove carefully, passing cars with solo male occupants slowly perusing the street, their drivers scanning the women who either sauntered along the sidewalk or stood alone or in pairs on street corners. Some of the women ventured towards the cars when they stopped at street lights. It was a strange array of shapes, sizes and ages in garish makeup, spandex, sequins, thigh-high boots – anything to catch the attention of someone who might be willing to pay for some short-term company.

Feeling slightly sick, she slowed her car to a stop as the light turned red at the next intersection. A vehicle with a male occupant pulled up beside Marcie's car. The man wore a business suit with his rumpled tie askew. He appeared to be in his mid-forties. Behind him, in the back seat, was an infant's baby seat. The man rolled down the window, motioning to Marcie to do the same. Marcie was curious. He seemed to be a typical businessman who had worked late, so she pressed the button on her armrest to lower the window on the passenger side. She waited for the man to say something.

His crooked smile and question gave away his intentions.

"How much, baby?"

Marcie's face remained expressionless. She turned back to face the street ahead and pressed the button to roll the window back up, willing the light to change.

The man tried again, his voice rising to be heard above the rising window. "C'mon. How much? I can tell by the car your rates will be high, but I can afford you. Just tell me. How much? You can come with me to the ATM, and then we'll go have some fun."

Marcie rolled the window back down. "Shouldn't you be home with your wife and kids? What's your wife doing now? Making supper and waiting patiently for you to come home from work so you can read to your kids and put them to bed? Don't mess that up. Go home!"

The light changed to green and as she pulled away and pressed the button that controlled the window again, she could hear the man yelling something about her having no right to judge him and that he would find somebody younger who was not a lesbian and oh yes, way better looking and not as fat. His diatribe was laced with obscenities. There was more, but the closed window successfully shut out the rest. She could not shut out the view of the man's raised middle finger as he roared past.

Marcie shook her head as she continued along the street. *The suit does not necessarily make the man.* A patrol car raced by on the opposite side, its blaring siren clearing a path and no doubt scaring the shit out of some of the drivers who assumed it was coming for them. The flashing blue light on the roof was a blur as it shot past. Another patrol car was stopped at a street corner, its light bar revolving and shooting periodic blue slashes across a pair of officers and the group of women they were talking to. Some local citizens marched together with signs shouting slogans at the prostitutes, urging them to leave the area.

As Marcie turned down a side street, the overhead lights illuminated fences and store walls defaced with graffiti. Marcie found herself wondering why some of the artists weren't doing something more with their talent. Gaudy signs advertised massage parlors, peep shows and strip clubs. As if that wasn't bad enough, she suspected that many were fronts for drug dealing and money laundering. She had trouble digesting it all. There were so many places that Shoni might have been taken if she had been designated for prostitution instead of domestic labor that the task of trying to find her was an insurmountable burden weighing heavily on her shoulders.

Marcie had just about resolved to return home when she remembered the photos in her bag. She decided to try. Two women stood at a street corner watching her car approach. Marcie knew they would be disappointed when they realized a woman was driving the car, but she would only take a minute of their time. Under the glare of the street light, she could see that one of the women was taller than the other, thanks to her stiletto heels, and a hot pink mini-dress barely covered her thighs. Her straight blond hair cascaded over her shoulders. The other woman wore a tiny jean skirt, a short top that flared out above her belly button, bright red lipstick and blue eye shadow.

Marcie parked at the curb. The two women hurried over to her car, unable to tell through the tinted windows that the driver behind the wheel was a woman.

The prostitute in the pink mini-dress wobbled on her high heels. Either her feet were sore from standing, or she was unaccustomed to the heels. The hookers stopped short at the sight of Marcie and started to turn away with a look that was difficult for Marcie to read.

"Wait, I just want to ask you a question. I'll pay you."

At the mention of money, the women stopped and turned back. The heavy overdone makeup and the hard life they led made them appear to be in their forties but Marcie felt they were probably in their late teens or early twenties. Looking at their vague, glassy stares and slightly off-balanced body postures, Marcie wondered if they were high on drugs. Well, how could you blame them, she thought? She might be, too, if she had to do their job.

"You a cop?" This from the girl in the jean skirt.

"No, I'm not a cop. I'm looking for a friend and I'm wondering if you can help me."

"We can't help. We're working. Go before you get yourself and us into trouble." This time it was the woman in the pink mini who spoke. Marcie detected a strong Eastern European accent.

The woman in the jean skirt mumbled, "In case you don't unnerstan' what she's sayin' here, if our boss finds you hangin' around wastin' our time, you gonna get yo' ass whupped, girl."

Marcie stared for a moment. Through their street slang and tough demeanors, she felt a sense of protectiveness toward these girls. There but for the grace of God could go I, she thought. "I won't take much of your time." She took two photos from her purse and handed them out the window. "Just look at this photo. Please tell me if you've seen her."

Marcie rummaged through her bag and pulled out some cash while the women peered down at the photos in the glare of the street light. She was about to hand the money to them when she noticed the women looking anxiously down the street. The side mirror reflected an old black luxury car rapidly approaching. It was accompanied by an intermittent thud of bass coming from the stereo.

The shorter girl nudged her friend and gestured back to their spot under the light while hissing to Marcie, "Get out of here. Go! Now!"

The urgency in the woman's voice was unmistakable. Marcie quickly shoved the cash out the window. The girl in the pink mini grabbed it and stuffed it in her handbag. She hurried back to her place, glancing down at the photo as she went. The other woman threw her picture on the ground and tried to saunter confidently back towards their spot on the sidewalk. Marcie pulled away just as the black car drove up to the space at the curb she had occupied only seconds before. She watched in her mirror as a short muscular man exited the car and strode over to the girl in the pink mini. She saw him grab the photo from her hands and slap the woman hard, causing her to stagger backwards before regaining her balance on her high heels. The photo ended up in pieces on the ground. The two women resumed their place under the street light once again, as if nothing had changed.

Marcie felt her face flush with anger. She wanted to go back and put her gun in the guy's face, but she knew how dangerous that would be. At this point, she could have happily pulled the trigger but she suspected there would just be another pimp and the women would likely resume their way of life. She couldn't think about their plight or the world they lived in right now. Her focus needed to stay fixed on Shoni.

Carefully Marcie drove up and down each block, handing out her photos. When she approached the various women, she was met with every emotion imaginable – sympathy, fear, derision, anger, sadness, belligerence – but no one acknowledged knowing or having seen Shoni. Marcie thought once she saw a fleeting recognition on the face of one of the women, but it was gone in an instant.

She had a few photos left as she turned onto a side street leading her back to the turnpike. She noticed a dilapidated building with a weather-beaten sign advertising massages at reasonable rates. She decided to go inside with her photo, and ask if anyone recognized Shoni. If not, maybe she could leave a photo with the business owner. Marcie parked her car under a street light for safety, threw the strap of her bag across her body, and entered the building. A bell chimed as she entered announcing her arrival. The smell of incense filled the room, and three young women in various states of undress occupied chairs along the wall.

The girls looked up expectantly as Marcie entered. They were all of Asian descent and each sported tattoos and very heavy makeup. Piercings glinted in the sparse light. Crossed legs extended from short dresses and swung back and forth like pendulums. All were barefoot. One chewed gum vigorously and noisily. Marcie couldn't imagine walking barefoot on the threadbare carpet that looked like it hadn't been treated to a vacuum for decades. She surmised the young women were the "masseuses."

An overweight woman peered over the counter at Marcie as she approached. It was dark in the room with the only light coming from a red bulb hanging above the counter, which cast a garish glow over everything. Soft music played in the background. The shadows cast by the light grotesquely accentuated the high spots of the woman's makeup that may have been applied with a trowel. The conversation started the same as it had all night.

"You a cop?"

The question came through dark red lips. The woman looked at Marcie through eyes outlined in kohl black, dark as a night sky. Marcie glanced at the girls who curiously returned her look. In the darkness, she thought that if the girls were over 18 years old, she would soon be walking on Mars.

Marcie reassured the woman that she was not a cop and handed her Shoni's photo. "Have you seen this girl, by any chance? I'm looking for her. I'm a friend." As she waited for a response, she noticed a hall trailing away from the counter with a number of closed doors. Large numbers from 1 to 4 painted on each door designated the rooms where the girls apparently conducted their business. Impassively the woman stared at the photo for a few seconds and then said, "Cute girl, but I ain't seen her. What's it to you, anyway? You should be careful, you know. You're just going to buy yourself trouble by going around asking questions in this neighborhood. Why don't you leave it alone? This girl is probably making a living somewhere. Let it go, sweetie."

Marcie sighed, thinking how many times she had heard that same advice already. How many people had said these exact same words to her? That number would soon be into double digits, for sure. She looked again at the girls lounging seductively in their chairs and held up the photo with her eyebrows raised. The girls all shook their heads quickly and smiled sweetly back at her. The smiles were as fake as is if they had been painted on. Marcie thought they were probably the practiced smiles they pasted on to make their customers feel important.

"Thanks for your time. If you hear anything about her, please let me know."

Marcie exited the building, thankful to get away from the mustiness that overpowered the strong scent of incense. She tilted her head back and rubbed the back of her neck. *This is like looking for a needle in a haystack – if I could even find the haystack.* She wondered if she had accomplished anything at all, other than getting at least one girl hurt and perhaps more.

She couldn't know that her evening was about to get worse.

As she turned the corner, three young men came into view beside her car. Their shapes were clearly outlined by the street light overhead and what they were trying to do was soon evident. One was working a bar into the window of her BMW, attempting to open the lock. The other two observed, pushing and slapping each other on the back and exchanging remarks. The men were all in their twenties with their underwear visible above the low-slung waistbands of their pants. They reminded Marcie of the punks in Tanzania. At the same time, the thought of the man slapping the young hooker earlier in the evening flashed through her mind. Marcie stood watching the scene for a few seconds as she felt adrenaline sharpening her senses. She could have called the police, but instead she walked purposefully towards them while sliding her hand inside her bag.

The man working on the door was oblivious to her approach. The two bystanders made no attempt to be quiet as they continued poking at each other.

The smooth, comfortable grip of her gun felt cool to Marcie's touch even though it had been wrapped snugly in her bag throughout the warm evening.

"Can I help you, gentlemen?"

The two bystanders jumped at the sound of her voice and turned to face her. The third man continued to pry away at the door. One of the three men moved ominously over in her direction, the downward movement of his hands punctuating each syllable as he spoke.

"Yo, get lost, bitch. Can't you see we're busy here?"

Marcie responded calmly by withdrawing the gun and pointing it in the face of the man who spoke. The short barrel was about a foot from his forehead. She said between gritted teeth, "Before you say anything more, I think you should know I've had a very bad evening so far. I would strongly suggest your buddy stop doing what he's doing or I will put a bullet right between your eyes. He will be next. I also suggest it would be wise to go back to auto theft school or wherever it is you improve your limited skills because your buddy there is taking way too long to unlock the door of *my* car."

The man who had been busy at the car door stood up. The one with the gun in his face slowly put his hands in the air. His face abruptly changed from laughter to a sneer. Marcie could almost smell the wheels grinding in his head, calculating whether or not she could handle the weapon. Her unwavering stance with the gun never leaving the spot between his eyes seemed to convince all three that she was serious.

He found his voice. "Okay, okay. No need to get violent, lady. We were just having a little fun here." They backed away from her car.

Marcie continued to aim the gun at the first man, the largest of the three, as she moved around the car to the driver's side. She quickly shifted the gun to her left hand and raised her eyebrows as she brandished the key fob with a flourish while pressing the button to open the door. The door locks unlatched noisily as if taunting the trio.

"Much easier this way. And the great thing is that it's legal." Sliding behind the wheel and keeping her gun trained in the direction of the three would-be car thieves, Marcie started the car and drove off, leaving the men to deal with their wounded egos. She doubted that they would be repeating this story among their peers in the foreseeable future.

Marcie tucked the gun back into her bag, turned the stereo up to ear-splitting levels, and aimed the car home. She took a few deep breaths to calm herself.

This had been quite a night, she thought to herself.

It was just as well that she had no idea what lay ahead.

Chapter 28

Marcie glanced at the clock on the stove as she walked into her condo. 1:30 a.m. – and she was wired. Pointing a gun in someone's face will do that to you, she thought. *I must be crazy. Anything could've happened.* She flipped on the light and tossed her bag onto the couch. She was satisfied on one level with her night's work. Most of the photos had been handed out. She thought she would probably not see any results but at least she had done something. She looked at her phone for about the twentieth time since she parked the car. No message from Nathan. It was late, so he was probably sleeping or maybe working the case. *And anyway, why would there be a message?*

She prepared herself for bed and lay down, trying to will herself to sleep. That run-in with the young punks had gotten her adrenalin racing. After tossing back and forth trying unsuccessfully to find a relaxing position, she realized sleep was not going to come easily. In fact, trying to sleep in the next few minutes was going to be impossible. It would probably just lead to another nightmare, anyway. Finally, she gave up and turned the bedroom light back on. She fluffed the pillows so she could partially sit up. Drawing her knees towards her chin, she picked up her cell phone. She checked her emails and responded to those that needed an answer. Next she scrolled through the latest postings on Facebook to find out who had spent their day stubbing their toe or entering into a complicated relationship.

She decided to take a chance.

She sent a message to Nathan.

Are you there?

She continued to scroll through the Facebook postings, ignoring most, when her phone chimed indicating a message had arrived.

Just got home. R u ok?

Marcie smiled at the tech-speak from the straight-laced FBI agent. She dialed his number.

Nathan answered on the second ring. He told Marcie how pleased he was to hear from her at this time of the night, and again asked for assurance that everything was okay.

Marcie said, "I'm fine. I just walked in the door and I can't sleep. I thought I should tell you what I did tonight. I hope you don't mind the late night phone call." She went on to explain that she had handed out flyers with Shoni's photo in an attempt to find out what may have happened to her.

Harris was not amused and for the first time since they'd met, he expressed frustration with her. "Marcie, you should NOT have been there. I'm all too familiar with the area you were in. We're looking at some of the people there as part of our human trafficking investigation. You shouldn't be going in there alone and particularly if you're stopping to chat with some of the hookers. Their pimps will not take kindly to someone nosing around asking questions! It's difficult enough for the police to do anything, let alone a private citizen who is poking around. Not only that, they could even think you're a police woman undercover. It could jeopardize our investigation *and* get you hurt or worse."

"I know that now, Nathan, I saw the pimp's reaction firsthand," Marcie replied, sensing the annoyance beneath his words. "A pimp did come up while I was talking to a couple of the girls, and I saw him slap one of them as I was driving away. It's just that I saw tonight on the news that arrests were made there recently. Based on what I saw, it didn't look like much had changed. Business appeared to be booming. Was the arrest part of your investigation?"

"No, those were bit players running that ring. They were trafficking domestic girls. It's great that the Tampa police were able to shut them down. That's what they should be doing. No, what we're looking at is an international ring headed by some very dangerous people. There's a lot of money involved, so they're willing to do anything, including murder, to keep their operation successful. We're still trying to find the head of it. It takes time, Marcie, and we don't want to move too quickly. We want to be sure we have enough evidence and information to shut down the entire operation."

"Okay, I understand that, but I had to do something, Nathan. I doubt that anything will come out of showing the photo around but maybe something will."

"Well, showing the photo around was not necessarily a bad thing, I suppose, but did you leave your contact information on it? That wouldn't have been a good idea at all. Tell me you just verbally gave your number to the people you talked to."

A shock wave traversed Marcie's spine. It was a moment before she could find her voice. She had to clear her throat. She realized she might have just made a terrible mistake. She said weakly, "Uh, I *did* put my name and phone number on the photo. I never thought, I guess. I just wanted people to be able to contact me if they had information about Shoni. All I did was ask if anyone had seen Shoni. Why would anyone want to track me down for handing out the picture?"

She could hear the tension rising in Nathan's voice as he answered her. "You don't know who you're dealing with, Marcie! You don't have a clue who these people are or how dangerous they are! You don't know the way they think. If someone believes you're asking too many questions or if you stumble across something that makes them think you're getting too close, they won't hesitate to do something to you or anyone else you're involved with. It's a lucrative market and they don't want anyone messing with it. *Please* don't distribute any more photos with your phone number on them. If you're threatened or see anything strange, let Detectives Baker or Finch know right away. Remember what happened to Irene? We don't know why she was killed but she's dead now and we're still investigating without any real leads. I'm not trying to scare you, Marcie, but you shouldn't have done what you did tonight. At least without telling me first."

Marcie's face flushed at the logic of what Nathan was saying. She realized she had done a stupid thing. Her bottom lip trembled.

Nathan wasn't finished. He didn't raise his voice, but his words chillingly hit their mark. "You aren't helping your own situation either. There are people here who think you might be involved somehow. If you get caught in that area of town, there will just be more questions. Do yourself a favor, Marcie. Back off. Leave this to us, and stop involving yourself."

Nathan's words echoed in Marcie's ears. They hurt more than she wanted to admit. She knew he was right, but the words still stung. Feeling cornered, she lashed out, saying louder than she intended, "So are you seriously investigating me? Is that what dinner was all about? Of course I remember what happened to Irene and don't ever think I will forget her. You *are* scaring me and I don't think it's necessary. You're right, I did something foolish, I shouldn't have included my contact information, but I was just trying to help. All I did was hand out some pictures, for God's sake. I think I'd better go. This conversation is over. Good night, Nathan."

Harris' voice took a more soothing tone. "Wait, Marcie. I just don't want anything to happen to you. I like you, and I want to make sure you stay safe so we can get to know each other better when this is over. Okay?" Marcie stayed quiet, so Nathan simply said, "Good night, Marcie. Try to get some sleep."

As if in slow motion, she put the phone on the nightstand and lay back with her arm over her face. Her thoughts rolled around in her head, one after another. *Oh my God, what did I do? He's right. I shouldn't have put my contact information on the pictures. Now anyone can find me. And I was so rude to him. Nathan has a job to do. He was just looking out for my safety, and I didn't ask him about his day. I didn't tell him about pulling my gun on the three teenagers. I must have been reacting to the tension of everything that has happened. How could I have been so stupid to put my contact information on the picture – and the way I reacted is even more embarrassing. He'll probably never call me again unless it's about business, and he would be right not to. Talk about overreacting! What an idiot I am.*

Hot tears rolled down Marcie's face. She thought about texting Nathan to apologize or calling him back, but she thought she should do that when she was more rested. She hoped he would forgive her.

She was just drifting off into a restless sleep when the phone chimed on the nightstand.

Chapter 29

Nathan!

Marcie bolted upright and pressed the button on the side of her phone so she could read the text message. She swiped the remaining wet spots from her cheeks with her other hand. Her phone displayed the incoming message – but it wasn't from Nathan. Four words widened Marcie's eyes and stiffened her spine.

Can you help me?

What? Could this be Shoni? Marcie's thumbs danced across the screen, barely touching it. *Who is this?*

Marcie waited, staring at the screen. She didn't recognize the phone number. The minutes ticked by. She wondered if the person at the other end was typing. Could it be Shoni? Or someone else? Or even a cruel hoax? Or was it the people Nathan had warned her about, trying to frighten her? She lay back on the pillow, her arm behind her head and her phone resting in her other hand on her stomach. A few more seconds passed before the chime indicated another message had arrived.

We talked tonight . . . with another girl on the street. Need help.

Questions flooded through Marcie's head. She typed: *Who are you? What do you want from me?*

This time the response came back quickly: *My name's Alina. Not much time . . . using a client's phone . . . he may wake up any minute. I want to get away. Please help.*

Alina? Sounds Eastern European. Was she the girl who was slapped?

Why can't you walk away?

Always watched, even my phone. They beat me. Need safe place. Please!

Marcie was digesting what she had just read when she saw that the person on the other end had added something. The message startled her to the core.

Maybe can help you.

Marcie typed: *What do you mean, help me?*

Might know where your girl is.

Marcie's thumbs flew over the phone's small keyboard on the screen. She scowled when her phone's auto correct feature took it upon itself to try to interpret what she meant and respelled a word. Cursing under her breath, she quickly revised the wording and hit send.

Don't understand. We need to talk. Can we meet somewhere? Is there a number I can use to call you?

She waited again for what seemed like an hour, but was really only minutes.

Finally it came: *Will contact with meeting place. DON'T CONTACT ME. NO POLICE. Dangerous. Please help me.* Then just seconds afterwards: *Must go, client waking up . . . must delete all messages.*

Marcie waited with her phone in her hand, but no more messages came through. She lay awake staring at the ceiling, pondering what she should do next. The tone of the conversation seemed real enough. Marcie shuddered at the thought of the woman sitting in the dark or in the bathroom furtively typing away and hoping the man in the room didn't wake up. Would the man discover that his phone had been used? If he did, then what would happen? Did Alina really know where Shoni was? Should she talk this over with Nathan Harris or Albert Baker? The texter had said no police.

Besides that, Marcie thought, she probably wasn't high on Nathan's personal list right now. His words still stung in her head, though she knew he was right. She really did need to forget about Shoni and what she was involved in. But she might be able to get some help for Alina. She decided she would show the conversation and the phone number to Albert Baker the next day. In the meantime, she decided the one person she knew who had the most experience on the subject of providing outreach services to women in crisis and who might be able to offer some advice was the professor at the school, Braden Maxwell. Even though he had the personality of a cactus, she made up her mind she would talk to him

about it when she saw him at class the next day.

Marcie was functioning on about two hours of sleep. Functioning meant only that she was awake. She had difficulty absorbing what was being said in class, and she felt nauseous. After class, she approached Professor Maxwell.

"Mr. Maxwell, may I have a word?"

"Ah, Ms. Kane. Of course, how may I help?"

Marcie tried to hide her surprise at his conciliatory tone, so different from the last time they had spoken. She decided to leave out any reference to Shoni.

"I got a phone call from a woman last night who said she was looking for help. She's a prostitute and she apparently wants to get out of the business. She asked if I could help somehow. Do you have any thoughts on how I could help her? She says the men she is working with are very dangerous."

"Really? Well, let's talk then." Marcie found herself in the cafeteria again with Braden Maxwell. On their walk there, they had talked generally about the course and how Marcie thought she was doing in the program. With coffees in front of them on the table, Maxwell got to the point. "So why would this woman call you? How did you meet her? You do manage to get yourself into situations, don't you, Ms. Kane?"

Marcie ignored the barb. "I met her earlier last night. I went out into her neighborhood to talk to some of the girls. Isn't that what we're being trained to do, Professor Maxwell? Aren't we supposed to help girls and women who need it?"

"Indeed you are, Ms. Kane," Maxwell said, adding, "I think your best bet is to get her to a women's shelter. If she's serious about turning her life around, that would be the best way to start. There are some good ones in the area. Is she in St. Petersburg?"

"I met her in Tampa," replied Marcie, "but I don't think it would matter to her where she goes." She sighed, taking another sip of her coffee. "But who knows if she'll even call me back. It sounds like she just wants to get away from the life she's in."

They talked for a while longer. Marcie was pleased that Maxwell was apparently taking a greater interest in her than last time. As they finished, he said, "Let me give you the name of a good case manager I know who can help you. Unfortunately I left my phone upstairs, so I'll have to call you later with the information. She could place the woman in a shelter in the St. Petersburg area where she'll be safe."

Marcie didn't want to pass up this opportunity or risk Professor Maxwell forgetting to make the call so she handed her phone to him and said, "Would you like to use mine? I'd really like to get the case manager's name as soon as I can."

Maxwell thanked her and motioned to his cup. "Are you interested in a refill? I can get it after I finish talking to the case manager."

"You go ahead and make the call. I'll get more coffee for us." Marcie picked up the cups as Maxwell was dialing. She went to the counter, thankful that he was willing to make the call while she was still there. She wanted to be ready if Alina contacted her again, which could be any moment. She was grateful for his contacts and that he knew a case manager to help Alina. With cream, sugar and coffees in hand, Marcie threaded her way carefully back to their table.

Maxwell was finished with the phone call when she returned. "Everything's set. If the woman calls you again and *if* she decides to meet you, give this case manager a call and she will set things up for you." He handed her a piece of paper with the contact information on it. They shook hands as they parted, and the instructor congratulated her on taking the initiative to help the woman. "Just be careful, Ms. Kane," he said as she turned to leave. "And good luck."

Marcie went about the rest of her day feeling tired but more optimistic. She found herself wondering if she would hear from Alina again. She didn't think she would but if she did, she would pass the information along to Baker along with the name of the case worker. She knew she would feel better having taken some action, but she was also satisfied that her involvement would be over. She was feeling pretty good about her decision.

Now if only she would hear from Nathan Harris.

Chapter 30

Marcie stopped by Mason and Sami Seaforth's after her courses finished later in the afternoon. The conversation and banter always flowed easily with her friends, and naturally they invited her to stay for dinner. She wanted to put Shoni, Irene and Alina out of her mind so she never raised the subject. When she looked at her watch, she couldn't believe it was 8:00 p.m. She playfully chastised them for keeping her up so late. She drove home in the setting sun and stopped at the grocery store on the way to buy a few supplies. She was putting the groceries away when the buzzer sounded, indicating she had a visitor downstairs. She pressed the button to ask who it was and the response surprised her.

"Flower delivery, ma'am."

Flower delivery? At this time of night? "Isn't it a little late to be delivering flowers?"

"You're my last delivery, ma'am. Lots of weddings, I guess. I tried to deliver them earlier, but you weren't home."

"Okay, bring them up."

Marcie darted to the couch where she had tossed her bag the night before. She realized Nathan must have hit a nerve about the dangerous people she might have disturbed as she pulled her gun out of the holster in her purse and shoved it in the waistband at the back of her jeans. She thought she was being a little ridiculous and probably paranoid. *The poor delivery man doesn't know he's in danger of getting shot.*

There was a knock at the door. Marcie peered through the peep hole. The man standing outside her door was dressed in the uniform of a delivery man and he was carrying a beautiful bouquet of red, pink and white roses. She opened the door and the exquisite fragrance immediately tickled her senses as the delivery man handed the bouquet to her. The logo on his uniform indicated he was from "Flowers for Every Occasion." She handed him a tip, and the condo was filled with the sound of cracking cellophane as she removed the wrapping from the flowers. The card she was looking for fell on the table. A warm feeling swam through her as she read, "Sorry if I upset you last night. I hope your day went well. Talk soon. Nathan."

What a thoughtful thing to do. Especially after the way I treated him. Marcie stood on a chair to find the vase that had been gathering dust on top of the china cabinet. It had been so long since anyone had sent her flowers to put in it that she'd placed the vase out of sight so it wouldn't be a sad reminder.

She washed the dust off the vase and happily occupied herself arranging the flowers until she was satisfied. A sense of buoyancy filled her as she fussed with the flowers, mixing and matching for maximum impact. She nearly floated with pleasure as she placed the vase on the coffee table. She knew she would take them into the bedroom with her that night and make sure she could see them easily from wherever she was in the condo the next day. The fragrance was not overpowering – just enough to freshen the condo – and the colors dazzled. Marcie thought Nathan had hit a home run with his choice.

Just as she picked up the phone to call Nathan to thank him, she felt it vibrate in her hand. She looked down to see who was calling. Once again, the number was not familiar to her.

"Hello?"

The voice on the other end spoke in a hushed tone. "It's me, Alina. Can you help me?"

There was that European accent again. Marcie was sure it belonged to the woman who had been slapped. She tried to hide the surprise in her voice that Alina had actually called. "Are you the person that texted me?"

The answer was a simple, "Yes."

"Maybe I can help. Can we meet to discuss it?"

"You don't understand. I have to get out of here *now*. It's too dangerous."

Marcie could sense the tension coming through the phone. "Okay, do you have time to talk now then?"

The woman's voice was an urgent whisper now. "No, you *really* don't understand. They're watching me. Can you help me or not?"

"Okay, I'll pick you up. But first you have to tell me about the girl whose picture I showed you. I think you do know her. Tell me what you know."

"Oh my God." She pronounced it "Gott." She continued with exasperation, "I might know where they take the young girls before they're sold." Then her voice rose in pitch. "They're coming. I have to go. Don't call back. Pick me up at midnight at this address."

Marcie ran to the counter with her phone squashed between her shoulder and cheek and fumbled for a pen in a woven basket. She scribbled the address on a napkin as the phone went dead.

Marcie sat motionless on the stool with her elbows on the counter and her chin resting on her clenched fists. She stared at the closed drapes, seeing nothing.

She tried to sort through the questions. What did Alina mean by "sold?" Who was threatening her? Who were the "they" that were coming after her? Her pimp? Her John?

Marcie wanted to discuss all this with Nathan. The woman had said no police, but Marcie had been down that road two years ago and had no intention of making the same mistakes this time. She also realized that she was starting to have feelings for Nathan Harris and she didn't want to upset him again. But after their blow-up on the phone, she had to face the fact that Nathan had a professional conflict because of her involvement with Shoni and Irene, and it was unfair to expect any kind of relationship would be possible. Still, maybe they could at least be friends.

Marcie dialed Nathan's number. First, she was going to thank him for the flowers and to apologize for the way she had acted. She also wanted to tell him about what had happened since she talked to him last. She needed his advice and calming influence. Most of all, she wanted to tell him about Alina. She could feel her disappointment when the call went straight to his voice mail.

"Hello, Nathan, it's Marcie. Thank you so much for the flowers. I'm sitting here admiring them. It was so thoughtful of you. I want to apologize for the way

I acted last night. I should be sending *you* flowers. There's something else I would like to talk to you about, too. I'd like your opinion. Please call when you get a chance. I hope everything is good with you. Thanks again."

She put her gun back in its holster in the bag and puttered impatiently around the condo until it was time to leave. Still no return call from Nathan. She wanted to discuss the situation with Nathan before calling Baker. She slung the strap of her bag over her shoulder and headed out the door, thinking about what she was going to do. She fully expected Nathan to call while she was in the car and he would tell her what to do. If she hadn't heard from Nathan, she would call Baker before she got to the address where she was supposed to pick up Alina.

She had been on the road for about half an hour, following the instructions from her GPS, when her phone rang. She glanced at the screen of her navigation system expecting to see that it was Nathan calling, but instead it was yet another unfamiliar number. Marcie's next thought was that it would be Alina calling from someone's phone, so she hit the button on the steering wheel to activate the Bluetooth.

There was an eerie silence on the phone for a few seconds until finally a deep male voice said, "Marcie Kane?"

The voice sounded distorted, as if the person was talking through a mask or with a hand over his mouth. When Marcie said yes, the caller continued, "The location where Alina wants to meet you has changed. You'll find her in a park." He gave Marcie the address. "You will have to look closely. She isn't feeling very well, so when you get there she won't be calling out to tell you where she is. In fact, she isn't feeling *at all*. You should probably bring a bag. But better make sure it's large enough for a body. Stop interfering or you'd better go pick out your own body bag because you're next."

"WHAT? Wait -"

He had hung up. There was nothing but silence now on the line.

An urgent blast from a horn behind Marcie's car reminded her she had taken her foot off the gas pedal and her car was coasting on the interstate. Still in shock, she let the car drift to the lane next to the median where she stopped and put on the four-way flashers. Stars drifted in and out of her vision, and nausea forced its way into her stomach. She bent over the steering wheel with her hands clutching her abdomen. This can't be happening. Was she responsible yet again for someone dying? She stared at the phone in her hand. She pressed the screen to bring up the call log, and the number was still there.

She leaned back in her seat, took a deep breath and dialed Detective Albert Baker

Chapter 31

Marcie wasn't sure how long she had been driving towards north Tampa before her GPS announced she would arrive at her new destination in two minutes. Her mind had been blank while the miles drifted by as her foot held the accelerator down. Flashing lights from emergency vehicles startled her long before she pulled into the parking lot. Red and blue shadows eerily dappled the walls of the houses and cars parked on the street.

It wasn't what she expected. It was an industrial area with factories. White smoke billowed from large smokestacks on either side of the road, but she was pulled towards the emergency vehicles jammed in the parking lot at the end of the street. It was like she had been carrying a weight on her shoulders since the phone call and a great sense of sadness overcame her. She leaned over the wheel as she drove slowly into the lot. Her hands trembled on the steering wheel. She didn't know for sure what she was going to find but her angry gut told her it would not be good. The caller had been clear about what he had done.

Marcie's eyes narrowed as she drew closer. It wasn't the entrance to a park. At the end of the parking lot was a heavy chain link fence with a large gate that yawned wide open. *Did I get the wrong address?* Floodlights lit up some huge pieces of dilapidated equipment, all of which lay dormant. Her car's headlights shone on a patrol officer who flagged her down as she pulled into the parking lot. She rolled down her window, and the glare of a flashlight momentarily blinded her. A dark shape was visible behind the light shining in her eyes. She introduced herself to the officer and let him know she was the one who had placed the call to Detective Baker. After checking her driver's license, the officer lowered the light and without saying a word, aimed it at a vacant spot beside a patrol car that was barely big enough for her vehicle. She squeezed her car into the narrow space and managed to leave just enough room to open the door.

The officer asked Marcie to follow him but said nothing else as they walked. Marcie's questions about Alina went unanswered so she gave up. The full moon and the officer's flashlight guided them through the opening of the gate, and their feet crunched on gravel as they walked into a large open area. High-powered flashlights held by emergency personnel bobbed and danced off the run-down machinery that soared into the sky. Temporary spotlights illuminated piles of dirt and gravel sporting tall weeds that grew unabated. A few dilapidated buildings stood at the foot of a large hill. The place was decrepit and forlorn, beaten down by a lack of human contact.

The officer said something into a speaker microphone on his shoulder. In response, Marcie could make out the large form of Detective Albert Baker emerge from behind one of the machines. His purposeful stride towards them identified him as the central figure among the cast of players.

Baker greeted Marcie as he approached. "Ms. Kane. We meet again."

Marcie said, "I don't understand. Is this the right address? The caller said she would be in a park."

Baker shrugged. "I don't know if you got the right address or not, but this *is* a park. It's an industrial park. This particular address is an abandoned gravel quarry. We haven't seen any sign of a woman here yet. What exactly did this caller say?"

Marcie recounted the conversation to the best of her recollection. She thought that Baker was looking at her skeptically. Even in the shadows cast by the various shapes surrounding them, she could see a frown on his face, reminding her that so far there was nothing substantiating her story. She finished by thumbing the screen on her phone to locate the number in the call log and handing it to Baker. Her shoulders quivered in spite of the heat in the night time air.

She said weakly, "That's the number of the guy who called. It sounded like his voice was distorted somehow, but you should be able to trace him back to the number." Pointing to the screen, she added, "This number above is the one Alina called on, but she said the phone wasn't hers."

Baker looked at the numbers. "We'll put a trace on them but if something did happen to this woman you speak of, and if the caller has any smarts, the call was probably made on a burner phone. The one Alina called on was probably her trick's cell, so we might be able to trace him."

The term burner phone was familiar to Marcie from watching TV. She knew it referred to a phone criminals used and threw away after making a call. It would be prepaid with cash so it was virtually untraceable; once the caller was done, the phone would be broken apart and the pieces would be scattered in so many places, it could never be whole again. Her shoulders sagged.

Baker continued, "So I understand you handed out some photos of the girl you met in Africa with your contact information on them. Is that true?"

Marcie felt her face flush again. "Yes, I did. But I never thought anything of it. I was just asking if anyone had seen her. I mentioned it to Nathan Harris and he told me how dangerous it was to do that, but it was too late. I never expected to hear anything from anyone. I was really surprised when the woman called."

"What did she say again?"

"She said she wanted to get away. I had spoken with her and another woman she was working the corner with. I was just trying to get information about Shoni, but I guess she saw me as an opportunity to get help. I'm pretty certain the caller on the phone was her. She spoke with a European accent just like the woman on the corner. I spoke with one of my professors at school about her, and he thought someone should try to get her to a woman's shelter where she couldn't be found. I called Agent Harris for advice, but he didn't answer. I thought I would hear from him before I picked up Alina. If he hadn't called, I was going to call you before picking her up. I told her I would meet her tonight at an address she gave me, but then I got the call from the man who implied she was dead. Look, I have the texts Alina and I exchanged."

Marcie scrolled through her phone once again until she found the text messages and handed it to Baker.

As Baker read the chain of text messages, Marcie looked towards the parking lot at the collection of emergency vehicles and then back at the police officers shining their lights in and around the gigantic bins and conveyor systems in a thus-far fruitless attempt to find anything. She wondered if there was any way this could be a hoax – that Alina could be standing on her street corner conducting business as usual and laughing at the wild goose chase she had sent the crazy woman on. Marcie didn't know anything about Alina. Her gut told her Alina was telling the truth but it could all be lies.

Baker said without taking his eyes from the screen, "So were you going to take a prostitute into your home – someone you had barely met? Do you really think that would be a wise decision?"

Marcie said nothing. She knew she had been making mistakes and Baker's comments did make sense. She had already decided she was trying to do too much. Maybe she was wasting his time and that of the whole emergency crew. Enough was enough. Baker and his crew had plenty on their hands without chasing shadows.

Baker stopped reading and looked up at Marcie. "What's this about her being able to help you – about maybe knowing where the girl is? Did she say what she meant by that?"

"We didn't get a chance to talk about it. She said she might know where the young girls are taken before they're sold, but she had to hang up before she could say more."

Baker's expression didn't change as he stared thoughtfully at Marcie. Finally, he said, "Okay, where's the street corner that Alina and this other woman were hanging out? We'll go and talk to her partner if she's there. I believe your story, but they might just be trying to spook you or have a little fun with you. I need the address where you were supposed to meet her originally too."

Marcie watched Baker write down the information as she told him and asked the detective to let her know if they found any sign of Alina. With the assurance that they would, Marcie walked slowly to the car with her head down. She pulled out of the parking lot and started towards home – but there was something she had to do first.

She headed in the general direction of St. Petersburg but she made a detour that took her into the heart of the prostitute corridor. She had no intention of stopping but she had to see for herself if she'd been deliberately misled in some sort of cruel joke. She turned in the direction of the street corner where she last saw Alina and her colleague.

At this time of night, the street was even drearier. A man lay passed out on a lawn. Another staggered down the street swilling from a bottle in a brown paper bag held to his lips. The gaudy signs hinting at any manner of perversions shone brightly, inviting passersby to take part. Males could be seen furtively coming and going from some of the establishments. Two blocks away Marcie saw two women standing in the glare of the streetlights. She was too far away to know for sure whether they were the same two, but one was dressed in a hot pink mini. The other woman appeared to be taller than Alina and Marcie could see even from that distance she was wearing shorts that exposed the lower curve of her buttocks. Marcie thought as she slowly approached that the woman in the mini could be Alina.

As Marcie drove through the last intersection before the corner where the women stood, she glanced both ways down the street perpendicular to the one she was on, checking for the large old luxury vehicle the pimp was driving. Seeing no sign of it, she proceeded in the direction of the women.

As Marcie drew closer, a heavy feeling draped over her like a blanket. The feeling was not dispelled as she quickly drove past the two women. A glance in the rear view mirror told her that one of the women was watching her car as she continued down the street.

Marcie was certain of one thing as she turned onto the interstate towards home. While it didn't confirm anything, neither of the two women standing on the corner was Alina.

Chapter 32

As she drove home thinking about everything that had transpired, Marcie thought she heard the familiar chime of a text message coming from the phone in her jeans pocket. Although she knew driving and talking on the phone was legal in Florida, she'd always thought the law needed changing, and that trying to hold a conversation while concentrating on shifting traffic was too distracting and dangerous. The message would have to wait. She hadn't heard from Nathan since she'd sent her text thanking him for the flowers, so she hoped it would be him. On the other hand, it was 2 o'clock in the morning so she was unsure why he would be contacting her at that time.

Marcie drove into the parking garage at the condo and coasted into her spot, nosing the car to within a few inches of the wall. Cars filled almost all the spaces up and down the rows and she expected their owners, except for the odd insomniac, would be slumbering in their condos, recharging for another day. As she walked towards the door leading to the basement lobby, she pulled the phone out of her pocket and started to scroll through the screen, looking for the new message.

Fatigue was overtaking her and it took a few seconds to find the message, but just as she went to open it, a sound alerted her to something unusual in the garage. Something was different. She could feel it. Marcie walked through the garage often enough that the sounds were as familiar as the smell of old leather. At night there was the drone of the overhead lights, the distant hum of the air conditioners that serviced the building, the rhythmic drum-like thrumming of the cicadas seeping in through the openings in the garage – they were all sounds Marcie expected to hear. Occasionally, the cables grabbing the pulleys to start the elevator on its journey up or down joined the other noises to form a discordant band. The sounds were so common that usually she barely noticed. But something different had just inserted itself. This one didn't belong.

Marcie stopped to listen, glancing nervously over her shoulder and scanning ahead of her. She examined the parked cars closest to her in the garage. She tried to peer beyond the shadows, but it was too dark. She listened intently, trying to understand what was different. Nothing was apparent, yet she could feel something in the air.

She thought that maybe it had been the squeak of her own running shoes echoing around the concrete walls and off the cement columns. She began walking again, quickly picking up her pace.

There!

Footfalls.

Heavy footfalls and moving faster than hers.

Marcie looked over her shoulder and started to run towards the door. At the same time, she reached into her purse to pull out her gun. But it was too late. She sensed the shape coming out of the shadows behind her. Just as she tried to turn around to see who was coming, something solid hit her and sent her sprawling in a crumpled heap on the hard concrete floor. Pain resonated like fire through her knee and shoulder as first one hit the floor and then the other. Air rushed from her lips as her lungs emptied.

The impact of the blow sent her purse flying out of reach and her phone skittered across the floor under a car parked nearby. Marcie spun around trying to see her attacker. She sat breathing rapidly, her fingers splayed on the cold floor, her knees drawn up to her chin in a defensive position. She inhaled deeply, gasping, but the muscles in her legs strained as she prepared to run or to fight to her last breath. She calculated the chances of getting over to her purse, pulling out her gun and firing it before her attacker did whatever it was he was planning. But it was too late. He approached her as she crab-walked backwards, farther away from her purse. She pressed her back against the garage wall, trying to push herself away, but there was nowhere else for her to go.

The man stopped and stared at her, apparently deciding what he would do next.

He was tall with a slender build in a dark brown leather jacket and blue jeans. He was that much more terrifying because his features lay hidden behind a sinister black balaclava. He cocked his head. He slowly raised his arm, but the gun Marcie was expecting to see was not there. He simply pointed at her and spoke, his voice muffled by the woolen cloth. "Stop interfering. Next time will be much worse." With that, he turned and disappeared into the shadows from which he had emerged a few minutes earlier.

Marcie watched him pass from sight behind the car and sat listening, slowly gathering herself. A distant car started outside the garage and she assumed it belonged to her attacker. She stood up, badly shaken by the events of the last few minutes. Her clothing was clinging to her. She brushed herself off and flexed her fingers and shoulder muscles to make sure nothing was broken. When she put weight on her knee, she felt the tightness of a scrape, but she knew she would be fine.

Marcie limped to her purse and threw the strap over her shoulder, grimacing as she bent down to grope for her phone under the car. She couldn't see it. She lowered herself to her hands and knees so she could peer under the frame of the vehicle. Her phone lay in two pieces with the plastic back a little farther away from the main part. Grunting from the effort, she retrieved both. The screen was cracked, but she was relieved to see it light up when she touched it. The phone still functioned.

Wobbling unsteadily, Marcie inserted her key into the lock of the door leading to the basement lobby and found the bench just around the corner. She sat and leaned back against the wall, her gaze staring into space. She sat unmoving for a few minutes, but finally she held the phone up to eye level and dialed to report the incident to Detective Albert Baker. His mumbled response told Marcie she had wakened him and a patrol officer soon arrived to take her statement and look around the building. Marcie was beyond tired. After the officer left, she had cleaned up the scrapes on her knee and shoulder and fallen into bed. Before she went to sleep, she deliberately switched off her alarm. Her class could proceed without her. She was quite sure she wouldn't be missed.

She drifted off into a troubled sleep, completely forgetting about the text message.

Chapter 33

The fact she was so tired didn't prevent a nightmare from intruding into her subconscious like a thief in the night robbing her of sleep. Once again she had tried and failed to save Shoni, but she couldn't quite remember the scenario. Pretty hard to put the positive spin advised by her psychologist on it when the details are unclear. Usually, her nightmares featured high definition with surround sound. Maybe it was some sort of breakthrough.

She had awakened around 9 o'clock, showered and now she was shepherding some fruit around on her plate with her fork. Her left elbow was propped on the table, carefully avoiding the cut she had suffered in the parking garage, and her head rested on her hand. She hadn't heard from Nathan. She had moved the roses from the bedroom to the living room and their splash of color brightened her mood considerably. But it didn't improve her appetite. She gave up on her breakfast and scraped the remains into the garbage with her fork.

Marcie decided she would call Nathan while she finished her coffee to let him know about being attacked. He had probably already heard it from Baker. She realized how exhausted she was, mentally and physically. She had had enough. It had started out simply enough. All she wanted to do was find out where Shoni was and help her if she could. The girl must be so scared. She was in a new country being forced to do God only knows what. At the least, Marcie thought the girl could use a friend. She deserved a chance and someone to help her.

Her knee tightened as she got up and limped to the sink with her plate and utensils. When she finished washing and drying them, she took her phone off the counter and was about to call Nathan's number when she saw the unread text message. *I forgot all about this.* She opened the message app to see who would have texted her at 2 o'clock in the morning. The message staring back at her sent a shockwave through Marcie that started in her brain and ended in her running shoes. She read it again and again as if in a fog. She checked the caller's number at the top of the text, but it was unfamiliar to her.

Who would send her this message? Was the message she was looking at meant to warn her about the man who attacked her? She looked back at the screen to confirm that her mind hadn't been playing a cruel trick. It was still there.

"Check the Hillside Inn. Watch out for Mr. Smith."

Now things had gotten completely out of hand. Someone wanted to scare her – and it was working. She had been assaulted and her life threatened. Alina could be dead and Marcie had been told she might need her own body bag. And now Mr. Smith's name had resurfaced. It was the name from Tanzania – the person with the eyes that the head teacher, Mrs. Adimu, had described. What was it? Oh yes, they would "pierce you like steel rods." She hadn't even noticed the eyes of the man who attacked her. Too many other things to think about. She never dreamed she would hear Mr. Smith's name again.

She settled her nerves and dialed Nathan's number. Once again, it went straight into voice mail. *Dammit!* She left a message. "Hi Nathan. I hope everything is okay with you. You won't believe what's happened to me since we last talked. Please call me as soon as you can. I really need to talk to you. Bye for now."

Marcie's next call was to Detective Baker, and her frustration level grew even more when she got the same result. Once again she left a message. "Detective Baker, it's Marcie Kane. I might have some information to share with you about the whereabouts of Shoni Batanga. Please call me as soon you can."

With both calls made, all she could do now was wait. She wandered into her office, turned on her computer, and typed "Hillside Inn" into Google. Immediately, she got a match. It was on the eastern outskirts of Tampa. It had mostly-positive reviews by Trip Advisor, and its claim to fame seemed to be its view overlooking a lush valley below.

The place certainly looked innocuous enough. It didn't look like the kind of place that would be a haven for prostitution. It seemed to be in a nice enough neighborhood. Marcie knew that the internet wasn't always reliable, but the pictures made it look like a hotel that anyone could take their family to.

A quick check on the balcony told her the sun was beaming down and the humidity had disappeared. She rode the elevator to the garage and looked nervously in all directions as she walked to her vehicle. Few cars remained in the lot. She heard bursts of laughter and lively conversation from people heading toward the pool with towels over their arms. It was hard to believe that just the evening before, she had been sprawled on the floor with somebody dressed like a terrorist hovering over her uttering threats. She wondered if there was still a little blood from her cuts and scrapes on the floor.

Marcie loved driving on a day like this. It was the kind of day when she knew her decision to purchase a convertible was the right one and lowering the top was exactly what she did when she got to her car. She turned the key, and tuned the radio to the local classic rock station. Driving with her top down and the radio on was a favorite pastime of Marcie's that usually allowed her to forget everything. She could certainly use that right now. But as if drawn by a magnetic force, she found herself programming the address for the Hillside Inn into her GPS instead. In minutes, Marcie was headed up the freeway ramp on the way to Tampa again. She couldn't remember having ever been up and down this interstate so many times over the course of just a few short days. But it gave her somewhere to drive on a spectacular day.

It was a leisurely drive – at least as much as it could be on the interstate. The baseball hat she stored in the center console for just such occasions kept her hair from her eyes. Eventually Marcie could see the Hillside Inn ahead of her, and just as the internet had described, it was an average-looking complex in a middle class area. As advertised, it sat on the edge of a valley that afforded spectacular views for the patrons. A large deck hung out over the greenery below, and by the tables arranged on its surface she assumed it was attached to a restaurant.

Marcie felt a stab of hunger and realized the few pieces of fruit she had eaten earlier that morning weren't enough to fill her up. Now that she had seen the Inn in person, she thought of turning around to leave. What good could she do here? Instead, Marcie turned her engine off and sat in the parking lot, thinking about why Shoni's captors would bring her here. All she could come up with was that the young girl was forced to do housekeeping duties now. At least that would be better than prostitution, anyway. Marcie was about to start the car to drive home when she looked at the restaurant, shrugged and decided there was no better place to grab a bite to eat than right here.

A large bus sat idling in front of the entrance as Marcie passed by. She wrinkled her nose as she thought she could taste the diesel fumes hanging thickly in the air. She stepped around a mountain of luggage arrayed like colorful beached whales on the sidewalk. The revolving door leading into the lobby resisted at first, but she was able to get it moving and enter the lobby. The elderly owners of the luggage chatted and laughed in a line, waiting for their turn at the registration counter.

Marcie made her way up the stairs and to the deck at the back of the Inn where she sat reading a menu in one corner looking out over the valley. She ordered a light lunch and a smoothie from the waitress and watched her walk back through the door leading to the kitchen.

As she did, a flash of white caught her eye. She turned her head further to the left to see a large white van pulling into the parking lot. When it stopped, the driver opened the door and walked towards the back. It must have been the movement that caught Marcie's attention. The van had side windows but they were darkened. Just enough light shone through from the other side of the van that Marcie could see shadows moving about in the back. The driver threw the left door wide first and then the right. Young women spilled out through the gaping rear doors like angry bees leaving a hive that had been disturbed. They were all dressed the same in light brown uniforms. Marcie guessed they were the cleaning staff coming to clean rooms for the elderly tourists. Kind of late, she thought, although she'd had to wait for a room to be cleaned on a few occasions herself.

She watched the girls hop down from the back of the van. From her vantage point, she could see they were mostly Asians. She would have expected young women to be chattering and laughing, but there was none of that. Maybe they just didn't like their jobs, but they just stepped out of the van and milled about, waiting for someone or something.

Marcie's meal arrived, and she started to turn around to eat, but something else caught her eye. The driver was speaking and gesturing to one of the young women while the others ambled towards a side entrance to the Inn. The driver was speaking animatedly, while the girl listened intently. Marcie sat forward on her chair. It can't be! When the driver turned the girl roughly by her shoulders so that she was directly facing him, Marcie saw that unlike the others, she was black. Marcie was too far away to be sure, but she felt in her gut that the girl she was staring at was Shoni.

Marcie grabbed her purse, threw some bills on the table to pay for the un-eaten meal, and raced for the door. She ran down the stairway to the main floor and fought her way through the crowd of elderly tourists still registering at the front desk. She excused herself repeatedly as she forced her way through a group chatting near the front door. She turned back to apologize over her shoulder once again as a tiny woman in a print dress and red hat whose creased face had been earned over at least 85 years raised her cane and loudly admonished Marcie for her rudeness.

Marcie pushed hard on the stubborn revolving door to get out into the front parking lot. As she tried to get the door moving, she could see the girl she thought was Shoni being ushered into a black car by the van driver. The girl seemed to be struggling as she was pushed into the back seat. The suction holding the revolving door finally released and Marcie emerged into the sunlight just as the girl locked past the driver's shoulder straight at Marcie running down the steps.

Marcie forgot about the pain from her scraped knee as she leapt off the step. She grimaced at the electric shock in her knee when she landed but as she recovered, her eyes connected with the girl's from across the parking lot an instant before the door slammed. The van driver knocked on the roof of the idling car and it shot off through the parking lot away from Marcie. A small face was pasted to the glass, looking straight at Marcie.

And in that moment, frozen in time, she was certain that the girl staring wide-eyed at her was definitely Shoni.

Chapter 34

Marcie's arms swung as her long determined stride took her across the parking lot to the van driver. She tapped him on the shoulder as he was climbing into his vehicle. He jumped. He turned and stared at her, his face a mask. The man was tall and slight with an angular jaw and large blue stud in his left ear. His eyes were dull grey and underlined by dark circles. His beard was scruffy. Marcie wondered if this was the legendary Mr. Smith. He had already slammed the back doors shut and seemed to be in a hurry to leave. He turned back and stepped hurriedly onto the first step while grabbing the steering wheel with his right to hoist himself into the driver's seat.

Marcie said, "Wait! I want to talk to you."

The driver settled into the seat with a displeased scowl and tried to pull the door shut, but Marcie grasped it with both hands to keep it open. She enunciated every word. "I said I want to talk to you."

The driver relaxed his hold on the door for a moment and glared at Marcie. "Look, lady, this ain't the hotel shuttle. Go ask at the front desk if you have questions." He yanked the door out of Marcie's hands and slammed it. He turned the key in the ignition with the other hand as the van fired up.

Marcie shouted through the closed window. "I want to ask you about the black girl that got in the limo. Who was she?"

The driver's eyes rolled skyward. The window lowered a few inches and he turned towards Marcie. "I ain't got a clue what you're talking about. These were the housekeepers for today's cleaning shift. That's all I know."

The window rolled back up and the driver peeled away from the hotel parking lot leaving Marcie covered in a cloud of dust and blue haze. As she hastily memorized the license plate number and reached into her pocket to enter it on her phone, the screen lit up with an incoming call.

She stared at it intently with a sense of relief flooding through her.

Finally.

"Nathan!" she said, "I've been trying to reach you." Marcie walked back towards her car holding the phone with her left hand while pressing the button on her key fob at the same time. She heard the door locks unlatch.

"I know, I'm sorry. I got your messages and I wanted to call. We're working hard on the trafficking case." Without giving her a chance to ask any questions, Nathan changed the subject. "Hey, I'm glad you liked the flowers."

"I loved the flowers! It was so thoughtful, especially since I was such a bitch. I overreacted, Nathan, and I'm sorry."

"Well, I overreacted, too. Of course people like these can find you if they want to whether you put your contact information on the photos or not. It's easy to track someone down nowadays with the internet. I was worried about you going into that neighborhood, but I admit I was being a little overprotective."

Marcie felt that if Nathan were standing in front of her right now, she would try to kiss him. But she knew that wasn't going to happen. She was sure his protectiveness was mostly professional. She could be a key witness in the case, and naturally he didn't want anything to happen to her. Nevertheless, she felt warmth rush through her and the fact that he thought enough of her to want to be overprotective for whatever reason caused her to flush.

Nathan continued in his professional tone, "You said you had some information that might be relevant to the case. Detective Baker has been keeping me informed, but I'd like to hear it from you. What have you been up to, Marcie Kane?"

Where to start, she wondered?

She began by telling him about driving to meet Alina and the phone call warning her that Alina was already dead in a park, only it was an industrial park instead of a nature park. She talked about seeing Baker there at the gravel pit. Then she told Nathan about the terrifying attack last night in her own parking garage. And finally, she told him how she had driven out to the Hillside Inn where she was positive she had just seen Shoni Batanga.

Nathan didn't interrupt her as she barely took a breath. She didn't want to forget anything and she thought in her haste she might. But it felt so good to be able to unburden herself to Nathan. She could feel the relief washing over her. Finally, she told him that she had received a message after she was attacked last night to watch out for Mr. Smith.

The phone was dead silent. Marcie said, "Nathan, are you still there?"

"Mmm, yes, I was just thinking." His voice seem strained, like he was about to explode again. But then he said in a concerned tone, "I haven't talked to Detective Baker yet this morning. Marcie, are you all right?"

Marcie retorted with exasperation. "Yes! I haven't been able to reach either you or Baker. All I got were your voice mails! I'm okay. It was just scary at the time. I got a scraped knee and cut elbow out of it."

"Don't downplay this, Marcie."

"I'm fine."

"Okay. Did you get a good look at your attacker?"

"His whole head was covered up. He was wearing a balaclava so, no, I didn't get a good look at him.

"Any idea who might've warned you about Mr. Smith?"

"None. I've been wracking my brain trying to think of someone who would connect Mr. Smith with me. I can't come up with anything."

"Well, at least we're starting to build a profile on Mr. Smith. We have descriptions given to us from Godfrey and Mrs. Adimu, the head teacher. We have the call made to you about Alina, although we don't know for sure whether that came from Mr. Smith. You must be getting close to something or they wouldn't go to such drastic measures. On the other hand, it looks like they just want to scare you off. The attacker didn't seem to want to harm you. They probably did it at your condo building to show you they know where you live and that they can get to you any time they feel like it. I guess they didn't scare you off if you're there at the Hillside Inn."

Marcie caught the sarcasm in his tone and reminded him that she'd tried to reach him unsuccessfully. "When I couldn't get you or Baker, I could've called

Finch, I guess, but I just decided to go see what the Inn looked like for myself. I didn't think that would be dangerous, especially in broad daylight. I never believed I would see Shoni. I mean, this hotel is full of elderly tourists and families! But Nathan, I'm sure it was her. If not, it was her double. She looked so frightened. Where would they be taking her?"

"You said someone told you that Shoni would be *sold*? That could mean they have found a bidder willing to pay their price for her. It could be anyone anywhere in the world. I don't think the van driver is going to be much help. My guess is that his job is to pick up and drop off the housekeeping staff. He was probably telling the truth when he said he didn't know anything."

Marcie said, "I wondered if the van driver might be Mr. Smith. He had grey eyes that could be considered 'piercing' by some people. He also had a scruffy beard, although I don't think anyone would consider it aristocratic as I believe Godfrey thought Mr. Smith's goatee was." Marcie stopped herself. "What am I doing? I'm just making wild guesses. None of it makes sense to me. Anyway, maybe this will help," and she recited the license number.

"Great job getting that license number," Nathan said, his voice rising urgently. "I need to go, Marcie. We'll track down the van as quickly as possible and question the driver. Please go home and try to keep a low profile. Detective Baker will contact you if he has questions."

"You know what, Nathan? I can do that! I know you're going to find this hard to believe, but I have absolutely no problem with going back to my normal, mundane life. This is getting too crazy for me. I feel like I've been a step behind since I went to Africa. I've come in after the fact with everything that has anything to do with Shoni and Irene. I'm quite willing to let you guys handle it. Is there some way you and I can get together sometime when you're in town and enjoy a normal meal without talking about guns and prostitutes and human trafficking rings? I think I would like that more than anything."

"Me too, Marcie. I'm not sure when I'll be back in the area, but let's see what happens, okay? Once we have this situation resolved, I promise I will make a special trip down just to see you and we can pretend we're two normal human beings. How's that sound?" He chuckled.

They chatted for a few more minutes before signing off and Marcie headed home. On the way, she realized just how tired she was. She thought that maybe tonight would be good time for half of one of the pills the doctor gave her and the decent nightmare-free sleep that surely it would bring.

Chapter 35

Marcie was about halfway home when her phone rang. The screen on her navigation system announced that the caller was the Tampa Police Department. She pressed the button on her steering wheel and heard Albert Baker's voice on the other end.

Detective Baker got to the point immediately. "I have some bad news about the woman who contacted you -- Alina. We kept searching that site where you were told to go, the old gravel mining operation. It's in the process of being turned into a nature preserve, and the hole where they formerly extracted the gravel is now full of water. Anyway, there's a trail that leads to the top of a ridge overlooking the pond, and it has to be a 75-foot drop straight down to the bottom. Well, we sent some divers in there once the sun came up, and they found the woman's body. It looks like she either fell or had been pushed over the edge and hit some rocks on the way down. For some reason, your caller sent you to the right location but he neglected to give you all the details about where her body could be found. I'm sorry to have to tell you this, Ms. Kane, but I knew you would want to know."

Marcie had drawn in a breath of air when Baker mentioned he was calling about Alina and hadn't exhaled until he finished. Her shoulders sagged as she listened.

Baker continued, "Her full name was Alina Dobrescu and according to her colleague at the corner, she came to the U.S. about two years ago. The other woman didn't want to say much, but she did say she thought Alina was killed because she was trying to get away – as a message to the other girls. We're going to be sweating her a little more to try to get more information.

"We traced the phone number Alina used to call and text you, and it belonged to some businessman. At first, he didn't want to talk at all, but when we threatened to tell his wife, he caved. Said he often hired Alina and she must have used his phone after he went to sleep. That ties in with the story she gave you. We don't think he had anything to do with her murder. He's just a john. He's a mousey little guy just looking for some action is all."

Marcie had remained silent until now. Her breathing was uneven. She said faintly, "So you mean if I hadn't talked to Alina, she would still be alive?

Baker hesitated before continuing. "I'm not saying that. She had apparently tried to get out of the business before and had been beaten for her troubles each time. Each beating was more severe than the one before it. It wouldn't have mattered if it'd been you or someone else. The end result would've been the same."

Marcie sagged with guilt, but just said simply, "Okay, thanks for letting me know." Then she told him about seeing Shoni at the Hillside Inn.

"You do realize that by not giving me the information you had about the Hillside Inn before you drove out there, you were potentially obstructing justice, right?"

Marcie blew air through her lips. "I did try to call you – there was no answer. I never dreamed that I would actually see Shoni at the Hillside Inn, but I'm certain it was her. I'm sorry if I didn't inform you before I went myself, but I can assure you, this is getting too crazy for me. I'm hoping you guys can find Shoni and deal with the guys that took her. With any luck and for the benefit of us both, you won't be hearing from or about me again."

"Well, if anything else does come up, make sure you let us handle it." Baker stopped before musing as if to himself, "It may not mean anything, but the gravel mining operation where Alina was found is on the same river that goes past that Hillside Inn you mentioned. Once again, I'm sorry to have to tell you about Alina. Take care, Ms. Kane."

She turned her vehicle onto the Pinellas Bayway and was only a few minutes from home when the phone rang again. She didn't recognize the number and was surprised to hear the caller announce his name.

It was her professor. "Marcie, it's Braden Maxwell. We missed you in class today."

Marcie thought it was odd that he would take the time to call her for being absent, but she guessed she paid more attention than most of the others in the class so it was possible that he would notice her absence.

"I just had a few things to take care of. Nothing serious. I should be there on Monday."

"How did you make out with the European prostitute? Did you hear from her again?"

Marcie said dully, "Her name was Alina and she's dead. Mr. Maxwell. The police found her at the bottom of a pond in a gravel pit. Apparently, her pimp or someone killed her because she wanted to get out of the business. I guess it was some kind of message to the other girls."

"I'm so sorry to hear that. She's not the first and she won't be the last, Marcie. It's one of life's hard lessons in this business, I'm afraid. These people are often very dangerous. Are you okay?"

"I'm fine. I just need some rest."

"Are you still following up on that African girl?"

"Nope, I'm done with that. The police can handle it. I feel like I was way over my head and with the threats I was getting and possibly putting people in harm's way with my questions, I think it's time to quit."

"Yes, sometimes it's best to let the authorities handle these things. Did you say you were getting threats? What kind of threats?"

Marcie sighed. "Someone attacked me from behind and shoved me down in my parking lot. I have no idea who it was. He was wearing a balaclava."

"Were you hurt?"

"A few scrapes, that's all."

"That's good to hear. It's definitely time for you to step away. These people obviously mean business. Anyway, I just wanted to make sure you were okay. You seemed to be getting in pretty deep. I don't recommend this kind of activity to my students, and I certainly hope you didn't get the impression from me that I thought you should continue to be involved. That certainly wasn't my intention."

"No, of course not. I appreciate your concern, Mr. Maxwell. See you in class."

"Please, call me Braden. Good night, Marcie."

Marcie clicked the phone off. Well, she thought, that was a little weird. First he calls to see if I'm okay because I missed class, and then he tells me to call him by his first name. The thought ran through her mind: I hope he isn't getting too interested in me on a personal level. Then she laughed out loud. I guess he just really *does* take his job seriously. She pulled into the driveway leading to her condo parking lot and checked her surroundings before getting out of the car. She put her bag over her shoulder and held it so that the gun was easily within reach. A flickering overhead bulb cast eerie shadows on her path to the door, making her trip across the garage that much more tense. It was probably the quickest she had ever reached the door leading to the lower lobby.

Chapter 36

Marcie woke on Saturday morning feeling refreshed. As she puttered about the kitchen, she reflected that she'd had a dreamless sleep. She had to admit the half pill helped, but the fact she hadn't had a nightmare was a huge bonus. It felt good. She had gone to bed with a clear head, having made her decision to let Nathan and Baker handle everything. She decided life was pretty good again, although she didn't know where she stood with Nathan. She wondered if he felt anything for her, but she understood that there were a few reasons why he was so reticent about getting personal with her.

She sat at the island in her kitchen and plotted her day. She had taken her time showering. She thought that she would start with a workout at the gym or a swim in the pool. She would figure out which it was going to be when she stepped out on the balcony to check the weather. A quick glance out the window when she opened the drapes told her the sky was overcast and not a pool day, so the decision was easy. Then she needed to shop for groceries, and maybe she might splurge and do some shopping for fun. Of course, if she did bring home something new, something of equal size would have to leave. That was her philosophy and the way she kept things manageable in her closet. Since she would be going to the gym and then shopping, she had chosen form-fitting denim jeans and a dusty rose casual blouse to start the day.

She stood up from the stool to put her dishes in the dishwasher when she heard a Skype call coming in on her computer. She rushed into her office, leaned over the chair that was pushed under the desk and jiggled the mouse until the cursor was hovering over the red "Video Call" icon. Her spirits soared. It was Nathan! In spite of assuring herself she looked presentable a few times already this morning, she checked her reflection one more time in the mirror above the desk before clicking the mouse that opened the gateway to allow Nathan's image to appear out of the ether. The next hour was spent chatting, and Marcie's plans went out the window. It was so easy to converse and laugh with Nathan Harris. It felt to Marcie like she had known him for a very long time. Relaxed and comfortable with each other, they covered a lot of ground in their conversation, revealing their respective likes and dislikes with food, movies, music, sports, books, even politics. Finally, the conversation got around to the case. Nathan said, "I'm happy you've decided to pull back from this whole situation. I know it's hard for you, but Marcie, we have the experience and resources to deal with it. We think we're starting to get closer to identifying what's going on, and even though I wish you hadn't been involved at all, your information has been helpful. By the way, I'm actually flying down to Tampa later today on business. That's really why I called before we got distracted by our pop culture preferences." He laughed. "Are you available and interested in going for dinner tonight?"

Without hesitating, Marcie said, "Of course, I would love to. Where shall we go this time? If you still trust my judgment, I can make a reservation for us. How does that sound?"

"Your judgment has been impeccable so far, at least when it comes to restaurants. Please do that, maybe for around 6:30? I'm looking forward to it. See you soon." His face disappeared from her computer screen as they disconnected their Skype call. Marcie realized that her heart was beating faster than usual. She ignored the implication that her judgment in other areas had been questionable, and just sat staring motionless at her computer screen. He was sending such conflicting messages. One minute he was firmly entrenched in his professional FBI agent demeanor, then the next minute he was warm and friendly and engaging, then suddenly he had his FBI hat back on, holding her almost at arm's length . . . She suspected that he did really like her and that she intrigued him. She felt that underneath, Nathan wanted to see her but his job and their roles in this case were getting in the way. She sighed and pursed her lips at the empty room. Well, one thing was certain: she was very excited about seeing him that evening. They would just have to see where it led. She knew herself, and she knew this was the first time in a long, long while that she had felt anything for a man. Nathan Harris was definitely worth the effort. She had carelessly expended her time on less worthy endeavors in the past.

Marcie was packing her gym clothes into her bag when her cell phone rang. When she answered, there was just a faint hint of breathing on the other end. Marcie was just about to hang up when a small female voice whispered, "Is this Marcie Kane?"

Marcie stiffened. "It is. Who's this?"

Marcie thought she knew the answer but it was difficult for her to believe so she held her breath waiting for a reply. Her suspicions were confirmed.

"It's Shoni Batanga. I . . . I . . . I think I saw you at the hotel yesterday. I'm in bad trouble. I've escaped from some very bad men and they're looking for me. If they find me, they might kill me. Please . . . can you help me?"

The last four words struck Marcie with a jolt. They were the same as the ones Alina had used. Marcie didn't want a similar fate to happen to Shoni.

"Shoni, I thought that was you at the hotel! I'm so glad you're calling me. I'll give you the number for the police department, a Detective Baker. He's my friend. Call him and he'll help you."

"No," came Shoni's whisper on the other end. "I can't. I don't trust the police. I know what they are like. They are so corrupt. They won't help me. They will just sell me back to these men who held me. I need you to help me. Please. I'm afraid of Mr. Smith, too. He hurt my friend Irene, and if he catches me, I think he will kill me. I can hide for a little while, but I don't know where to go. I can't hide for long."

"The police aren't the same here in this country, Shoni," said Marcie, trying to reassure the frightened girl." I understand your reluctance, but you *will* be safe with them. You can trust the police here."

There was panic in Shoni's voice. "I *don't* trust them. My friends in my country tell me about bad experiences." She was still whispering, her small voice was wavering and she sniffed every few seconds. She was close to breaking down.

Marcie could sense over the phone that the girl was terrified.

"Okay, Shoni, don't panic, I'm going to help you. But how did you get my number?"

"We all sleep together in a small room. A girl who works as a prostitute, I think, had my picture with your phone number on it. She said you passed it out on the street. That's how I knew you wanted to help me."

Marcie sighed. "Can you tell me where you are?" Shoni recited an address, one that Marcie realized was on the other side of the city. "All right, Shoni. I'm going to leave now and come to you. It's going to take me 40 minutes to get there. Do what you have to do to stay safe. I'll be there as quickly as I can. I'll watch for you, but please watch for me, too. I drive a blue car."

Immediately after hanging up the phone, Marcie placed a call to Detective Baker.

When Baker answered, she told him about her conversation with Shoni and where she was supposed to pick her up. She added, "Detective Baker, she has a deep mistrust of all police because of her experiences in Tanzania."

Marcie got the impression Baker was about to say something, but was refraining. She wondered if he was tempted to make a comment about her promising not to get involved any more and leaving it to his department. But instead he said, "It sounds like she's going to hide if she sees a police car coming. That's not going to help her or us. So listen, here's what I think you should do. She's obviously terrified. She's not going to go with anyone but you. Go and meet her as you've planned. Then bring her here to the station and we will debrief her and find a safe place for her to stay until we get this sorted out."

"I don't think that's going to work. She'll freak if I take her to a police station. I'm telling you, she has zero trust of the police. I really don't know what she would do. She's just as likely to bolt. What if I bring her back to my place and you send over a female officer to talk to her – preferably in plain clothes?"

"That won't fly, either. You've already been attacked at your condo. If you're being watched, what's to prevent someone from attacking again and grabbing Shoni? If that happens, we may never find her – and you could end up getting killed. Tell you what, go ahead and pick her up. We'll have an unmarked car follow you. Just a second."

Marcie waited and listened as his breath became a little louder, as if he was making an effort to hold the phone and do something else at the same time. His voice came back on. "There's a Best Western a few blocks from where she said she would be. Take her there." Marcie wrote down the address.

Baker continued, "You're still driving a BMW convertible?"

Marcie was already walking out the door. "Yes, it's a metallic blue Cabriolet. Here's my license number. Please make sure your guy is there."

"You may not see him, but he'll be there. I'll have him follow you to the hotel to make sure nothing happens. I'll wait to hear from you. We'll decide what to do after that. Your idea of Shoni meeting a female officer is a good one. We'll have a case manager experienced in working with girls trying to get out of the sex trade there for the meeting as well." Baker paused before adding, "Good luck, Marcie. Be very careful."

"Wait, Detective Baker. I have a number for a case manager that my teacher, Professor Maxwell, gave me. Do you want it?"

"No, we do this all the time. We know the good ones."

Marcie said, "Okay," and hung up. She adjusted the shoulder strap of her bag as she reached the elevator. The gun inside was just heavy enough to be a reminder to Marcie that it was there. She pressed the button for the elevator and waited. The numbers slowly paraded by. As she waited, she shook her head at how she could not seem to get away from this. Every time she resolved to get out of it, somehow she got dragged back in. Finally, there was an audible ding and the elevator doors opened to take her to a meeting with the girl who had been invading her thoughts since the night they met.

Chapter 37

The sky opened up on the way to Tampa, and Marcie's wipers struggled to keep the rain off the window enough that she could see. Car lights broke eerily through the downpour and Marcie hoped that Shoni was somewhere out of the rain. The trip took longer than it would have in good weather and Marcie pulled onto the street where Shoni said she would be. The area showed signs of trendiness with its small retail outlets and healthy living stores. Marcie realized it wasn't far from the Hillside Inn. She slowly approached the designated intersection, hoping to see Shoni burst out of a doorway. There was no sign of the girl.

Marcie wondered if Shoni had given up because she was late. Or worse yet, she could have been recaptured. She realized that the phone call with Baker had taken some time and the weather delay hadn't helped. It was probably an hour and 15 minutes ago since Shoni called. Marcie peered through the rain for any sign of her. The large rain drops pounded like hundreds of tiny hammers on the roof of the car and left large puddles on the streets as the drainage system failed to keep up. Street signs vibrated in the wind and the lights hanging over the street swayed precariously. Shreds of paper floated in the rivulets on the streets or danced spasmodically in the wind.

Distorted lights shone through the rain that mottled the windows of the stores, but the only other signs of life were a handful of cars and a street person huddled on the sidewalk. Marcie felt a pang of sorrow. He sat on a piece of cardboard hunched over with his head resting on his knees. An old coat draped over his shoulders afforded the only form of protection against the elements. The scene reminded Marcie of the tarp she had been under in Africa hiding from the men who were determined to kill her. A shudder ran through her at the thought. The man had to be drenched and he must be freezing in the rain. She suspected the local merchants wouldn't let him in their stores because of his appearance. But she had to focus on finding Shoni.

She looked in her side mirror to see if she could see the unmarked police car. There was no sign of that either, but she wasn't surprised since Baker had promised they would stay out of sight to avoid spooking Shoni. Marcie didn't know what to do. She wouldn't know which store to start with to ask if they'd seen the girl.

She drove an extra block down the street, widening the circle she was driving in and slowly turned the corner. Even if Shoni was hiding in the shadows of an alley somewhere, she should be able to spot Marcie's car. Still nothing. Marcie had made a complete circle and was approaching the spot where the street person huddled against the storm. She decided she would at least stop to offer him some money so he could get out of the rain. She slowed the car and rolled the passenger side window down. Water immediately dampened the seat. Suddenly, movement on the sidewalk caught her attention.

The bundle that she thought was a street person had sprung into a whirl of activity. The coat flew off revealing a small girl. The girl ran for Marcie's car and yanked on the door handle but it held fast, locked. Marcie quickly pressed the button to unlatch the passenger door and the girl quickly got inside and slammed the door.

Shoni said, "Go!"

The scent of the girl's wet clothes assaulted Marcie's nostrils as she pressed the accelerator. She rolled up the window. Water dripped onto the floor from the girl's soaked clothing. Shoni's body shook in the passenger seat and Marcie could see clenched teeth through the girl's parted lips. Marcie switched off the air conditioner and turned on the heater in the car as she merged into the traffic on the street.

Shoni surveyed her surroundings and cast a glance over her shoulder.

Marcie said, "I'm so relieved to see you, Shoni. Are you okay?"

The girl nodded but she could barely stop her teeth from chattering long enough to utter, "There was a big black car circling like you were. I think it could be them."

Marcie thought it was probably the unmarked police car but she said simply, "Could be who?" She looked in the mirror and saw a number of cars behind, including a black vehicle a few cars back. She asked again, "Are you okay?"

"Yes, I'm okay now. Do you know where Irene is?"

"Uh, we can talk about that when we get to the hotel I'm taking you to." A glance in the rear view mirror told Marcie the black car had moved ahead of another vehicle before pulling back into the lane she was occupying. Marcie thought it would be the policeman wanting to make sure he didn't lose them.

Words spilled from Shoni's mouth. "She's dead, isn't she? I saw Mr. Smith hit her. She was sick and she told him she had a disease. She called it sickle cell disease. She told me about it. She said she needed medication or she would get very sick and maybe even die soon. She tried to escape but she got caught. Mr. Smith said she was more trouble than she was worth. He called her damaged goods. He hit her hard on the side of the head with his fist and she hit the other side of her head on a sink when she went down. She didn't move. I was so scared. I did nothing. I should have done something, but I couldn't. I was afraid the same thing would happen to me. They took her out and put her in the back seat of a car. That's the last I saw of her."

Shoni sniffed repeatedly as she told her story. Marcie was surprised the girl wasn't sobbing, but she had probably seen so much in her home country that she had built some sort of immunity. Or perhaps she had already cried every tear.

The black car was four cars behind.

Marcie decided that Detective Baker's case manager should be the one to deal with the subject. "Let's get you to some place safe and then we can talk about everything that's happened. Did the men who held you captive touch you?"

"One wanted to, but Mr. Smith told them to leave me alone. He said bad things would happen to the men if they touched me. He said he would get lots of money for me. I think they sold me last night. I knew I had to get out or bad things would happen. That's why I escaped. They would have sent me somewhere. "

The black car was now two vehicles behind.

Marcie's phone rang and she immediately pressed the button to answer. When she heard Baker on the phone, she glanced at the navigation screen and was thankful to see the caller was not identified. She didn't want Shoni to know she was talking to the police. But the navigation screen also told Marcie she had made an error. She hadn't had time to plug in her phone and the one bar left told her the battery was nearly dead. She had a charger in her glove compartment, so she would ask Shoni to reach it as soon as she got off the phone.

Baker said, "There's a problem, Marcie. The guy we sent out got rear ended at a light on the way over to your location." His frustration became very clear. "Some asshole behind him didn't realize it was pissing rain and slid into him. We sent another car, but he's still on his way. Do you have Shoni?"

Then who the hell is in the car behind us?

"Yes, I do, but there might be another customer looking right now . . . uh, looking at the car." She hoped he understood her cryptic message and that Shoni didn't.

Apparently he did. "Really? Okay, just take it easy. Stall if you have to. Our man will be there as fast as possible to take care of the guy following you. When that's done, go to the hotel we talked about. One of my people will be there in plain clothes waiting for you."

Marcie disconnected.

They were on the entrance ramp to the interstate. The car was right behind them now, just feet from the rear bumper of Marcie's car.

Marcie looked at Shoni, pointed to the seat belt that was dangling over the girl's right shoulder and had two words for her.

"Buckle up."

Chapter 38

The black car closed fast as they pulled onto the interstate. Marcie looked in the rear view mirror, but the darkened windows in the car behind prevented her from seeing how many people were in the car. She sped up but the black car kept pace.

Marcie glanced at Shoni and the girl's eyes were as wide as an owl's. She was staring over her shoulder at the car rushing toward their bumper. Marcie had to get her phone onto the charger so she could let Baker know when they got to the hotel. She pointed at the glove compartment. "Shoni, could you reach in there and hand me the phone charger?" Shoni leaned forward to press the button to open the latch. At the same time, the grille of the car following them filled the rear view mirror just before it smashed into the back of Marcie's car. Shoni's hand never reached the latch. Her body was slammed back in her seat. The BMW lurched forward, and Marcie felt the back end reeling from side to side.

What the hell?

Marcie knew if the driver of the other car wanted to send them careening across the highway into oncoming traffic, he could do it. She had to get away.

She pressed the accelerator and sailed around a slow-moving vehicle in front of her. The car behind did the same and was closing the gap again. What was she going to do? Where was the damn police car? She couldn't wait for him to show up. She had to do something. She quickly checked the navigation system and saw that an exit was coming in about a mile. If she could get off at the next exit without the black car, they might be able to disappear into the traffic. At the speed they were travelling, the exit would arrive very soon.

She cut left across two lanes of traffic to the lane nearest the median and tucked in beside a car to her right. The black car was right on her bumper again as if connected by an invisible chain. She slowed her speed to keep pace with the car beside them, and their heads snapped back against the head rests as the black car jarred them again. The woman driving the car next to them stared with her mouth agape at Marcie and Shoni. Shoni was leaning with her back rigid, her hands firmly gripping the seat and her head forming an indentation in the head rest. The woman in the car beside them frowned and looked down and to her right. Marcie guessed she was fumbling in her purse to find a phone to report the incident on the interstate. As the woman looked down, her car slowed.

NO! Keep moving! Marcie slowed down to maintain the same pace as the car beside hers. She knew she was risking another jolt. Frustrated motorists behind were becoming annoyed at the cavalcade and horns blared. The exit was quickly approaching. It was three lanes to the right of Marcie's position now, and precise timing would be required. Marcie looked past Shoni through the passenger window to see a disgruntled driver roar past on the right of the petrified woman beside them. That appeared to clear the second lane over. The outside lane closest to the exit was completely open – or so Marcie hoped. That could change instantly, but she had no choice. It was now or never. Time seemed to stand still, and Marcie realized her next manoeuvre was going to require a lot of luck and at least a prayer. What she was about to do could be suicidal. It was nearly time. Another bumper-to-bumper jolt swayed her car again, and shrill horns erupted from the shocked motorists around them.

One more look in the right side mirror of her car told Marcie that with luck and some perfect timing on her part, they just might make it. A car had pulled in behind the woman in the next lane, effectively boxing in the black car. *Please, please stay where you are for a few more seconds.*

It was time. *Now!*

Marcie slammed the accelerator all the way to the floor and felt her car surge ahead of the vehicle beside her. She yelled, "Hang on!" as she yanked the steering wheel to the right and pushed down on the horn as hard as she could. Her right back bumper must have scraped by the woman's fender by inches as Marcie's car started a hazardous angular journey across three lanes of traffic. She could hear car tires sliding on the wet pavement and the sickening crunch of fenders bending.

Time hung suspended in the BMW while the chaos outside the vehicle could be measured in fractions of seconds. They made it across the first two lanes of traffic when the sound of an air horn shattered the silence in their car. Marcie's eyes widened in terror as a tractor trailer she hadn't seen coming loomed in the lane nearest the exit, bearing down on them. It was headed directly at Shoni's side of the BMW and closing fast. The truck's motor complained with shuddering moans as the driver desperately geared down. The air brakes huffed and the big rig's eighteen wheels bounced erratically on the pavement, trying to slow down the enormous vehicle. Even on the wet pavement, smoke erupted from the protesting tires and the trailer vibrated and swung violently from side to side.

Marcie had pulled the wheel to the left the second she heard the horn. It was instinct – the will to survive. The truck nudged her back fender and ground to a halt. The sound of metal on metal from colliding vehicles hung in the air like fingernails on a blackboard. Marcie had aimed her car directly for the exit, but her actions to avoid the semi truck and the rub by the big vehicle on her fender had altered her angle. Her car swayed wildly as it rocketed straight at the apex of a triangular metal guardrail separating the ramp exit from the interstate. Shoni's hand was on the dashboard as she leaned forward, a silent scream separating her lips. Marcie jerked the wheel hard to the right to avoid the guardrail, sending the car into a fishtail with the rear of her car making a valiant but impossible attempt to catch the front.

Centrifugal force mashed Marcie against the door. Shoni's arm stretched across her lap, her hand holding her in place as she hung onto the armrest while the car slid sideways towards the barrier. All four wheels scrambled to grab onto something as Marcie spun the steering wheel back to the left, desperately trying to regain control. She realized she had overcompensated as the car started to spin in the opposite direction, but it finally rocked on its wheels and settled down. The car thumped into the barrier, then thankfully straightened out.

Marcie once again stomped her foot to the floor and the car shot forward. She drove with one hand as she punched buttons on the navigation system. Her heart was pounding, trying to leap out of her chest. She hadn't had time to be concerned while she was wrestling with the car but now she felt faint. She called up a list of hotels on the system. She needed to get Shoni to a safe place and call Baker to let him know where they were. She couldn't circle back to the Best Western that Baker had chosen. It was too close to where she picked Shoni up. The rear view mirror was becoming her best friend as she looked for any sign of the black car. He wouldn't be able to get off the interstate until the next exit, so Marcie had bought some time – but not nearly enough. There was no sign of their pursuer yet, but she knew it wouldn't be long until he found them again.

A beep emanated from her pocket. Her heart sank. It was two tones alerting her that her phone was shutting down. The battery was dead.

She couldn't take the time to pull over and plug it in now. It would have to wait until they got to the hotel. Marcie decided the best strategy was to head back to St. Petersburg. Shoni's breathing had settled back to normal and her eyes had shrunk to their normal size. Marcie drove at the speed limit, continually checking all the mirrors to make sure no one was following them. She knew her battered car would attract attention and that the police were probably already on their way to the commotion that had just occurred on the interstate. She was also quite sure the car that had been following them would be at the next exit by now and possibly heading back their way.

"Are you okay?" she asked Shoni. The girl simply nodded. She seemed to be in shock. Marcie patted her leg and said, "I'm sorry about that. We don't usually drive like that here. I just had to get us away from the black car."

Shoni was breathless. "I thought driving in Dar was crazy. I have never experienced anything like that." She looked at Marcie with a small smile that caused her to burst out laughing. Marcie's body was vibrating from the experience and it felt good to share a laugh. She held up her hand and Shoni responded with a weak high five.

Marcie decided the best thing would be to get the girl talking. "Watch for the black car on the side streets. I'll watch behind. So, how did you escape?"

Shoni's head turned from side to side as she looked down the streets perpendicular to theirs at each intersection. Without looking at Marcie she said, "All the girls stay together in one room. There are four of us. Three of the girls work at night and I was left alone after they took Irene away, but they guarded me. One of the girls had a piece of paper she got the night before, and it had my picture and your name and number on it. I recognized your name. You told us you were from this area, but I was so surprised and so happy to see your name. I watched and the men who guarded us got careless because they thought we are weak. One time they just stood outside smoking and left the door unlocked. When they weren't looking, I ran out the door to the street. I ran and ran and I saw them looking for me. I learned to stay safe in my country. There are lots of bad men there. I borrowed a nice lady's phone and called the number on the piece of paper you handed out."

Marcie marveled at her young friend. She had lived so much in such a short time. "We have to find a safe place now and get you some dry clothes. You must be very cold. Keep watching for anything that looks suspicious. I'll find us a hotel where we'll be safe."

Marcie drove along the side streets, occasionally taking a detour to see if anyone was following. It appeared that they had lost the black car and anyone else who might be trying to follow. Finally, Marcie asked the question that had been bothering her since this all started.

"You could have ended up anywhere in the world. How did you end up here?"

It wasn't that Marcie distrusted Shoni. But it did seem like a wild coincidence that Shoni and Irene would end up in Tampa, of all places. She wanted – no, she needed – to hear the whole story.

Chapter 39

Shoni started, "Mr. Smith came to the school just after you did. Remember how I asked if you would take me to the United States? You told me that I should keep studying. I should have listened to you, but Mr. Smith said he would take me where I wanted to go. He told me to meet him at the gate of the school after midnight and I did, but I took Irene with me. That was a big mistake; I should not have taken Irene."

"Can you describe Mr. Smith for me? What does he look like?"

"He is tall and has a small beard, but it's his eyes that you would notice first. He has the eyes of a wild animal on the hunt. I have seen those eyes on an animal tracking its prey – the eyes of a predator."

Those eyes again. Marcie wondered why Shoni agreed to go when she sensed the man was dangerous. "Okay, continue your story."

"Mr. Smith seemed nice at the school, although his eyes scared me. We were taken by taxi to a house where there was a big awful man and we had to wait there. When Mr. Smith showed up, he took us to a nice hotel in Dar es Salaam where we stayed overnight. Mr. Smith slept in one bed and Irene and I in the other. He told us that when we got where we would be going, we would have jobs working in restaurants and that we would get an education. He said we would meet lots of boys and we would find a nice boy to marry. He ordered in a nice breakfast the next morning but I started to think maybe I had made a big mistake. I told Mr. Smith that Irene and I should go back to the school, but he said he would take us to Tampa Bay because that's where he lived. He said it would be easier to get a job there. I remembered you said you lived near a place called Tampa, so I thought it would be perfect."

Marcie thought of an expression Nathan had used. He had said that the FBI classifies pimps into two categories – "gorilla pimps" and "Romeo pimps." Gorilla pimps will use violence and take girls from the streets if there is a potential for making money. The Romeo pimp is skilled at seeing what vulnerable girls need. Nathan said they will use every honey-ladened technique possible to lure the girls, and it doesn't take much to appeal to a 16 year-old girl's sense of adventure and romanticism. Mr. Smith sounded like the latter – at least until he got what he wanted.

Shoni continued her story. "He locked us in our room and went out to get some papers and airline tickets for us so we could travel. He said we were very special and we would do very well in America. He gave us some stories to tell anyone who asked us and he was always with us. Even when we went to the bathroom in a public place, he would stand outside and wait for us. When we waited at the airport, a lady asked me where I was going and what I was going to do when I got there. I had to pretend I didn't understand and Mr. Smith answered for me. The lady was very suspicious. I don't think she believed him but he grabbed me by the arm and pulled me away from her. He grabbed me so hard, it hurt me.

"When we got to Tampa, we were given jobs cleaning hotel rooms. It was such hard work and long, long hours but he told us that we had big debts to pay. We owed him for the papers he purchased so that we could come to America, and for the airline tickets. The total amount was so high I don't think I could ever pay him back. It was thousands of American dollars. He gave us practically nothing – just enough to buy a little food or some girls used it for cigarettes. He wanted to give us drugs, but I refused. Some girls accepted the drugs and then they had to pay for those, too. Some of the girls took a lot of drugs. He said he would sell me to someone else and that would pay my debt to him, but then I would owe the person who bought me. He said I would work for this other man until I paid off the debt. I know he was going to sell me for sex.

"As I said, I saw them hurt Irene. I'm so, so sorry about Irene. I will never forgive myself. I knew when they hurt her and took her away, I had to leave somehow. I waited for my chance. I learned how to pick locks back home, but I just had to wait until they got careless. When I saw your name, I knew I had to find you. Did I do the right thing?"

Shoni's eyes widened again as she related her story and the question left Marcie with a lump in her throat. She wanted to stop the car and give the girl a big hug. "Of course you did the right thing. You and I have friends who will stop Mr. Smith. You have been through so much."

"Oh, I have been through nothing. One of the girls I was staying with was Mexican and she came to America in the back of a closed truck with many other people. She said there was no air in the truck and many of the people died. And when I was in Africa, I heard stories of people trying to get to Italy on a boat and it rolled over and many drowned. They were all trying to find a better life. I am very fortunate and happy to have found you."

"If you heard the stories of people drowning, why did you try to get out of your country?"

Shoni was visibly relaxing, comfortable in Marcie's company. "You have to understand, Ms. Kane, there is no future for some of us there. We have no money to further our education. Our families have died of HIV/AIDS. We have no one to keep us there. Our area is very poor and there is very little hope. The only thing we can do is sell small items to buy food. But my friends and I can do more. We just need a chance."

Marcie swallowed hard at the impassioned plea of her intelligent young passenger. She felt pride at Shoni's courage and determination. Shoni was bright and thoughtful and she was the type who would take any opportunity to better herself, no matter the risk. That's what had placed her in this vulnerable situation. But it had cost Shoni dearly. Marcie was determined to help her.

Marcie pulled the car into the parking lot of a Ramada Inn near St Petersburg. The hotel looked new and the landscaping along the driveway entrance was impeccable. But it was barely noticed by the occupants of the car as they drove in. Marcie told Shoni that they would stay there overnight and decide what they should do after that.

She parked her car out of sight and as far from the entrance as possible. She told Shoni to keep her head down, and she would do the same. As they exited the car and walked hurriedly towards the front door of the hotel, Marcie checked all the nearby streets for any black cars that might look suspicious. She saw nothing. It seemed like they had lost their pursuers. They entered the hotel, and Marcie signed the registry for a room with two double beds. Shoni's hands clenched together under her chin couldn't hide her damp hair and the wet t-shirt hanging heavily from her shoulders and clinging to her breasts. The clerk behind the counter had a questioning look as she glanced first at the girl and then at Marcie.

Marcie responded by saying, "She had a soccer game this afternoon. Who knew the rain was going to come down like this? They should have canceled the game, but you know how soccer coaches are. They want to get every possible game in."

The woman nodded with newfound understanding and sympathetically handed Marcie the room key. When they entered the room, Marcie started the shower for Shoni. It was then that she realized she still hadn't plugged in her cell phone before they came upstairs. Baker was going to be frantic. She could see him putting out an all-points bulletin on her car. She said to Shoni, "You have a hot shower. Stay in it as long as you want; you don't have to worry about the water running out. When you're done, wrap yourself in a towel and get into bed. I'll go out and get us some food and find you some fresh clothes. You must be starved." She immediately regretted her remark because she thought Shoni was probably accustomed to feeling hungry. "I'll be back in about half an hour. Don't open the door for any reason or answer the phone. When I knock, I'll tell you it's me, okay?"

Shoni nodded. "Am I really free, Marcie? Is it over?"

Marcie put her hands on Shoni's shoulders. "It is, Shoni. You'll be okay now. You're going to be safe. Listen, I'll be back soon. Go and have your shower and get warm. And when I leave, please put the chain lock on the door for extra security."

Marcie threw her arms around the girl and Shoni hugged her back with such intensity it was like she didn't believe that everything was finally over.

Marcie adjusted the shower temperature, tossed a kiss to Shoni and locked the door behind her.

Chapter 40

Marcie was aware of a mall about two miles from the hotel. She darted out the door of the hotel and sprinted to her car as quickly as possible, just in case someone was watching. The sight of her battered vehicle made her heart sink but she knew cars could be repaired. After driving for a few minutes, she checked the mirrors again and pulled into the mall parking lot. She plugged the phone into the charger.

She quickly did her shopping, buying some water, fruit and snacks and picking up some t-shirts and pants for Shoni. She wasn't exactly sure of Shoni's size, but she would take the girl shopping properly when Marcie was sure she was safe. She had noticed a restaurant on the way over and would pick up something more substantial to eat there. Shopping took about 20 minutes, and it was time to call Baker.

Marcie hurried back to her car and tapped the key fob. The torrential downpour from earlier had weakened to a drizzle, but it was still enough to soak through to the skin. She heard the familiar chirp in response indicating the doors had unlocked. Another car wheeled into the parking spot next to hers. It was something that happened every day in every parking lot in the world, but she was on high alert because of everything that had happened. A quick glance from the corner of her eye told her it wasn't the black car from the interstate. She juggled the bag of groceries on one knee so she didn't have to put them on the damp ground and quickly reached forward with her hand through the string on the shopping bag holding the clothing to open the door. She sensed someone approaching from behind. She started to turn around when a hand firmly grabbed her shoulder and an arm reached around in front of her.

She heard the tiny hiss of a small aerosol dispenser and her eyes caught fire. She dropped her packages and grasped at her eyes. She couldn't open them. Panic shot through her. Had someone poured acid on her face? She wanted to rip her eyes from her head to ease the burning sensation. Her nose and the area surrounding her eyes were boiling. Her body shuddered, forcing her to lean forward. She took a deep breath causing her to ingest the spray that hung in the air into her lungs. She coughed uncontrollably as spasm after spasm shook her.

A hand roughly directed her away from her car. She heard a door open. She couldn't see, but she felt a hand on her head, roughly pushing it down and forward and a second hand launched her onto the seat of an unfamiliar vehicle. Her head thumped against the door on the opposite side of the car. She screamed between coughs but it came out as a hoarse rasp and anyway, the door had slammed shut. She might as well have been trying to scream in space.

Then a door in front of her opened and she heard someone slide into the driver's side. The spasms had slowed. She tried to open her eyelids but it just increased the pain and water leaked down her face. It was like someone had ground sand into the back of her eyelids. She wondered if she would ever see again. What had this monster done? The strength with which she had been shoved into the car told her the person was male and she caught a whiff of a man's cologne that triggered something in her brain. She had smelled it before. What did he want? Why was he doing this? Marcie tried to calm herself. Her breaths came in hyperventilating gasps. She fought to control her nausea and slow the coughing.

A voice came from the front seat as the car started moving. "Relax. I sprayed you with Oleoresin Capsicum. Pepper spray. You won't be able to see anything for 20 or 30 minutes and then you'll be fine. You might feel sunburned for awhile, but you'll get over it. Please don't throw up in my car."

It was like Marcie had been struck with a hammer. She had the strangest sensation that she knew that voice, had heard it before, only this time it was flatter and devoid of emotion. She tried desperately to open her eyes but immediately slammed them shut. The light shot a thousand tiny needles into her eyes and she couldn't bear to keep them open. At least the coughing had diminished and her breathing had slowed.

She sat slumped in the corner of the back seat. She couldn't do anything in this state. She couldn't see, so even if she did try to escape, what would she do? She decided to listen to what her captor had to say and bide her time. Her hand felt beside her and brushed across the seat. *Where's my purse?*

The voice again. "If you're looking for your gun, I threw it and your purse in the front seat of your car. I warned you to leave things alone. You know, you've been a real nuisance. You just wouldn't let it go. I have to give you credit for trying to save that girl. She came to this country willingly, though. Then when you caused the pileup on the interstate that was just plain stupid. Do you know how many people could've been killed? I'll bet the police are still trying to sort that mess out." He chuckled.

Marcie said nothing. Again came the sensation that she knew this voice, had smelled this same cologne. Her brain was having trouble dealing with it. She made an effort to straighten out in the seat and sit up but another round of spasms shook her and bent her forward. She forced herself to keep her hands away from her eyes although she desperately wanted to rub them. She still couldn't pry them open. The physical challenges of her eyesight had trumped the emotional fear of the unknown, but new thoughts wormed their way into her head. If the man was being truthful, she would soon be able to see again. *But what did this person have in mind? Where were they going?*

They rode in silence for a few minutes and that gave Marcie's mind the chance to clear a little. This had to be about Shoni. She hadn't had a chance to call Baker. More than anything, she wished she had gone ahead and called him with her phone on the charger. If only the battery hadn't died, she thought, but she couldn't concern herself with that now. It was too late. She felt bad for Shoni as well, but knew she was a resilient young lady who could handle things herself for a little while. As long as they didn't discover where she was until the police found her, Marcie felt Shoni would be safe.

"Where are we going?" Her voice was barely audible. She wished there was more strength behind her question. She felt weak and helpless.

"Oh, don't worry, you'll recognize it when we get there. You've been there before." The voice remained lifeless.

Somewhere I've been before? Marcie tried to guess where that might be but it was difficult to concentrate on anything except her eyes. The burning was lessening. She needed to see the person in the front seat to confirm her suspicions. Then she would pick her spot to deal with him.

Marcie reached across her lap, concealing her left hand under her right arm, and tugged on the door handle. Maybe she could jump from the car. The door was locked. She sighed. Now that's rich. A mechanism designed to keep children from falling out the back door was keeping her captive. He had engaged the child safety lock.

She thought she could hit him hard enough to incapacitate him as he drove but that could get them both killed. Maybe she could try a surprise attack at a stop light. She might be able to climb out through the front door if she could hit him hard enough. Or maybe shove him through the driver's side door. But she still couldn't see. She could just as easily run out in front of an oncoming car.

He seemed to read her mind. "Don't think about trying to jump out. You can't open the doors from the inside. And anyway, I will have no problem shooting you in the back. See what I have?" His throat was dry and a laugh came out more like a cackle. "Oh sorry, you can't see right now. Well, listen."

Marcie heard two distinct clicks. From her gun training, she recognized the sound of a magazine sliding from a hand grip as it was ejected and the click when it was reinserted. It could have been a Beretta 9m. It was a popular gun because of its reliability, especially in the military. She had fired one many times at the range with He Who Shall Not Be Named. But there was something else that caught her attention. The car had slowed and the road noise was different. It wasn't the hiss of the tires on the damp pavement anymore. It was the distinct sound of gravel popping under the treads. He said she had been here before. *Oh no, it couldn't be.* With a growing sense of dread, Marcie became sure she knew where they were. It was the gravel pit in the industrial park, the spot where Alina had been found dead.

She heard the rustle of a waterproof jacket, like her captor had scraped his whiskered chin against it to look over his shoulder at her. When he turned back, she heard the same sound. He said, "I have good news and bad news for you.

Which would you prefer to hear first?" When he didn't get a response he continued. "I'll give you the bad news first. The bad news is that you appear to be a person who reacts badly to pepper spray. People react differently so it has a lesser effect on some. Plus you got it directly in the eyes, so it will take longer for the effects to wear off. The good news for you is that I won't have to hit you with it again.

"I'm going to stop up here and if you behave yourself, you won't get hurt . . . at least for now. I want some information from you. This can be over with pretty quickly. Now, I'm going to come around to your side and unlock the door. Don't try to fight. I'll shoot you in the kneecap if you try to run. Do you understand?"

Marcie nodded slowly. The gunman did as he said he would and let her out of the car. She was able to look through narrow slits enough to make out a gun pointed directly at her. The face she could barely make out did not match the voice she thought she had recognized. The man had facial hair, which appeared to be in the shape of a goatee. She remembered that Mr. Smith had been described as having a goatee. And he was described as being tall, just like this man. Confusion swept through Marcie as she tried to place the face with the voice. She was sure she recognized the voice, but maybe she was wrong. She desperately hoped she was wrong. Surely he could not betray her like this.

She heard a door dragging on the ground as it was roughly pulled open. She was shoved into a small disagreeably musty and damp shed.

The door shut and she heard the click of a lock.

She was being held captive.

Shoni lay naked in bed in the hotel room with the covers drawn up to her chin. Her clothes were spread around the room drying on the chairs. The hot shower Marcie had suggested had warmed her. It was a luxury she had never experienced before. At home she was lucky if she got a wash in the morning with lukewarm water heated over a fire. First, she had to carry the water in a jug on her head a very long distance. Then she had to boil it for drinking water. Whatever was left, which was very little, could be used for washing. The scarcity of water was always such a concern at home. Here, the water poured out of the shower head endlessly. Even when she and Irene were introduced to the shower when they were traveling with Mr. Smith, he said they had to be quick. She wondered then what it would be like to stand under the luxurious spray for an eternity without having to worry about anything.

But now she was cold again. If she could shrink under the covers more, she would. It had been two hours since Marcie left. She said she would be right back. Where was she? Had Marcie abandoned her too? Something must have happened. Shoni thought she had connected with Marcie and her instinct told her that her new friend was a good person. But she had been wrong about Mr. Smith. Maybe her instinct had been wrong again.

Marcie had told her before she left not to open the door to anyone and not to answer the phone. Marcie said she wouldn't be gone long. Shoni didn't know what to do. It seemed as if the room was becoming colder. She wished she could disappear but she knew in her heart that was impossible. She covered her ears, willing the sound to go away.

A man was pounding and calling her name from the other side of the door.

Chapter 41

Marcie blinked rapidly to clear her blurred vision. It seemed to help, and each time she did, she was able to pry her eyes open just a little wider. Her eyes still stung, and the skin on her face and nose felt like she'd been standing in direct sunlight without protection for about a month, but if she could believe what the man said, the symptoms would soon disappear. She inhaled deeply to calm herself, but the sharp burning sensation in her lungs caused her to cough involuntarily for a few seconds each time. But compared to the way she felt 20 minutes ago, this was pretty good. She judged it must be late afternoon or early evening.

She appreciated the dullness of the room, as it gave her eyes a chance to adjust. She examined the room and there wasn't much to see. She decided it was a shed of some kind where tools were stored when the gravel pit was active. Any tools that had been there once had been long since removed. The little bit of light in the room was provided by spears piercing the darkness through cracks in wallboards that had warped over time. Dust particles danced unimpeded in the tiny spotlights.

The word "dank" crept into Marcie's subconscious. That was the only way to describe the heavy air of the shack. It was old and musty. It had a dead carcass aroma like there could be a deceased mouse or two lying in a corner. There had been a window, but it had been boarded over from the outside. Marcie tested some of the boards but they were unforgiving. She tried to stick her fingers through the tiny cracks but even though the boards had warped, they were not rotten. The only furniture was a cheap plastic lawn chair in the room, the kind that everyone buys for their patio until they can afford something better. The nausea hadn't subsided completely so Marcie decided to sit for a few minutes longer.

She knew when the time came she would have to act quickly. She didn't know what her captor wanted, but he hadn't made much of an effort to hide his face so Marcie knew he wouldn't be letting her go. She suspected his intention was that she'd end up in the same pond as Alina. The only way to prevent that was to get close enough to him to use her martial arts training. She would pick her spot and act.

She thought she had heard her captor drive away earlier, but footsteps now crunched on the gravel outside. Someone was pacing and talking. The scent of cigarette smoke drifted into the shack. It actually smelled pleasant as it overpowered some of the mustiness in the small room. Marcie tried to confirm whether there was one person or two. She was sure the footsteps belonged to a single individual. It didn't seem to be a phone call. It sounded more like the person was talking to himself.

Marcie felt she would soon know how many were outside, but the numbers were about to increase. Lights bounced through the cracks in the boards signaling an approaching car. This definitely was going to be a far bigger problem if she had to deal with more than one person. The car stopped close to the shed and a car door slammed. The man with the monotone voice exchanged some angry words with his counterpart. Then he entered the shed carrying a plastic chair similar to the one Marcie was sitting on.

Marcie stared at the silhouette that had stopped just inside the door. His body shimmered in the doorway. His features still lacked clear definition because of the light behind him, but she was even surer now by the shape of the man. That it could be him was unfathomable, but she was sure. Her mind reeled from shock. He shut the door behind him and moved closer, dragging the chair with him, but he still remained in the shadows. He set the chair ten feet in front of Marcie's and she could see the outline of a gun nestled in his lap. By the way he was holding it, Marcie was quite sure his finger was through the trigger guard. He slouched casually in the chair, one leg extended, as if they were about to have a morning coffee and talk about the weather.

His voice had neither pitch nor intonation. "Your fighting skills precede you. You did very well against my rather large and muscular forger in Tanzania.

I'm not about to give you a chance to take a swing at me. Besides, there's a man outside who has been ordered to shoot you if necessary."

Marcie opened her mouth twice to speak but no words came out. She shook with rage, "What are *you* doing mixed in this? And *why*?? I trusted you. I took you into my confidence. I believed you could help the girls. You're in a position to make such a difference."

He rose and came closer to Marcie. Close enough that she could see. He stared at her with eyes that lacked any morality. They were as dead as his voice. But they were as others had described. They could indeed see right through Marcie. They weren't the eyes of the man she knew.

"Ah, so you can see through my modest disguise. I knew you would be able to, but it's amazing what they can do with contact lenses and some facial hair. Today, I'm Mr. Smith, the man you've heard so much about. Tomorrow, I will simply be Braden Maxwell again, everyone's favorite lecturer and college professor. I can come and go as I please and no one's the wiser. As long as people don't get too close it's impossible to tell who I am. Clever, don't you think? Unfortunately for you, I'll have to kill you now since you recognized me."

Marcie snorted through her nose. "I don't think you ever intended to do otherwise. Do you really think I wouldn't recognize you? Was that you in the black car on the interstate?"

"No, it was the man who's standing just outside the door. He was pretty impressed by your manoeuvre, by the way. Of course, you could've got innocent people killed, but it was still very impressive driving. He was just trying to get you to pull over. I was only a few cars behind and saw it all. If you had pulled over, none of that would have happened. You managed to create enough chaos that it blocked the interstate for awhile."

Marcie extended her arms with her palms up. "Why? Why is Shoni so important to you?"

The man's demeanor darkened. It was clear to Marcie that his patience was waning. His voice thinned. "Do you have any idea what young girls are worth on the open trafficking market? I sold her to a brothel in the United Arab Emirates for a lot of money. They bought her only from a photo. But I have to produce the girl. I don't get paid if I don't deliver and the deal will be ruined. I could even end up dead. These are very serious men. No one will buy another girl from me if I don't produce Shoni.

"I thought I had two girls I could sell with Irene and Shoni, until I found out Irene was damaged goods. She had that damn disease. Plus, she kept trying to escape. I should have sold them when I was in Tanzania but there's a better market for girls sold from the States, no matter what their nationality. Then I had to get rid of Alina. I find if the girls see what happens if they try to escape, it settles them down for awhile. Shoni said she wanted to come here to Tampa, so it was easy to get them here. I understand now it was because of you. And you . . . you're a royal pain in the ass, you know that? You could've saved us all a lot of trouble, Marcie Kane. And you would've done very well in your chosen field. You could've saved a lot of young girls. But did you listen? No! Well, it's too late now. Tell me where Shoni is and I will make your death as painless as possible."

Marcie bunched her right fist and prepared to launch herself at her captor, but he quickly moved back to his chair. He admonished her like a child. "Don't waste your energy, Marcie. That won't get you anywhere."

Marcie thought that if she could keep Maxwell talking as much as possible, maybe Baker would discover her car and therefore, Shoni. If it was dinner time or later, Nathan must be wondering where she was by now. She just needed to keep this guy busy and talking. And if she could get him close enough to him . . .

She said softly, her voice barely above a whisper, "I called the police after I plugged my phone into the car. They will already have Shoni."

It had the desired effect. He leaned forward. "I didn't hear that. Speak up."

She repeated what she had said, only this time even softer. He threw his head back in anger. "Really? You think I'm going to come near you so you can disarm me or something. I wasn't born yesterday, Marcie." He cocked the gun and aimed it at her leg. "I will put a bullet in each of your arms and legs if you don't speak up." He casually lifted the gun and sighted down the barrel, aiming it at her legs.

Marcie spoke up. "Okay, I said I called the police and they were on their way to pick her up. They'll have her in their custody now. They'll figure out who you are and you'll be put away where you'll never be able to hurt girls again. If you cooperate, though, maybe the police might show some leniency." Her voice remained level but fear was forming tiny droplets of water that dripped down her face and soaked her armpits.

"Too late for that. And I think you're wrong about the police having Shoni. I'm pretty sure Shoni wouldn't trust the police any more here than she would in her country. Distrust of the police is pretty prevalent in Tanzania, didn't you find? But if she is with the police, I have no further use for you. Stand up."

"What – what . . . what are you going to do?"

"I told you, I need to know where she is. Let's go for a walk. What's the matter? Not quite so brave now?"

Marcie glared at him but she got up from the seat. The gun was now pointed at her head. She slowly walked towards the door with her captor behind her. It must be how a convict feels on his way to the electric chair. She thought of Shoni and her friends. She thought of everything she had to live for. She knew he was planning to shoot her and dump her in the pond so there was no better time than right now.

She spun around and stepped to one side away from the gun. A well-aimed punch caught Maxwell in the throat and he went down gasping for breath. The gun skittered away, and she kicked it further into the corner. Whipping back around towards her adversary, she aimed a kick at his face but he recovered enough to grab her foot as he rose from the floor. His momentum pushed her backwards and she lost her balance and crashed against the side of the shed. Marcie's back hit the wall first, propelling her head violently against the wall. The impact stunned her, but she heard the door to the shed open and a new figure entered the room. The man who had been standing outside until now lifted Marcie from the floor and a big fist slammed into the side of Marcie's head.

For Marcie, the sparse light that had been in the room faded to black.

Chapter 42

Marcie awoke to see ground moving beneath her. *Am I having a nightmare?* The humid Florida air that became almost visible after a day of rain hung heavily in the night. She blinked her eyes rapidly and quietly drew in three sharp breaths. Her head was pounding and the area just above and beside her eye hurt like hell. *What is happening to me?* For a few seconds the ground came and went as she drifted in and out of consciousness. Enough moonlight shone through the clouds to illuminate the gravel passing by on the trail beneath her face. Her toes scraped on the surface. Tall blades of grass glistened as the ground passed by on either side of her, as if on a conveyor belt. Her hands hurt, and it took a few seconds to understand why until they dipped down and scraped in the gravel.

She slowly came to the realization that this wasn't a nightmare, at least not one from which she was about to wake up. She was being carried face down up an incline. Cobwebs filled her head, but instinct told her not to let her captors know she was awake. She knew she needed a chance to get away, and she also knew subconsciously that the element of surprise had to be on her side. She forced her mind to think back on what happened. She remembered a big man coming through a door but nothing after that.

She remembered nothing before that, either. Her mind was so foggy. At least she was alive. She took that as a small piece of encouraging news. The men carrying her grunted at the effort of supporting her body up the steep incline. She knew she must feel like dead weight, and she concentrated on making herself as heavy as possible, tightening her muscles and pushing down on her arms. Maybe if they were tired when they got to the top of wherever they were going, it would give her some small advantage. She just needed them to lose concentration for a few seconds and she would make a run for it – if she could somehow make her legs work.

But she was having so much trouble concentrating. Was it possible these men were taking her to safety? She couldn't be sure, but it didn't feel right. She tried again to remember what had happened but nothing was clear. She didn't know who these men were or why she was with them. She only sensed that she was in a very dangerous situation and she had to escape.

The men dragged Marcie uphill for a few more minutes. Her knuckles felt raw from scraping on the gravel and her toes burned from being dragged through the rough pebbles covering the hard ground. She managed to remain perfectly still while making herself as much of a dead weight for the people carrying her as she could. If they were trying to save her, she would ask for forgiveness later. But she was pretty sure that wasn't their intention.

The men's breathing became more labored the further up the incline they went. The steepness of the climb, the heavy humidity and her body's weight were taking their toll. They apparently finally reached the top and they unceremoniously dumped Marcie on the ground. One of the men roughly turned her onto her back with his boot. The way they were treating her confirmed her danger, but she still couldn't remember who they were or why they were doing this. As she turned, sparks flew in her head but through a slit in her eye she was able to see a man propped on a rock a few feet away. To her unclear eyesight, his shape took on the appearance of an apparition in the dark. He had a gun in his hand pointed towards the ground. He was slumped over, drawing heaving breaths.

She felt a fleeting hint of recognition. She should know him but hard as she tried, she couldn't quite grasp it. Marcie sensed more than saw that she was on the edge of a precipice. There was nothing but blackness below. She knew there were two men but were there more? She searched in her memory banks but they weren't co-operating. Her head was pounding.

"Wake her up." It was the man sitting on the rock.

The accomplice leaned down and slapped her face hard. Fireworks erupted in her head. She tried to push herself up on her elbows but the shooting stars were replaced by a wave of vertigo and she fell backwards with her arm over her eyes.

The man on the rock said with frustration clear in his tone, "Marcie, you have one chance to make this easy on yourself." She looked under her arm and squinted. The gun was pointed at her. "Tell me where Shoni is or my friend here will throw you over the edge. There's nothing but jagged rocks between the top and the water, thanks to the construction company that emptied this pit. You will undoubtedly break a few bones on your way down. You will not be able to move, and you will drown. It will be most unpleasant for you. For the last time, where is Shoni Batanga?"

"Who are you?" Marcie's words came out in a slur through barely parted lips. Her arm was still over her head.

Maxwell snorted. "Who am I? You don't know who I am? Did he hit your head too hard or are you pretending to have amnesia to save yourself? I'm quickly losing patience."

Marcie heard him speak but he might as well have put the alphabet in a blender. She understood nothing. She tried again. "Why are you doing this? Who's Shawna?" Marcie's own words echoed in her head, causing her to nearly lose consciousness.

Maxwell looked at his accomplice. He wasn't sure whether she was faking it or not.

"It's not Shawna, it's Shoni and she's the girl you've been trying to save." His voice was rising to a near fever pitch. "*Why am I doing this*? You think I earn enough as a lecturer and consultant? They pay peanuts. Selling the girls is a lucrative business."

Marcie drew one leg up and moaned as she tried to put some words together. She knew she had questions, but she couldn't formulate them.

Maxwell's words were rushed. "You must've shut your phone off or something because I lost track of you and Shoni for awhile. When you came back online I was able to track you to the mall. Unfortunately for you, you left Shoni somewhere. I have people looking for her now. In case you were wondering how I found you, I took the liberty of placing a hidden tracker in your phone when I borrowed it that day in the cafeteria. While you so graciously refilled my coffee and I was supposedly setting you up with someone to help Alina, I was actually installing the tracking app. You almost caught me doing it when you came back sooner than I thought. Don't know how I would've explained that.

"Anyway, I told you in the garage that night at your condo to leave it alone. I tried to warn you, but you wouldn't listen. You're too hard-headed. Now look where you are." His voice changed. "Stand up. We're wasting time here."

Another jumble of words that meant nothing to Marcie, and she lay unmoving in the dirt with her hands over her eyes. She thought if she moved, she would either throw up or pass out.

Maxwell's accomplice leaned over and put his hand under her arm, roughly dragging her to her feet. Marcie swayed on rubbery legs, bent over at the waist. She had to lean on her captor. The effort of standing brought another round of nausea to her stomach, and she stumbled from the dizziness in her brain. She had trouble focusing on her adversaries.

She mumbled words that were barely audible. "I have no idea who you are or where that person is."

"Okay, this has gone on long enough. I thought I could talk some sense into you, but apparently not. In a way this doesn't surprise me, Marcie. You seem to have this insane desire to protect some girl you barely even know. Even though you're going to die for it."

Coldly, Maxwell looked at his accomplice. "Toss her over the edge."

Marcie closed her eyes. She didn't have the strength to move, and her head was spinning. It was as if she were drugged, uncomprehending of anything around her. She tried not to collapse. She wanted to die with dignity, without showing fear. And then suddenly, for some unknown reason, her mind began to fight back, struggling for clarity and her ultimate survival. As Maxwell's accomplice moved around behind Marcie to shove her forward, a single thought became crystal clear. This maniac was actually going to kill her.

Chapter 43

Dizzy but conscious now, Marcie struggled against her captor. Her strength was no match for his. She squeezed her eyes shut and put all her effort into digging her heels into the ground, but the cliff's edge was coming ever closer. She tried desperately to break his hold on her, but she was too weak and he was too strong. She twisted her shoulders back and forth but he only tightened his grip. Every movement brought more dizziness and nausea. Cool air rising from the bottom of the pit washed over her.

Desperately Marcie kept fighting, pushing back against the big man shoving her roughly toward certain death. She heard the other man say impatiently, "You shouldn't have hit her so hard. She's useless to us now. Pick her up and throw her over. Enough's enough. Let's get this over with."

She felt the man let go of her arm and reach down under her legs to pick her up. Just then a sharp sound shattered the still night air. Marcie fell hard to the ground. She was lying on her back, her legs angled beneath her. The shock of the fall set off another fireworks display in her head. A low moan escaped from her lips. She forced her eyes to open and moved her head slowly and painfully to the side to see the man who had been pushing her lying crumpled face first on the ground beside her, blood dripping from a bullet entry wound in the back of his head.

Someone yelled, "FBI. Braden Maxwell, put the gun down."

Marcie thought she should know that name and the voice who was saying it, but her brain turned everything into a foggy sludge. Nothing made sense. She staggered clumsily to her feet, reeling from fear, the blow and vertigo. Her head hurt worse than ever. She swayed perilously close to the edge. If she fell now, no one could save her. Marcie felt the ground give way beneath her feet and she started to lose her balance, tipping headfirst toward the rocks below.

Suddenly she felt a strong arm grabbing her, pulling her away from the abyss. Someone had saved her! Her body slumped, her legs giving out. She leaned against her savior.

And then she felt the cold barrel of a gun placed against her temple.

Braden Maxwell shoved her body in front of his, gun at her head. He had saved her from crashing on the rocks and tumbling, her body shattered, into the water at the bottom of the quarry only to use her as a hostage. He yelled, "Back off. Drop your gun and turn around! She dies if you don't let me out of here. Just do as I say. I'll take her down the hill and let her go there."

Marcie hung from Maxwell's arm. His hold was harsh. She thought she was going to pass out. She needed to focus. Her head felt like a hyped-up carousel spinning out of control. The moon slipped from behind the clouds just in time to expose a man appearing from the shadows, his gun held in both hands at eye level and aimed directly at them.

"I'm Special Agent Nathan Harris of the FBI. It looks like we have a stand-off, Maxwell. Put the gun down. You can't win this one. If you give us the information we want about who you're selling the girls to, we'll go easier on you."

"I can't do that. Without that girl, my life isn't going to be worth anything to those people. They bought *her* and they won't accept anyone else. That's the way they think. I have nothing to lose now. I have to disappear. I *will* kill Marcie before you have a chance to do anything. Step aside and let us go down the hill. You'll never hear of me again."

Marcie's mind was slowly clearing but her pounding head still made it difficult to comprehend what was happening. The curtain of fog raised in her mind just enough to know she should recognize the man standing in front of her with his gun aimed just over her shoulder. She thought he was on her side but his face drifted in and out of focus.

Nathan Harris took a step closer, but Maxwell pressed the gun more firmly into Marcie's skull. She could smell the fear on her captor. He was a caged animal that would do anything to save his life.

Nathan said, "Okay, you win, Maxwell. I'll let you go down the hill. Leave Marcie at the bottom of the hill and go."

Marcie could feel Maxwell tense up. He screamed, "IT'S NOT THAT EASY! How many people do you have waiting at the bottom? Is there a sniper somewhere waiting to pick me off as soon as I let Marcie go? I've changed my mind. She's coming in the car with me. Don't follow us – and don't send anybody to chase us, either. I'll drop her off when I'm ready. Then I'll disappear."

Nathan's next words were spoken with the calmness of someone talking to a friend in a conversation over a cup of tea. "There's no sniper. I shot your friend. I came here by myself. I've called the police and they're sending backup. If you're going to go, you'd better do it. I'll put my gun down and step aside and you can go. I don't want to see anything happen to Marcie."

Maxwell's feet shifted in the dirt but his head was directly behind Marcie's, ensuring Nathan had no clear shot. Marcie could feel his entire body trembling against her back. She wasn't completely aware of what was going on, but she knew the gun against her temple could go off at any second.

Maxwell said nothing for a few seconds and then, finally, "I have a better idea. Throw your gun over the cliff. Then step over by the edge and stay there. One move towards us and Marcie dies."

As if following orders, Nathan moved closer to the edge. He thought of trying to get Marcie's attention to move so he could take a shot at Maxwell, but he wasn't sure she would even see his hint. She was hanging from his arm. She looked groggy and confused. And it was dark. The odds weren't good.

Nathan's gun sailed into space over the edge of the cliff.

Maxwell took his arm from around Marcie's throat and shoved her violently towards the edge of the cliff. As he did so, he leveled the gun at Nathan and fired.

The moon once again looked out from behind the layer of clouds.

The last thing Marcie saw in the semi darkness as she rolled towards the edge of the cliff was the FBI man leaning forward grasping his chest and about to crumple to the ground.

Chapter 44

Marcie felt herself rolling like a runaway log. She had no control of her limbs as momentum carried her closer towards the edge. Her mind was still fuzzy, but memory flooded back from the deepest recesses. It was the endless nightmare, the one in which she grasped for Shoni and at the very last second, just missing her. All her nightmares had a similar ending, but that particular one was especially vivid as she skidded towards the edge. In that nightmare, she remembered watching Shoni tumbling end over end into the abyss. NO! This couldn't be happening to her.

And from the deepest part of her being, Marcie's survival instinct took over. She flung out her hands in a last-ditch attempt to prevent herself from suffering Shoni's fate in the nightmare. She clawed at the earth with both hands, her fingernails lifting from her fingers, grasping for anything that would prevent her fall. Her momentum carried her relentlessly forward and she felt her legs slip over the edge. The ground gave way from under them, and she was about to start into a freefall. Her hands scrabbled frantically at the loose dirt, her fingers leaving a trail, searching for anything that could stop her fate; and in the last split second before she started her descent, she felt her hand grasp something. It was an embedded tree root protruding from the ground. There wasn't much to hang onto, but the tree root was thick and firm.

The only question was, could she hold on?

Marcie hung in mid-air. Time stopped. She heard nothing. She didn't know where anyone was. She could feel the cool dampness drifting up from the water below. Her free arm dangled helplessly. Her muscles trembled. How long could her weakened body hang on? She tried to swing herself upwards to grab the root with both hands but the movement just caused her hand to slip. She tried again but her grip loosened even more. All she could do was hang there, and hope against hope that something would save her life. It seemed hopeless. The day's rain had made the tree root slippery, and she knew she couldn't hold on much longer. She prayed she would be knocked unconscious on the first rock she hit on the way down, so her death would be merciful.

Her fingers were losing their grip. She drew up her other arm, flailing weakly for something – anything – as she began to slide towards oblivion. A scream rushed into her throat. Suddenly, she felt a strong hand clamp over her wrist. It couldn't be! Why wouldn't this diabolical maniac just let her die in peace? But the hand was pulling her upwards towards him. Another strong hand reached beneath her other arm and carefully pulled her back up onto solid ground. She was pulled forward and far enough away from the edge that she couldn't feel the dampness anymore. The man rolled her onto her back and held her with his warm cheek nestled against hers. Relief settled over her like a warm blanket as she was comforted by the man leaning over. He was whispering something in her ear that she couldn't understand, but a quiet peacefulness settle over her. She tried to focus her eyes on the face above her but it was only a blur. Before she could say anything, the world tilted on its axis in her head and she passed out.

The sun had finished spreading its palette of colors across the ocean as dusk slowly settled over the neighborhood. Three weeks had passed since Marcie's near fatal brush with death and although the headaches had subsided, she was still ultra-sensitive to sound and light. She removed the sunglasses that covered her eyes and set them on the table beside her chair. She rested her head against the back of the lounge and closed her eyes. Her beloved stereo sat unusually silent in the living room. Laughter erupted from the kitchen as dishes clattered.

Without opening her eyes, Marcie said as loudly as she could from the balcony. "Don't break my good china." She winced and groaned quietly at the sound of her own voice.

Nathan's voice came back. "If you weren't being so lazy, you could protect your good dishes yourself." More laughter.

He came out on the balcony and set a plate of nachos down beside Marcie before taking a position in the chair opposite hers.

Marcie asked, "Is Shoni joining us?"

"No, all she's been talking about is building a virtual civilization in that computer game. She's determined to find a way to build one that will stand the test of time."

Marcie chuckled. It was her best friend Sami's favorite game and since she had taken a liking to Shoni, she'd showed her how to play it. "Well, she better enjoy it now. Next week we'll be taking her back to Africa. I'm so happy she's looking forward to going back. I didn't know how she would take it but she said she wants to go back. I think she feels she owes a few people an explanation, like Mrs. Adimu and Irene's family. I'm sure going to miss her, though."

"Yes, she's quite a young woman. I'm sure she'll stay in touch, Marcie. She really looks up to you. She also *has* to go back – she doesn't have proper documentation to stay here, anyway. I was happy she said she's looking forward to finishing her schooling and doing something for the kids in her own country. If she wants to get the right paperwork, she can always come back to the U.S. some day. She's been through a lot, but she's so incredibly fortunate. It could've been much worse without you. On another note, what did the doctor tell you today?"

"He said concussions are always unpredictable but I'm progressing. The headaches aren't as severe, and the dizziness is getting much better. And the best part is that since Shoni's been around, no more nightmares." Marcie stopped for a moment. "Nathan, I'm really happy you joined us for dinner before you go back to Atlanta."

"Why, thank you. I'm glad your memory has come back as well as it has. Sometimes these things take a long time, and sometimes the complete memory never comes back. I was very worried about you. I was thinking you would forget who I was and I would have to convince you I was one of the good guys all over again." He chuckled. "I'm looking forward to accompanying you two on the trip to Tanzania next week. It's too bad I have to go back to Atlanta tomorrow, but duty calls. Fortunately, duty is also calling me back to Tanzania, so the timing is good."

Marcie nodded. "How's the bruise on your chest?"

"It's much better, thanks. I'm just thankful for Kevlar. Maxwell shot me at such close range, it left quite a mark, but at least it wasn't a hole."

"Well, if it had been a hole, I would've been swimming with the fishes in the bottom of that pond, so I owe Kevlar a big chunk of gratitude too. Speaking of Maxwell, have you heard anything?"

"Still no trace. He's in the wind."

Nathan had been reluctant to talk about it, but tonight he continued for the first time. "By the time I regained my breath and found you hanging over the cliff, he'd run down the other side of the hill and disappeared. I thought I heard a boat start up when I was helping you. We think he had one waiting for him. I guess he thought you still had Shoni hidden away somewhere. The police did some great work tracing your phone to your car in the parking lot at the hotel. Shoni was pretty reluctant to let Detective Baker in, but he finally convinced her before he had to get the staff to open the door. He said she was dressed in a towel and holding a lamp in her hand to use as a weapon when she let him in and she was scared to death. Her clothes lay drying on furniture all over the room. I've been waiting to tell you specific details until I was sure your memory was back to stay. I thought it might be just too much for you otherwise, hearing that we hadn't caught Maxwell yet."

Marcie nodded slowly. "There is one thing that's been bothering me recently though, Nathan. I hadn't thought about it much before, but I've been wondering who it was that warned me about the so-called Mr. Smith? Do you know?"

"I don't know for sure, but I think it was the woman who was working the corner with Alina. She spoke highly of you, by the way. She thought it took a lot of guts to do what you did and she was pretty impressed. Going into that part of town and handing out flyers the way you did. I didn't tell her I thought it was pretty naïve of you to think you could hand out your phone number to everyone in the city without getting into some kind of trouble."

Marcie poked him in the ribs and a groan rose from his lips as she connected with his bruise. She said, "All right, all right! I think I've been chastised enough. Remember what happened last time? You upset me so much you had to send me flowers. If you make me mad enough, you just might have to do that again to make it up to me."

"Well, I did notice the empty vase on the table. It could use a refill, couldn't it?" He smiled.

Marcie bit down on a smile. She had regretted having to throw out his first bouquet of flowers, but dead petals were dropping all over the table. She had left the vase out as a reminder but wondered inside why: a reminder of how much she'd enjoyed his initial attention or a reminder instead of what their relationship could be if Nathan's career wasn't his sole focus in life. She decided to stay on neutral ground and keep the conversation on the case. "I still don't understand why someone like Braden Maxwell would be involved into something as horrible as this. He had a good job. He was respected. He seemed genuinely interested in helping downtrodden women and really concerned about global trafficking. It just seems so out of character for the man I knew from school."

"I can't explain it completely either, Marcie. I just know that many of the biggest trafficking consumers are developed nations, and men from all sectors of society support the trafficking industry. There is no specific profile for the 'typical' client. Men who purchase trafficked women are both rich and poor, Eastern and Western.

"In many parts of the world, prostitution is perceived as a victimless crime. Men don't make the connection between that and the slave trade. In western society in particular, there's a commonly held perception that women *choose* to enter into the commercial sex business. It's simply not the case for the majority of women in the sex trade, and specifically in the case of trafficked women and girls who are coerced or forced into servitude.

"That doesn't explain why Maxwell did it, but it does explain the business somewhat."

Marcie yawned. "Well, I guess it'll be one of those unsolved mysteries, at least until you catch him. You know what? I'm going to have to go to bed. I can't seem to stay awake as long as I could before the concussion."

"Okay, but there's something I want to say before I go."

Marcie felt her heart jump. Trying not to look hopeful, she gazed deeply into Nathan's eyes, waiting for him to continue.

"Marcie, I know I've been sending mixed messages about how I feel about you. I've grown really interested in you and if it weren't for this case that we're both involved in, I would be getting a lot more involved than you've seen me do so far, believe me. But I can't. Until Braden Maxwell is caught and dealt with, you're a potential witness. I can't be seen to be involved with someone close to a case I'm working on. It could be seen as a conflict of interest and destroy the case. I guess what I'm trying to say here is, well, Marcie, if you are still available when this is all over, I would very much like to spend some real time getting to know you better. You might not believe this, but you're the first woman I've had any interest in for a long time." He sighed. "I'm not asking you to wait, but I wanted you to understand."

Marcie looked across the water so that Nathan couldn't see that her eyes were glistening. He might not understand the reason for her tears, but the truth was, she would wait as long as it took.

Finally, she looked back. Nathan's mouth was downturned and he was hunched forward. Marcie wiped her eyes and suppressed a smile at the hangdog expression on the usually staid FBI agent's face. She leaned towards him, turned his face towards hers and kissed him lightly on the lips. Then she pressed her cheek against his and whispered in his ear, "Hurry up and catch that son of a bitch, Nathan Harris."

Chapter 45

The next morning Marcie was still feeling the emptiness that overcame her as soon as Nathan had closed the door behind him the night before. She tried to lift her spirits by thinking about their trip to Africa in a week. She realized how much Nathan meant to her, and she was pretty sure he felt the same even though he couldn't tell her. He made her feel comfortable and safe, and she hadn't felt that way for a long time. Marcie had sensed his reluctance to leave her last night. She was sure it was a struggle for him, just as it was for her. But he didn't have to worry; she would wait for him all right. He was more than worth waiting for.

Nathan and Detective Baker had decided that Shoni would be best served by staying with Marcie so the African girl had been at the condo since Marcie got out of the hospital. Shoni still did not trust the police although Baker had used his limited charm to coax her to open the door at the hotel. She had been frightened enough by Marcie's disappearance that she was willing to give Baker a chance.

Even though Maxwell was still out there, Marcie felt safe at the condo. Detective Baker had arranged for a patrol officer to be stationed at the entrance to the building until they took Shoni back to Africa, plus the building had its own security system. She and Shoni had enough groceries that they didn't need to go out.

Marcie cleaned the last of the breakfast dishes as she listened to the sounds of the virtual civilization growing on the computer in the office. Shoni was intelligent and caring and Marcie was convinced that the teenager would be a world leader someday, wherever she chose to do it.

Shoni hadn't been up long that morning. She slept in as any normal teenager would, but when she was awake, she filled the condo with a joy and exuberance that Marcie knew she would miss when the girl went back to her home.

Nathan was true to his word because the flower delivery man had just called and was on his way up to her condo. The patrol officer must have cleared him and Nathan must have ordered them from the airport. What a thoughtful gesture on Nathan's part, she thought, and she'd just finished washing the vase when there was a tap at the door.

A quick look through the peep hole told her the delivery man had arrived. He was standing on the other side of the door holding a big bouquet up so that Marcie could clearly see it. She looked closely and he was wearing the uniform from the same floral shop as the previous delivery man. The bouquet was huge and colorful and Marcie was excited to let the fragrance into the condo. This time it was for no special reason. Heat radiated through her as she swung the door open.

A forceful blow to the chest staggered Marcie. Her shoulders immediately tightened and she struggled to draw a breath as the delivery man shoved her backwards and slammed the door behind him. The lock clicked. The flowers tumbled to the floor, exposing a gun aimed at Marcie's midsection. The man was wearing the contact lenses and false beard, but there was no disguising his appearance this time. His eyes were bloodshot as if he hadn't slept in days, and his cheeks were sunken. A baseball cap shaded his swollen eyes. The name tag on the lapel belonged to the person who had delivered the flowers earlier – but the man in the uniform was unmistakably Braden Maxwell.

His voice was raspy and his speech slow. "I was surprised when I saw you coming into your building a few days ago, Marcie. You must have been returning from the hospital. Yeah, and that FBI guy, too. I was glad to see him leave last night. I've been waiting a long time for this. You two are certainly resilient. When I shot him, I thought that would be the end of him, but he must've been wearing a vest or something. I know I hit him. And you. I guess I didn't push you hard enough towards the cliff."

"What . . . do . . . you . . . want?" Marcie was having difficulty drawing a breath. Her thoughts wandered to her gun. She realized she had made a big mistake by not carrying it the way she had the last time a delivery man showed up. She had decided to leave it where it was in the drawer until she recovered completely from the concussion.

"Same thing I've always wanted. I want the girl, I want Shoni. I told you there are some very dangerous men who paid good money for her and if I don't deliver, I'm dead. I know she's here. I saw her come in with that detective and I haven't seen her leave. I've been watching constantly. Where is she? In the bedroom?' He called out hoarsely, "Shoni, come out, come out, wherever you are."

Marcie didn't reply and she hoped Shoni wouldn't say anything either. She was trying to think quickly of a way to disarm Maxwell. But then she heard the girl call out.

"I'm in here."

The voice seemed to come from Marcie's bedroom. That was strange. The girl was working on the computer game in the second bedroom when Marcie last saw her.

Maxwell waved the gun in Marcie's direction and said loudly, "You'd better come out. I'm about to kill your friend here if you don't."

Silence.

Tick. Tick.

Only the hands of the clock above the stove moved.

Maxwell and Marcie stared each other down like gunfighters on the streets of a Texas town in the 1800s.

Tick. Tick.

Marcie's eyes never wavered as she calculated her next move.

Maxwell's eyes narrowed. He called out again. "Shoni, get in here NOW."

Something had to happen.

Then small short footsteps shuffled down the hall carpet. Shoni emerged with her head down. She looked so tiny and vulnerable to Marcie with her shoulders slumped and her hands behind her back.

"Well, well, well, nice to see you again Shoni. I'm glad you've decided to join us voluntarily."

Shoni's arrival drew Maxwell's attention from Marcie for an instant, the distraction she needed to attack. She lunged at him. She fought like a caged animal in those few moments, unleashing a torrent of punches and clawing at Maxwell's eyes while stomping on his instep and wrestling with the hand holding the gun. She tried to push his hand towards the floor but he too was in a life and death struggle and his superior strength prevailed. She tried to jam her finger into the trigger guard of the gun to prevent him from firing but he forced his finger onto the trigger.

He was trying desperately to bring the gun up level with her stomach. He was snarling incoherently but he was winning. The gun inched up Marcie's torso but she fought furiously to protect herself and Shoni. She had lost Shoni in too many nightmares, but this was real life and she was about to lose her again if she couldn't stop Maxwell.

They stood struggling hand to hand for what seemed like an eternity, but Marcie was losing ground. She hadn't recovered fully from the concussion and she was smaller and weaker than her opponent. As Maxwell continued to pull the gun upwards, he applied his weight to force her back. Marcie staggered and felt her legs give way as the back of her knee contacted the ottoman in the center of the room. She fell over the piece of furniture and landed with a thud on her back, momentarily winding her. She quickly scrambled to a sitting position, but she realized it was hopeless. He had the gun trained solidly on her. She did the only thing that was left to do. On impulse, she shielded her head with her arm and just as Maxwell brought the gun up to sight down it for a fatal shot, Marcie yelled, "Shoni, run!!!!"

The gun roared through the confines of the condo and the sound reverberated around the room, temporarily deafening the occupants – except for one. Braden Maxwell would hear no more. Marcie froze in disbelief. Was it possible *she* was still alive and *Maxwell* was lying on the floor? Smoke drifted from the barrel of Marcie's gun that now dangled from Shoni's trembling hand. Shoni stared at Maxwell's inert form as his blood began to pool on the carpeting.

Shaking hard, Marcie willed her legs to move and she kicked Maxwell's gun towards the balcony. She crossed the room and put her arm around Shoni's quivering shoulders, pulling her close. She pried Shoni's fingers one by one from the gun and tenderly guided her towards a chair in the living room. The girl let out an uncontrollable sob. As her body collapsed into the chair she bent over, wracked by tears. Marcie knelt beside her as Shoni gasped convulsively, her shoulders shaking. After a few minutes, Shoni regained control and looked at the body with tearful eyes. She looked back at Marcie and with a quaking voice, she stuttered plaintively, "That – that was for Irene."

Marcie held her wordlessly, then leaned over to pick up her phone and dialed 911.

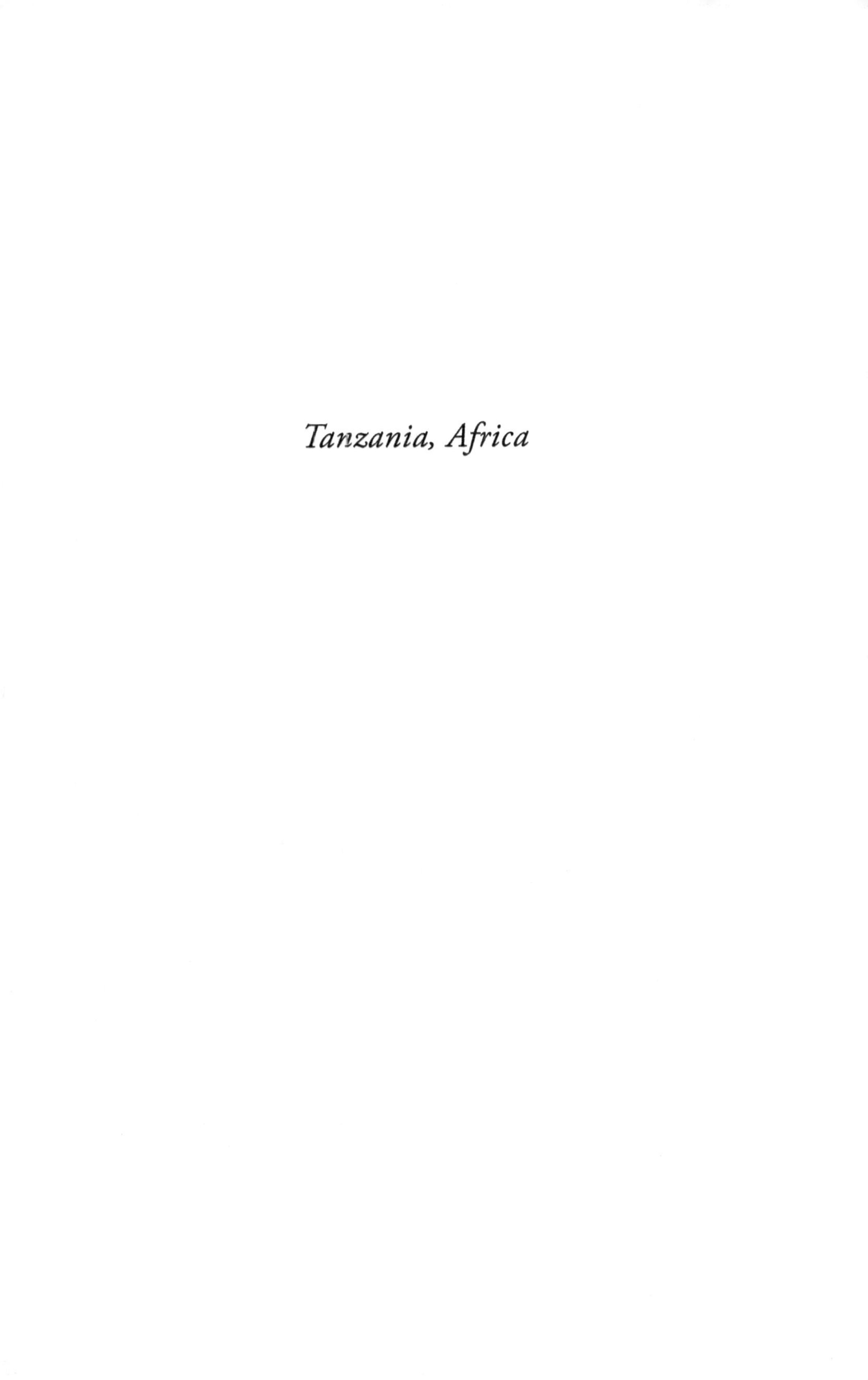

Tanzania, Africa

Chapter 46

Marcie and Nathan were savoring their meal in a hotel restaurant in Dar es Salaam with a very special guest. Godfrey the taxi driver had joined them, and they were filling him in on some of what had happened since Marcie had last seen him. Some – but not all. There were certain details that he didn't need to know.

Godfrey had asked a lot of questions about the events that had transpired in Florida. He was especially curious about how on earth anyone could sell girls on the internet the way people sell cars or cattle. Nathan tried to explain.

"If you haven't done much with computers, Godfrey, you may not know how things work. People on the internet use web browsers to gain information and look things up. These days, you can find anything at all on the internet with a simple tap of a computer key and online access. But there's something called the deep web or dark web that most people never see. It can't be found through traditional search engines. It's built with layers upon layers of access codes and top-secret security software that make it impossible to access, that is unless you're part of a particular group that controls it. These dark web sites are havens of illegal activity; and it's how people engaged in illegal activities globally communicate with each other about drugs and terrorism, among other things. It's also how they establish lucrative markets to sell girls from one country to another."

Godfrey stared with his mouth open, his vacant eyes betraying that everything Nathan had just said had sailed over his head and cleared the outfield fence. But he recovered, nodded sagely and said, "So now you can shut it down?"

"That would be ideal if we could, Godfrey, but it doesn't work that way. It's not that easy. It's like a ball of snakes, a slithering mass of codes and software that's always changing. If there's a hell in the internet, the dark web is it. We're getting closer to shutting down the organization that Braden Maxwell was part of, but his role was to recruit and supply the women. We have a lot more work to do to uncover the men who are purchasing these women. And no matter what we do, unfortunately others will pop up."

Godfrey shook his head in amazement before changing the subject. "And Shoni actually *shot* Mr. Smith – or Maxwell, I think you called him?"

Marcie took over. "Yes, she said she saw me put the gun in my drawer one night. I didn't realize she had noticed, and I would have been upset if she'd touched it under different circumstances. But she saved my life! I hugged her so hard I thought I was going to break her bones. It turned out her shot was fatal."

Godfrey nodded, his lips pursed. "But how did Mr. Smith get into your house? Surely you must have suspected he might show up one day?"

Marcie frowned slightly, looked down, and cleared her throat. "This is something that's been bothering me a lot. If I had just kept my wits about me, I could have anticipated that he would come back, and if I'd had my gun at the door, this could have had a much different ending. I guess I was just so excited Nathan had thought to send me flowers – or so I thought – and Maxwell or Smith was wearing the same delivery man's uniform as before. It looked so normal that I let my guard down and opened the door without thinking. Detective Baker found the real delivery man unconscious in the back of his van and the patrol officer who was watching the building had been shot. Fortunately, we were told they'll both recover. Still, I have to admit I was pretty naïve and stupid to just let him in like that."

Nathan picked up the story. "She's being kind. It was my fault. I told Marcie I would be sending her flowers, so it wasn't much of a leap in logic for her to let him in. Besides, Maxwell had disappeared off the face of the earth. We couldn't track him down anywhere, and we honestly didn't think he would come out of hiding. We weren't the only ones looking for him, either. Since he hadn't been able to get his hands on Shoni, there were some very dangerous people ready to kill him if they could've found him. Basically, Maxwell or your Mr. Smith had nowhere to run at that point, so he figured his best bet was finding Shoni and taking her with him."

Marcie sighed. "At least it's over, and we can all start rebuilding our lives. I'm just glad when I didn't show up for dinner that Nathan had the foresight to think I might have been taken to the gravel pit where they found Alina. If he hadn't shown up, I would have been at the bottom of the pond just like she was."

Nathan elaborated. "At first, I was surprised when Marcie didn't show up for dinner. Then I thought she had stood me up." He chuckled wryly. "But while I was waiting, Baker called to tell me they had Shoni and that Marcie hadn't returned to the hotel. I realized something was wrong and took a chance that Marcie might've been taken to the gravel pit. It turned out I was right, thank God!"

Nathan shrugged like it was just another day at the office, but Marcie noticed a small smile forming at the corners of his mouth. Marcie was happy in more ways than one that the case had ended as abruptly as it did. Her close call brought Nathan back on the first flight from Atlanta. He had managed to secure a short stint of administrative leave. Since then, he hadn't left her side.

They all sat for a moment quietly contemplating how the situation could have unfolded much differently with far more disastrous results. The room buzzed with conversations from the other tables. Finally Marcie broke the silence. "I had a long chat with Shoni on the plane on the way over since you-know-who was sleeping." She winked at Godfrey. "She was so happy to get back to see her classmates, and they were thrilled to see her. There's one boy named Samuel who was especially happy to see her. It took some doing to convince Mrs. Adimu to agree to let her back into the dormitory, but I think even she was happy to see Shoni come back, though she may never admit it."

Marcie hesitated, her fingers smoothing a ripple in the tablecloth. "I know what happened will stick with Shoni for the rest of her life. She may never forgive herself for talking Irene into going with her. Hopefully, visiting Irene's family will help relieve her guilt and they can stay in touch."

A hint of tears appeared at the corners of Marcie's eyes. She stopped playing with the table covering for a moment and then brightened as she continued. "Shoni and I spent time during the flight talking about what she wants to do, and I think she really does get it. She wants to finish school and get a real education so she can go out and make a difference in the world. She wants girls to be equal to boys in her country, and she believes everyone should be able to go to school and feel safe. She has seen a lot of violence against females in her country, and she wants somehow to be part of changing that. It will take time, but Shoni is wise beyond her years. I'm pretty sure she will stay in Africa and work toward those goals."

Godfrey nodded. "It's the Tanzanian way. We say, 'Do not mend your neighbor's fences before seeing to your own.'"

Nathan put his arm around Marcie's shoulders and pulled her closer. "What Marcie is not saying is that she is committed to funding Shoni's education. Marcie and Shoni have a bond that will never be broken. I think they'll be seeing a lot of each other in spite of the miles separating them."

Marcie looked into Nathan's eyes and the corners of her mouth turned up in an uncontrollable smile. She added, "I also told Shoni never to ask anyone else if they would take her somewhere. She said she'd learned her lesson."

Godfrey nodded. "I should hope so."

As Marcie leaned on Nathan's shoulder and watched Godfrey stir his coffee, she said, "How was Malaika when you saw her?"

"Oh yes, that little girl is something else. I think she will be the mayor of that area before she's 10 years old."

Marcie smiled at the thought of the young precocious savior who had helped her escape from Deop the night Godfrey was beaten so mercilessly. "We'll go and see her tomorrow. There are some other things we have to do, too, like going to Zanzibar – oh, and Nathan owes me a tour of Amsterdam." Her tired eyes flicked to Nathan and she was rewarded with a grin. "But now I think it's time for me to go upstairs. I still get tired easily. You two can stay and chat if you want."

Nathan threw his arms back in an exaggerated gesture and yawned widely. "I think this African air has worn me out. I'm going to have to a call it a night as well."

Godfrey shook his head knowingly and winked at Nathan. "You know in Tanzania we have a saying. It's not specifically about love but I think it applies. We say, 'Little by little, a little becomes a lot.'"

Nathan got up from the table with his hand in Marcie's. With the other hand, he warmly patted Godfrey on the shoulder.

"You know what, Godfrey? I think that's the wisest proverb I've heard come out of your mouth yet."

BARRY FINLAY

Photo by Ron Melanson

Barry Finlay is the award-winning author of the inspirational travel adventure, *Kilimanjaro and Beyond – A Life-Changing Journey* (with his son Chris) and the Amazon bestselling travel memoir, *I Guess We Missed The Boat*. The award-winning novel, *The Vanishing Wife*, is his first thriller. Barry was featured in the 2012-13 Authors Show's edition of "50 Great Writers You Should Be Reading." He is a recipient of the Queen Elizabeth Diamond Jubilee medal for his fundraising efforts to help kids in Tanzania, Africa. Barry lives with his wife Evelyn in Ottawa, Canada.

Contact the author:
Author Website: **www.barry-finlay.com**
Fundraising website: **www.keeponclimbing.com**
Facebook Page: **https://www.facebook.com/AuthorBarryFinlay**
Twitter: **https://twitter.com/Karver2**

Thank you for reading *A Perilous Question*. If you like what you read, please consider leaving a review at your favourite online book retailer.

9 780099 389 1 052